WHITE SKIN MAN

John
BAKER

WHITE SKIN MAN

ORION

First published in Great Britain in 2003 by Orion Books
an imprint of The Orion Publishing Group
Orion House, 5 Upper St Martin's Lane, London WC2H 9EA

The city and places in this novel owe as much to the imagination
as to the physical reality. The characters and institutions are all fictitious, and
any resemblance to real people, living or dead, is purely coincidental.

A CIP catalogue record for this book is
available from the British Library

ISBN (hardback) 0 75284 748 1
ISBN (trade paperback) 0 75284 749 X

Typeset by Deltatype Ltd,
Birkenhead, Merseyside
Printed and bound in Great Britain by
Clays Ltd, St Ives plc

For Anne

I would like to thank Anne Baker, Simon Stevens, and Rob Watkinson for their valuable and helpful criticism. For my time spent with a group of asylum-seekers in Hull, I would particularly like to thank Saleh-Kerem Omed, Azad Curche and Jankin-Haji Rachid. It is also necessary to say that any offended sensibilities are the responsibility of the writer alone.

'Draw your chair up close to the edge of the precipice and I'll tell you a story' – F. Scott Fitzgerald

'Prejudices are what fools use for reason' – Voltaire

'Political language – and with variations this is true of all political parties, from Conservatives to Anarchists – is designed to make lies sound truthful and murder respectable, and to give an appearance of solidity to pure wind' – George Orwell

1

A View From the Bridge

Earlier she'd walked past Paragon Station and through the town to the statue of Victoria. The old queen had been guarding Hull's central public lavatories there for a hundred years.

That day Katy Madika was trying out her new Nikon digital SLR. Katy had been inside Prince's Quay capturing images of shoppers validating themselves. She'd changed the Compact Flash card, and was on the footbridge that spanned the dock, looking for something different. The town's intellects and literati had infiltrated the street café on the other side of the dock and there was an abundance of colour and the hum of political palaver.

The water below the bridge reflected a young woman whose blonde hair skimmed her shoulders. There was a hint of make-up at her eyes and lips, a jade choker around her neck. She was wearing a sleeveless cotton top from French Connection, faded Paul Smith shorts and scuffed boots.

'How do I look?' she'd asked Daniel as she'd left the house. He'd placed his index finger to his cheek and rested his chin on the third finger of the same hand. 'Kind of Jodie Foster,' he'd said. 'Away from the set. You're not dressed for the fans. This is the real you on a day off. A day to yourself.'

She knew what he meant. The nightmare of her body after Chloe had been born was over. Everything was back in place, the muscles toned and only a few grams of fat in her entire system. She didn't need to rely on designer clothes to get her through the day. Katy Madika was fairly well designed herself. At 50 kilos she was the same weight now as when she had been a student at the University of Edinburgh.

Katy scanned the old buildings on Prince's Dock Street and came to rest on the profile of a man sitting at a table outside the Euro Café. Thin guy with thin hair, early twenties, prominent nose with a hook. Light-blue linen suit and deck shoes with no socks. Zoom in. There he was in full colour in the viewfinder, his head swivelling to the left as if he'd felt the lens brushing against the surface of his skin. Sallow complexion, as though his head and neck had been dipped in a stagnant pond.

Katy held it there. She wanted the guy's hand in the picture. People were attracted to faces but hands said more. Katy had a shoe-box full of photographs of the hands and feet and faces of the lepers that Daniel and she had cared for at the colony in Orissa. A catalogue of hands reduced to broken stumps, half-eaten noses and feet with missing and distorted toes.

She flicked the camera into continuous shoot mode and waited for the guy with the hooked nose to lift the cup to his lip. In a couple of seconds the camera had taken a dozen shots. One of them caught him narrowing his eyes, sipping coffee and at the same time scratching his nose with the index finger of the same hand.

Orissa in the Bay of Bengal held a special place in Katy's affections. It was where her eyes were opened to the reality of the wider world. The place where her innocence was trashed and the horror and majesty of the human condition were revealed. In Orissa Katy came of age. In the tiny leper colony on the coast she met and fell in love with Dr Daniel Madika and began to recognize the special thread that set her apart from ordinary people.

The hook-nosed man left his table and wandered away along the street. He lifted his arm in an expression of gratitude to the harassed waitress, smiling to himself when she failed to notice. Katy followed him unconsciously. Perhaps he would pose for her again or some other subject would present itself down by the marina.

There were few people around once they left the bustle of Prince's Quay and the Euro Café, and as they approached the river, a silence fell like light rain.

The man crossed Castle Street and passed the empty nightclubs along the side of Humber Dock, stopping before Minerva Terrace to talk to another man by an ancient cannon that poked its nose over the mouth of the dock. Katy veered off to the right and looked through her viewfinder from the bridge over the lock gates. She scanned the water, looking for a tramp or some other vessel that might make a photograph. In her mind's eye she saw the wake of a boat like a fold in the river. But there was nothing close enough to be interesting and she swung the camera back to the couple of men, the only figures around, and clicked five times in succession.

A shadow fell on the scene and Katy looked up over the camera at the back of one of the men in a white gabardine raincoat. The man was wearing a Panama and leaning on the cannon, obscuring the face of the hook-nosed guy. Katy heard two dull explosions, one following the other. They sounded controlled, as though they had taken place under water. But at the same time they were more immediate than that, closer.

The man with the Panama walked away from the cannon, leaving the young, hook-nosed guy slumped over it. Katy zoomed in and stared through the lens. Thick strings of blood uncurled from the man's head into the pale brown morning and dripped in clinging globules to the pavement.

Katy Madika felt her knees go. The sky seemed to shift down, the bridge beneath her feet lost its secure mooring on the old dock. Consciousness and space and time and imagination coalesced together into an unstable alliance. Katy, out of horror and shock, pinned down the world around her, filtering out sound in an effort to simplify and grasp the situation. She watched her feet move on the boards of the bridge but they made no noise. It was like watching an old black and white movie, complete with the distant hiss of the projector.

She grabbed the bridge parapet with both hands and looked over to her left, in the direction the man with the Panama had walked. He was still there, standing with his legs apart on the corner of Wellington Street, his hands deep in the pockets of his raincoat. He was looking back, but not at the body of the man haemorrhaging lifeblood onto the cobbles around the mouth of the dock. He was looking at Katy, his eyes, like those of a lizard, flicking swiftly between her face and her camera.

The man in the Panama took a step towards Katy and a rush of adrenalin brought life and strength back into her legs. She turned and fled back the way she had come, past the marina and into the anonymous glass and plastic façade of the shoppers' paradise.

She ran through the main deck, dodging happy consumers laden with the prizes of an advanced capitalist society, past the central atrium and out by the Carr Lane exit. Over the road Queen Victoria stood on a plinth with a pigeon on her head. Katy glanced behind to confirm that she'd lost the man in the Panama, then she ducked into the Ferens Art Gallery.

Quiet in there after Prince's Quay, not a hint of muzak, and space everywhere; cool air, lofty ceilings, marble and oil paint, the breath of times gone by. A couple of guides chatting in whispers by the desk, reassuringly attired in uniform. An armless torso in the corner, a porcelain head on a display stand, and no trace of blood.

In the washroom she leaned against the tiles and closed her eyes. Her heart was pumping hard, priming her organs, keeping the whole system on alert. Katy concentrated on her breathing, remembering the ante-natal lessons, regular breaths in and out. Don't panic. Chloe had been born so quickly that she had never got around to thinking about the breathing. The baby had knocked once and slipped easily into the world with never a doubt that it held a place for her.

Katy fought to obliterate the picture of the snakes of blood gushing from the man's head, the still and intimidating image of the assassin standing with his hands in his pockets on the corner of the street.

He was a big man, rendered shapeless by the raincoat. But as he took that step towards her Katy had watched the coat flap open and in the horror of the moment her photographer's eye had taken in the symmetry of his body. Long legs and arms attached to a steady, V-shaped frame. Above strong shoulders his head was squared, his hair dark, almost black. There was a wispy moustache and the impression of blue eyes, though he was too far away for Katy to see the colour.

She drank handfuls of water from the tap. She filled the washbasin and immersed her hands in it, ensuring that her wrists were submerged, bringing the cold liquid up to her face and neck. She patted herself dry with paper towels and inspected the image in the mirror.

She was making him up already, the assassin, reconstructing him.

4

She had witnessed the killing only a few minutes before and already she'd given the man blue eyes without it being possible for her to see what colour they were. What else had she added? The moustache? Could she be sure about that? And if her imagination was capable of adding these details, where did the invention begin and end?

Was there a man in a raincoat? Was that blood issuing from the hook-nosed man's head? From the perspective of the ladies' room in the Ferens Art Gallery all that she had witnessed seemed remote, like a dream or a nightmare. But the idea that it might not have happened unsettled Katy in a more real and immediate way than when she had witnessed it unfolding in front of her. If she had not been at the scene of a brutal and horrifying murder, if she had imagined it, then she was capable of swamping and replacing external reality by a brain malfunction, a kind of synapsal upheaval. And that loss, of the certainty of her perception, was infinitely worse than to have witnessed a murder.

But she was hysterical. The horror of the event had rocked her sense of self. She would need help to interpret it. In the meantime she could return, now. She could walk back the way she had come, through Prince's Quay with all the shoppers, go out again onto the bridge, past the marina. Only minutes had passed. The body would still be there. Or if it wasn't there, there would be an ambulance, paramedics, police. There would be commotion enough to recognize that she hadn't invented it. That what she had witnessed was horrifying and unthinkable, and yet nevertheless real.

Instead she went to the gallery's café and ordered a large cappuccino. Apart from the youth who was serving at the counter the place was deserted. She took the drink and sat at a corner table. She pinched the end off the paper vial of sugar and sprinkled it onto the foam of the coffee. She brought the cup to her lips and remembered the hook-nosed man doing exactly the same thing, and despite herself she narrowed her eyes and scratched her nose with the index finger of the same hand.

There was something about the episode that was like a movie set. The hook-nosed man was a bit-player, someone who was not going to feature in the unfolding narrative. He didn't have a speaking part. The big man in the raincoat could have been a De Niro character, one of the gangsters he played, wholly evil. And Katy was Gwyneth

Paltrow or Julia Ormond, an innocent bystander sucked into the plot by chance. Someone who had no training or experience of the dangers of the criminal underworld but who would survive by her pluck and invention.

Katy wasn't sure if she was beautiful enough to hold down the part, if she had the confidence to maintain the suspense at every twist and turn of the plot. There was something deeply unpleasant about the way film-makers always used a beautiful woman in her part. Katy had argued regularly with friends that they should use someone less striking, someone more ordinary. But people didn't want ordinary, they wanted excitement.

Not this much, though.

Anyway, she was stuck with the part now, like it or not. She was the heroine. And she wasn't ordinary. She was not always sure that she would describe herself as beautiful, but she was not ordinary. She was special and when she walked along the street, men looked at her. They always had. And women too.

Katy knew what she should do next. She should go to the central police station on Queen's Gardens. Either that or she should return to the scene of the crime and talk to the police, who would surely be there by now.

Another sip from the cappuccino, and it was while there was still contact between the cup and her lip that the man in the raincoat came into the café. He walked in slowly, casually, something exotic about him, as if he were a tourist from Chile or Argentina. If Katy hadn't witnessed his destruction of the hook-nosed young man she would never have guessed at the violence that ran in his blood.

His smile was enigmatic as he pulled out the chair and sat at her table. There was no doubt that the smile contained joy, but it did not indicate that he was happy to see her again. It was a smile of triumph, a smile for himself, for his own genius and fortitude in tracking her down.

He put his hands on the table and something heavy in his coat pocket slipped off his knee and swung the skirt of the coat down low, almost to the floor.

Katy wet herself. The ring of muscle at the mouth of the bladder relaxed involuntarily and her urethra was flushed with urine. Her underpants and shorts absorbed it and she immediately brought it under control. But still, there was no going back. It had happened.

He took the leather strap of her camera between finger and thumb and gently pulled it towards him over the table. Katy hung on to it for a moment before relaxing her grip. She watched it go. She glanced up and saw that the smile was still there, on his face.

'I'm going to take this away with me,' he said. Not a trace of an accent. 'You never saw me and nothing happened out there.'

Katy looked at him. The dampness around her crotch was worse than anything he could do to her. She'd have given him the camera if she could have been spared peeing her pants in the art gallery.

'Did you hear what I said?'

She nodded. Nothing had happened. It was all a dream.

The man got to his feet and walked to the door, the strap of the Nikon gathered together in his fist. He glanced back for an instant without the smile and then he was through the door and gone. Only the echo of his footsteps on the marble tiles.

Katy shifted uneasily on her chair. She was still sitting there twenty minutes later when the youth in charge of the café came to collect her cup. He was older than she had thought, more professional. 'You want another one?' he asked. 'Or something to eat? Got some nice cake.'

Katy shook her head. She let him take the cup but she retrieved the paper napkin. After a few minutes she stood, wiped the small damp patch on the chair and headed for the street. In her hand she clutched the Compact Flash card, which contained the images she had photographed from the bridge.

2

Flying Away

Stone Lewis had lived with Ginny Bradshaw in Hull for a year and two months; first in his tiny flat on Spring Bank, and then for the last four months in a bigger one on Spring Bank West, just over Botanic Corner, opposite the cemetery. Up-market, but not too far. It had been the best period of his life. No question. The worst time had been the long stretch in prison.

The cemetery on the other side of the road was full, had been for years, and there were parts of it that had run wild. Old tall trees and impenetrable thorn thickets, red-eyed wildlife peering out in the gloom of a summer midnight. Stone would walk there some evenings, decipher the inscriptions on the ancient tombstones and occasionally stumble over a fallen angel.

He hadn't slept again last night. Two nights in succession now, stressed because Ginny was going to LA for ten days. He had a surfeit of energy, which was in direct contrast to his mood of the week before, when he'd been barely able to drag himself out of bed. Stone lived his life between these extremes, managed it fine most of the time.

He scraped the razor along his cheek and listened to Ginny in the bedroom as she packed her bags for the LA trip. She was singing a melancholic Adriana Varela song in Spanish, a modern tanguero ballad. She'd heard it once, maybe twice, but already she'd memorized the lyric and internalized the melody, the beat and the delivery. Earlier, before the news broadcast, while Stone was working on the computer, she'd been belting out a rap number from a Marshall Mathers album. She cast her cultural nets far and wide and came up with an eclectic mix of the world's songs. With the ability to speak several languages she could devour almost anything that came along.

During the day she would be at her workshop where she designed and made ceramic jewellery; brooches and pendants, which she delivered to the posh shops in London and Leeds.

And if she's so great, so talented, so wonderful and intelligent, what's she doing hanging around in Hull with me? Stone would ask himself. And the answer was so obvious, so simple and true that he'd sometimes miss it and set himself to shaking. He'd asked his Aunt Nell the same question and she'd shrugged and told him he must be doing something right for once in his life.

'Enjoy it, Stone,' she'd told him. 'Nothing lasts for ever. When a woman decides to love you it's a special thing, but it involves you in an obligation. That kind of thing, you have to rediscover it every day.'

'I think I'll wake up and she won't be there.'

'Maybe that's how it'll work out,' Aunt Nell said. 'But she's here today, looks fairly settled.'

Aunt Nell was Stone's wise woman.

Ginny was mustard; you didn't have to be too bright to see that.

She came up behind him and shoved him to one side so she could share the mirror to make up her face.

'You don't need all that stuff,' he told her. 'You look good enough without it.'

He didn't expect her to reply. She glanced at his reflection with that I've-heard-it-all-before look, her Vietnamese features employed in a classical European attitude. She said, 'If I go out without make-up I feel naked. It's important to feel right. If I'm not comfortable I don't function properly in the world. Ergo, waste of a day. If I get my make-up right I go out and work effectively. Simple logic. Anybody could work it out.'

'Simple fact is,' Stone said, readjusting himself in relation to the mirror, trying not to cut his throat with the razor, 'if you've got a great complexion, good skin, all your features are in proportion and other women look crap next to you, then you don't need make-up. Also, if all that is true and you cover it with make-up you're gonna end up looking worse than before you started.'

Ginny smoothed the foundation and reached for an eyebrow pencil. 'D'you remember the Beatles song, "I Want You"?'

'You wanna talk about something else?' Stone asked. 'Change the subject? Make-up not stimulating enough for you?'

'Was it sung by Lennon or McCartney?'

'John Lennon on the official recording, but they say there's a version by McCartney. The full title is "I Want You (She's So Heavy)", and it's the longest Beatles track.'

'Longer than "Hey Jude"?'

'Yeah. Lot longer.'

'What about "Revolution Number 9"?'

'Maybe not as long as that, but close.'

'What's it about?'

'Longing and despair and going screaming mad.'

'You think I won't come back, don't you?'

'Not all the time. Only when I think about it.'

'You're crazy, Stone. I'll be back next week. You're my life.'

'Your cross, more like.'

She laughed. 'That as well. But I never wanted it easy. I want it real.'

'Lennon said something very similar.'

'I want you, Stone Lewis.'

'I know. Somewhere deep down there's no doubt. I'll be here, waiting. I'll keep the flat tidy, get drunk every other night, stay out of trouble, only take drugs occasionally. If I get desperate I'll abuse myself.'

She looked at him through the mirror, her make-up perfect except there was far too much of it. He put his arms around her from behind, clasped his hands together under her breasts. 'Is that all?' she said.

'Yup.'

She craned her neck to look back at him. She said, 'I don't want you to run away.'

'But *you* are,' he reminded her. 'Five hours from now you'll be on a plane to LA. When I get home tonight the flat'll be as empty as a preacher's promise.'

She turned to face him. 'I'll be away for ten days, Stone. Don't guilt-trip me for this. I'll miss you just as much as you miss me. I'll e-mail you every day.'

He looked down at her. 'Yeah,' he said. 'Do it, get it over with. Just remember it's a round trip.'

3
Omega I

Mort removed the swastika stud from above his eye and replaced it with an eagle in silver and black ivory. He inspected the row of dead piercings along the edge of his right ear. Somebody who didn't know they'd been there wouldn't notice them now, even the last one, which had gone septic and dripped gunge down his neck for a month. Might've lost his ear if old Dr Wilkinson hadn't noticed and given him the antibiotics.

'We don't want you to end up like Van Gogh, do we, Mortimer?' That was Wilkinson, he didn't say much, but when he spoke you could expect a gem. Some were so precious you didn't know what he'd said. Van Gogh was this foreign geezer what'd chopped his ear off and given it to a tart. Ginner had looked it up on the web and he'd printed a picture of the guy with one side of his face bandaged up. Gaz said that was typical of Johnny Foreigner; to give a tart his ear instead of his dick.

Gaz was sharp as well; but not in the same way as Dr Wilkinson. Mort had seen the doctor out with his family in Pearson Park one Sunday. His wife was a plump woman like one of those organic chickens in Tesco, short with tiny chicken-wing arms and a nose that could have pecked for a living. They had two kids with them, one of each, about the same age (fourteen? fifteen?), could easily have been twins. They had bright designer T-shirts and matching technical shorts and brand new Nike trainers. The old man must've been selling the family heirlooms to keep them two in clobber. Mort wondered what it would be like if Dr Wilkinson had been his father, or if he'd had a father at all. Would anything have been different? He expected he would have been controlled and he didn't know if he'd have liked that. Except for his wildest impulses, he liked things the way they were.

Way back when they'd been at school, Geiger Counter, the maths teacher, said that Gaz could go places if he used his brain. Which was the main reason Gaz didn't use it. 'Why the fuck would I want to go places?' he'd say. 'I'm better off here with me mates.'

There was more than one way of going places, anyway. Geiger Counter probably knew that; him being a teacher and everything. There was going places like in geography and there was going places politically. All three of them had done that. Everything that happened was going places, like when Gaz got his car or Ginner his motorbike. Neither of them had Mort's responsibilities, a mother who couldn't move out of her bed unless you put a rocket under her. If Mort'd been truly single he'd have scored himself a motorbike or a car, maybe both.

At least the eagle stud was black ivory and silver, if you believed the guy in the shop. Mort didn't care anyway. If the guy'd told him it was stainless steel and plastic he'd still have bought it. He hadn't bought it because of what was in it, but because of what it looked like and the power it represented and because it was made in Britain, if you believed the geezer in the shop. Well, why not? He was white and English, talked with the same accent as Mort and his mates. Seemed like a straight enough guy, not a shirt-lifter or an illegal. Not a Paki. Not a Jew.

Alice was shouting from the next room: 'Mort, give us a hand, will ya? Mort, d'you hear?'

Mort straightened himself and took a last look in the bathroom mirror. There was a small nick out of it up near the right-hand corner. He pushed his face up close, snorted and gobbed. When he stood back it was as if it wasn't a mirror at all. His own image was still there but in the background, reduced by the line of phlegm rolling down the glass. He caught it with his finger and led it to the washbasin.

'Mort, are you listening to me?'

He tore a strip off the bog-roll on the lino-tiled floor and smeared what remained of the mucus over the surface of the mirror. He ran cold water on the paper and wrung it into the basin, using it to carve a clear window in the glass. When he'd finished he polished it with the hand-towel. Good as new.

In fact, the mirror was the best thing in the bathroom. The walls had been painted yellow once, but someone must've got fed up with that because they'd started to paint green over the yellow and then had second thoughts and given up. Would've been better if they'd left it yellow. Mort couldn't work out who it was had done that. It had been like that as long as he could remember. Maybe it was Alice, when Mort was a kid and Alice could still walk and climb up ladders and paint walls? Maybe it was Alice when she was still having ideas about things? When she had a life.

Or it could have been one of her boyfriends, when she was still having them. Stupid bastards. Long time ago.

Mort had spent his entire life in the house in Greek Street. When they were kids Gaz had lived further down, near Hawthorne Avenue, and Ginner had lived round the corner in St George's Road. But Gaz and Ginner had their own places now because they didn't have a mother like Alice. Gaz's mother was dead. He'd had her cremated and kept her in a small plastic urn under his bed. Ginner's mother had remarried again after her divorce from his father and she was living with the new guy in Gloucester. Ginner thought the new guy slapped her around but he said it was her own fault for having sex with a southerner.

Alice had shuffled to the edge of the bed and got one of her huge legs over the side.

'What the hell d'you think you're doing?' he asked.

'I thought you'd gone,' she told him. 'I need me bag changing.'

'I tell you when I'm going out,' Mort said. 'You know that. I always tell you.' He lifted her leg, which felt like a ton of cold lard, and put it back under the duvet. He unhooked the bulging colostomy bag from the side of the bed and replaced it with an empty one. A few drops of piss dripped to the carpet during the changeover, but not enough to worry about.

'Thanks, love,' Alice said when he'd done with smoothing the duvet. 'You're a treasure.' When she'd finished speaking Alice left her mouth open. Mort wanted to tell her to shut it, but he held back because she didn't know it was open. Alice thought she was like everyone else and it was just her legs that had gone. She didn't realize that she was twice the size of other people and that she was losing her marbles.

Mort knew if he told her to shut her mouth after she'd finished speaking he'd be opening a subject that could take the rest of the week to get through. Alice would want to know what else there was about her that wasn't like other people, and with everything he pointed out she'd take on that sorrowful, reproachful look she kept for those occasions. The look that said Mortimer was an ungrateful and untruthful son who had never appreciated the time and effort his mother had invested in him.

He didn't want to start that off, open the heavens and allow all those old recriminations to come raining down on him. She might well be a cripple but her tongue was a professional athlete.

Still, it wasn't right, Alice's mouth being open like that. There should be some safe way to get her to keep it shut. Soon as he had a minute to spare Mort would get his head around it.

He wanted to die when he was thirty-five years old. He'd told Ginner and Gaz that if he was still alive on his thirty-fifth birthday he'd get drunk like on all his other birthdays, then he'd go out and top himself. 'Get a neat motor and take it up as fast as it'll go,' he'd said. 'Maybe hundred and twenty, hundred and thirty on the motorway. Drive it into the side of one of them bridges like Diana done.'

'You could drive it over the central reservation,' Ginner had said, 'into oncoming traffic. Take out some old bugger on his way home from work.'

They'd both looked at Gaz, because it was his turn to say something, but he'd been quiet for a long time. In the end Mort had asked him: 'What you thinking?'

'You could take a bird with you,' Gaz'd said. 'Tell her you're gonna go for a ride in the country.'

Yeah, there was lots of possibilities. It starts off with Alice's mouth being open and before you know what's happened you're thirty-five years old and dead on the motorway with this sexy woman clinging to your neck and you've taken out an old couple who were coming home from their daughter's wedding. All around cars and lorries are piling up and there's sirens going and lights from helicopters and the television news crews are drifting around the scene. Down the line there's an explosion as a petrol tank blows to the sky and suddenly both lanes are alight with tank after tank igniting and more and more fuel spilling over the road.

The fire chief and the chief of police are talking together, a safe distance from the carnage. 'What the hell started this?' the police chief asks.

'It was a guy called Mort,' the fire chief replies.

'Mort,' says the police chief. 'My God, we're gonna remember that name for a long, long time.'

Alice touched his leg with her bloated fingers. 'What're you doing today, chuck?'

'We're meeting up at Ginner's place, work on the computer.' He brought a bottle of Bell's and put it in her bedside cabinet. The empty from yesterday he put in the bin in the back yard. Then he brought half a dozen assorted packets of biscuits and a wonderloaf and a jar of strawberry jam and put them in the cupboard as well. Finally he found a packet of turkey slices and a jar of pickle to add to the store. 'That do you?' he said.

'Should do, chuck,' Alice said. 'I won't starve.'

Mort went to the bathroom for another pee and then upstairs to find his shoes. From the bureau in his mother's old bedroom he took a picture of Alice when she was about thirty and another picture where she had him on her knee. He looked about four years old. It was taken in a studio and the reds were too bright. Mother and son both seemed to be wearing lipstick.

Ginner was going to scan them and add them to www.whiteprojekt.co.uk. They were for the section on Real White British Family History, which had been Mort's idea, but which needed expanding from the single photograph of Gaz and his grandfather playing crazy golf in the rain in Withernsea.

The photographs were just a start. Eventually the section on Real White British Family History would stretch back and help people to establish who their ancestors were. Make sure there was no shit genes in there, dragging you down, undermining the purity of your blood, the lifeblood of the race.

Ginner had asked them what they would do if they found a couple of Jews and a nigger in their ancestry, and Gaz had just laughed. But Mort was still thinking about it. What would he do if there was

16

something way back, beyond living memory, that proved he was carrying, say, a fucking Arab's blood inside him? He wouldn't tell anyone, that's for sure. And he wouldn't be able to marry and father kids in case one of them came out wearing a turban. One of them curved swords tucked in its nappy.

But Mort didn't intend to marry or father kids, so the problem would die with him. He'd be the last of a corrupted line. Nature itself (herself?) would have sorted the problem.

They were getting lots of hits on the website already. There had been another round of factional splits among right-wing groups and in Hull, Mort and Gaz and Ginner were on their own again. There were two other groups in town and they were talking to one of them. Seemed like there were issues where they could join forces and others where they'd agree to differ. Politics were supposed to bring people together, give everyone a platform and a leadership, but it seemed the opposite happened most of the time. Nationally, the latest formations were around Omega, a dedicated terrorist organization so secretive that even Mort and his friends didn't know who the leading players were. Ginner and Mort had fantasized about joining Omega, going out there on the streets, forcing the bastards back to their own countries. Something big had to happen. Everyone knew that. And it would, it was coming. The country and the movement had been asleep for far too long. Drugged by boredom and the incessant whining of liberals and communists.

In the photograph of Alice with Mort on her knee she was a real stunner. There was no connection between what she was now and what she had been then. Mort couldn't see one, anyway. Not even in the eyes. Her eyes in the photograph were looking forward, sparkling with the possibilities that life was throwing at her. But her eyes now were fixed most of the time, looking into the middle distance to a place that didn't exist. What bridge was it that had brought her from there to here? Some kind of unholy structure out of God's jokebook.

'You gonna bring your old mum some Chinky food when you come home?' Alice asked when he was ready to go.

'Yeah, course. Sweet and sour?'

She nodded. 'A double. With chips, some of them prawn crackers, spare ribs and crispy noodles.'

4

Different Coloured Skins

Katy walked home. She couldn't take the chance of sitting on a bus stinking of pee, meeting someone she knew and having to make small talk while one of her neighbours wrinkled up her nose and tried to identify the smell. Most of the journey was uneventful. Later, when she tried to recall it, there were no images available apart from the smells of cooking from the bakeries and cafés along Spring Bank and Princes Avenue. On the corner of Victoria Avenue she was accosted by a couple of red setter bitches who were not satisfied by sniffing her crotch but wanted to lick it too. Katy stood with her arms in the air and her eyes closed until the dogs' elderly owner managed to pull them away. Martha and Julia, damn silly names for dogs.

Daniel and Chloe were out. Of course. Daniel at work. Chloe at the nursery in the park. When she'd left this morning Chloe was sleeping in her pram, and Daniel was reading one of his adventure stories, Forester or Patrick O'Brian. Katy's husband was an intelligent man who excelled at everything he turned his hand to; his academic and clinical qualifications were impeccable. But his fantasy world was composed of rigging, sailcloth and painted oceans, the backdrop to a life of blackguardly pirates, courteous heroes and ringleted heroines in crinoline dresses. And this was a man whose paternal grandfather had been a Bakonga chief near Kinshasa, a little over a day's walk from Stanley Pool.

Daniel was two people. He was the man he thought himself to be and the man who couldn't conform to that vision. Katy had two separate personalities as well, so the marriage consisted of the input and inter-relationships between four of them. The church, in its insistence that marriage was the union of soul and soul, was wrong. In addition to Katy and Daniel's two central personae there were a myriad of slighter personalities, each of which had their day from time to time. Chloe, as she grew, would be faced with a picture of marriage between her parents that consisted of multiple relationships all spawned by the same two individuals.

Katy stripped off and ducked into the shower, taking her shorts and underpants with her. She left them on the floor tiles, letting them soak up the suds that washed from her body, occasionally squelching the liquid from them with her foot. When she'd finished she rinsed the soiled clothes in the hand-basin and hung them on the line outside the kitchen door.

She wondered if other people who had peed in their pants would do the same, or if they'd throw the garments away. Incinerate them or put them in the waste bin. She thought she might not wear them again, that they would remind her of the hook-nosed man being shot and the man with the Panama stealing her camera, threatening her.

She began shaking. First her hands, and it was as if the trembling followed a fault-line in her body, up her arms to her head and shoulders and then down her torso and into her legs. It became so violent she couldn't stand and she let her body slide down the wall and sat with her legs splayed out in front of her. She was gritting her teeth, feeling the tears coursing down her cheeks and dripping off her chin onto the lapels of her silk dressing gown. Time lost meaning as she slumped there watching her own legs chattering on the floor in front of her.

Katy wondered if she was cold and realized that she couldn't actually tell. If she relaxed her facial muscles her teeth began chattering too and her body felt clammy and numb. At the same time there was a line of sweat on her upper lip and her forehead, and already she was damp under her arms and between her legs.

After a while the shaking eased, but as she got back on her feet she was overtaken by nausea and a hypersensitivity to noise. Far off someone was playing a radio and she was aware of the sounds of her own body, her breathing, the movement of her feet on the kitchen tiles. Katy gripped the edge of the kitchen work surface and made a conscious effort to regulate her breathing. She told herself that she must regain control. In her mind's eye she could see herself, far off, almost beyond reach.

Do something practical, she told herself. Anything.

Perhaps she should put the Compact Flash card into the waste bin. Get rid of it before the man in the Panama came looking for it. She must have been mad to hold it back. He'd be bound to look inside the camera to destroy the evidence against him. And when he didn't find it he'd come looking for her. Everyone in the house would be at risk. Chloe and Daniel as well as herself.

Katy could see the scene in her mind's eye. The carnage that would be left after the man in the raincoat came to call. The broken bodies of herself and Daniel. He wouldn't need to kill Chloe; she was too young to be a witness against him. But Katy's daughter would never know her parents. She would have an institutionalized childhood. Throughout her adult life there would be a dark area of trauma, which she would never understand and which would scar her perception of each day.

What to do? Katy didn't know. She could recall similar scenarios in films or television. In fiction she would lodge the Compact Flash card with a solicitor in a sealed envelope: *To be opened only in the event of my death.* An insurance job to keep the would-be assassin at bay. Or she might be the greedy type who would try to sell it to the guy in the Panama, get herself killed in the process.

She knew what Daniel would do. He'd take the thing to the police station. Their family would be whisked away to some remote location, their names changed, and for the rest of their lives they'd be looking over their shoulders from the dubious safety of a witness protection programme. A mixed race couple can't hide for long. They're too visible. Especially when they're as blonde as Katy and as coal-black as Daniel Madika.

Katy found a clothes-peg on a shelf and annihilated it while standing at the kitchen work-surface. She twisted the central metal spring out of shape and broke each of the two small stems of wood in two. She stared at the result; function and meaning reduced to purposeless rubbish in a matter of moments.

She was glad Daniel and Chloe were out, that she could have this time to herself. Though she hoped the shaking wouldn't return, or the feeling that she could do nothing to stop it.

For some reason she was beginning to look at herself and her family differently. She had never before realized how much Daniel and she depended on each other to void their respective realities. They were forever watching themselves, using the idealized icons of film and television to gauge how they were faring in the world. Their lives had become a nightmare of measurement. Were they attractive enough? Did they have the right friends? How did other people see them? These were constant questions, not always asked but ever present in their life together, an anxious breeze that blew through every day.

Katy had been blind to this element in her life until she had stepped onto the bridge at the mouth of the dock. It was as if the bullet that had shattered the brain of the hook-nosed young man had also opened up her own mind. As if her own preconceptions had bled out on to the cobblestones, leaving behind a vacuum that could now be filled with a consciousness of the real.

Had there been a single point, she wondered, a moment in her marriage to Daniel, when things had begun to go wrong? Because when she had first met Daniel Madika everything seemed to be right. She from her enlightened, liberal, middle England background; and he from good, solid immigrant parents who had not stinted a moment of their lives to ensure that their son had every advantage of morality and education.

Daniel and Katy's skins had been different colours. They were not conformists, sucked into the complacency and hypocrisy of the second millennium. Katy and Daniel were anything but that; they were pioneers, outcasts who had decided to take on the world with no weapons other than their love for each other.

So where had it gone wrong? Where, at what point, had their belligerence and non-conformity been undermined and metamorphosed into the restless anxiety and materialistic self-consciousness of their present lives?

Katy didn't know the answer. She only knew that their habit of scoffing at convention had become a cliché, an aspect of convention itself. She and Daniel had, without realizing it, slowly transformed each other into the kind of people who played at life, anxious only about how they appeared to others.

She walked upstairs to their bedroom, untying the belt on her red silk dressing gown as she went. She draped the gown over the edge of the bed and opened her wardrobe door. She chose a pair of white drainpipe trousers, which came to just below her knee, a sky-blue shirt of Daniel's and a pair of tennis shoes.

When she inspected the result in the mirror she recognized the clothes but her own face seemed to have altered radically. The bones hadn't changed, the general features were all intact. But the expression was new. This was a Katy she had never seen before, someone she had not thought to meet. Her expression was of vulnerability and of the knowledge of that vulnerability. The Katy who had gone out that morning to capture the world in digital images had herself been plucked out of life like a fish on a hook.

And she didn't know for certain if she would ever get back.

Daniel would not cope with this situation. Katy doubted that she would manage on her own, but her husband, on whom she depended for everyday problems, would not rise to this occasion. She would have to involve someone else and her unconscious mind had already sifted a name from the past. A woman with whom Katy had not been in contact for some time, but who now, if only because Katy believed her to be capable of grasping reality, would be the first person to hear the story of the hook-nosed man and his assassin in the Panama.

That woman was Eve Caldwell. Fifteen years older than Katy, Eve was divorced, bi-sexual and had been a lifelong member of the Labour Party until it was hijacked by the Blair faction. Now she ran an Internet café down by the river, System.ini, which was, by all accounts, a hotbed of revolutionary opinion. Katy smiled. That was Eve, and always would be. A freedom-fighter of the old school who believed that prisons were tools of political oppression and that humanitarian socialism was an inevitable result of the capitalist system.

It would be good to see Eve again. They had been close at one time, before Katy had met and married Daniel Madika, but during the last two years their paths had not crossed as often as either of them had wished.

Katy left the house and caught a bus back to town. She had an image of Daniel lodged in her head, and she couldn't shake it free. It was a reflection of the look on his face when Chloe had been born.

There had been Daniel and herself and the tiny baby between them. Katy had felt a surge of warmth as she looked at their future together. But when she glanced at her husband there was something else in his face, something she had never expected to encounter in him.

Admittedly, he was young, and she had just presented him with Chloe, an unknown and hitherto unimaginable addition to their happiness. But still, she was shocked by Daniel's look of sheer desperation.

5

System.ini

Eve Caldwell was talking about bridges and chasms. Something Stone'd never thought about before, not in this context anyway, bridges and chasms as symbols between social or economic groups, or perhaps as a symbol between a group and its objective. The Humber Bridge was there, of course, a couple of miles along the road, and Eve had incorporated a reference to it in the rough draft of a speech she was preparing for some conference. But she was after something less concrete and was trying to remember the name of the river that runs through the Underworld.

'Dunno,' Stone said. 'I never heard of a river in the Underworld. What is it? Like Hell?'

'Hades, yeah. It's one of the Greek myths. There's this river, and if you drink the water you forget everything. You don't know who you are or where you've been or what you're supposed to do next.'

Stone laughed. 'We used to get these pills in the joint, had exactly the same effect. Little green things you sucked and the world seemed like it was moving backwards, away from you. You forgot everything, your name, the walls, it was like floating for a couple of hours. We called 'em Long-gone Greens.'

'Hades had these rivers, there was one called Styx, where the dead were ferried across, but that's not the one I want.'

'Hey, listen,' Stone told her. 'Y'know this place we're in now. This room we're sitting in, surrounded by all these terminals. Y'know what you can do in here? You can log on to Google and type in "river" and "Hades" and "Greek myths", something like that, and the databases of the world'll be ransacked until they answer your question. Wanna try it?'

'Hey, you listen,' Eve told him, moving to the closest terminal and punching in the password. 'I'm the boss in here. It was me started this business and who taught you how to find your way around. So don't dis me. OK?'

'Yessir, boss,' Stone said, doffing an imaginary cap. 'I'll get together the coffee makings while you're looking for all those rivers. I've already cleaned everything twice, counted the float, made sure it didn't somehow get smaller.' He glanced at the clock. 'Only a couple hours to go. Don't look like we're gonna get too many more customers before home time.'

'But you never can tell,' Eve told him.

'Not in this life, no.'

Stone watched her smiling to herself as she waited for Netscape to hook her up to the web. One of the best moves in his life, he told himself, was coming to work for Eve Caldwell when he'd finished serving his time. Without her he'd probably be back inside by now. Aunt Nell had been important, too, and his mother, and hooking up with his Vietnamese girlfriend, Ginny. But Eve offering him a job had been pivotal. Stone had now taken on the running of System.ini for two days a week, bringing in Heartbreak, his aunt's boyfriend, when the place was busy, but otherwise managing the business alone. It was a doddle. He only wished it would make enough money to take him on full-time.

Eve wanted to bring him in as an equal partner, in the first place because she was an idealist who believed that employing someone was a form of exploitation. Secondly, she said if Stone ever took it into his head to go start his own business she would be stuck up the Swanee without a paddle. But Stone didn't find either prospect appealing. Being a partner would bring too many worries, take his mind off the job. And he would never start in competition with Eve. You don't bite the hand that feeds. If you do that you align yourself with scum.

Morality and business; beauty and the beast. Eve didn't think the two could ever work harmoniously together. Stone wasn't so sure.

Google came up with an answer. 'Lethe,' she said. 'The river Lethe. "The souls of the dead, aching with thirst, would be tempted to drink from it. Part of the training of initiates was the endurance of thirst, because one drink from the spring of Lethe caused them to forget past incarnations. They were left no wiser that the rest of humanity, always born without memories of previous lives.'"

'Like a spiritual lobotomy,' Stone said.

'Yeah, I guess. Doesn't say anything about a bridge, though.'

'Could have been a ferry.'

The door opened and a young blonde woman came in. Hair skimming her shoulders. White drainpipes with tennis shoes and a man's blue shirt. You had to look. She was a whole social class away from Stone and with a body you could only dream about, but she seemed out of sorts.

She ignored Stone. 'Eve, I need to talk.'

Eve glanced at Stone and he raised his eyebrows and said, 'Yeah, do what you have to. If I get a rush I'll shout.'

Eve led the way behind the counter, to the tiny office she used to cook the books for the Inland Revenue and the VAT man. There was room for a desk and two chairs but the door had had to be sacrificed, and whenever two people were together in there the air supply seemed inadequate.

Stone couldn't think of a good enough reason not to listen.

'You want something to drink?' Eve asked her visitor.

'Thanks. Not really.'

Silence.

Eve said, 'How've you been?'

'Oh, you know. It's not easy with a baby. I love her, but ...'

'That's not why you came?'

'Chloe's fine, Eve.'

'Tell me. What's wrong?'

Silence again.

Katy said, 'Who's the guy?'

Eve hesitated, lowered her voice a fraction. 'Stone. Stone Lewis. He works for me, part-time.'

'With tattoos?'

'With tattoos, yes. There's something wrong with that?'

'On his face? No wonder you don't have any customers.'

Stone took a deep breath. Maybe he should go in there and sort her out. There was one tattoo on his face; the teardrop under his left eye, and then there was the swallow on his neck. And he didn't like the way this conversation was turning out.

Eve said, 'You came here to talk about my staff, my marketing plan, what?'

'No, I'm sorry, something's happened to me. I don't know what to do.'

Stone settled down inside himself and listened as the blonde described the events of her day. As the story came out he found himself making small, arbitrary adjustments to it, imagining the woman had a tendency to elaborate. It was often a problem with new people, how much to accept what they said and how much to merely suspend disbelief until you could corroborate it from another source.

What was disconcerting about the blonde was that she seethed with dissatisfaction; it came through on her breath, the way she caressed the words with hard edges and let the softer ones pass her by.

'So what do I do?' she asked when she had finished her story.

A middle-aged man came into the café and asked for a terminal. Stone had to show him the basics and missed snatches of the conversation in the back room.

'I can't go to the police, Eve. Not now, not yet. He was so sure about me ... I know he'll come after me. There's Chloe to think about, and Daniel. If there was just me it'd be different ...'

'What if the guy kills someone else? He's got to be unhinged.'

'If I go to the police I don't know what he'll do. He enjoyed frightening me. It was all there in his look, how he could take my life apart fibre by fibre, and he'd be laughing while he did it.'

'All the more reason to get him out of circulation, Katy. And the quicker the better.'

A couple more customers came into the café and Stone watched them prowling the terminals. So she was called Katy. Seemed like the name was too good for her, as if it had been designed for someone else.

'I thought you didn't believe in prisons.'

'I don't believe in prison for fifteen-year-old shoplifters, Katy, or for women who break the law to feed their kids. But this guy sounds like his brains are fried. You can't leave him on the street.'

'The police could have picked him up,' Katy said. 'Anything could've happened.'

'Unlikely though. From your description he's not the kind who'd give himself up.'

'No, I can't face it. Not at the moment. I'll watch the news tonight. If they appeal for witnesses I'll come forward. But I don't want to get involved.'

Stone imagined Eve's tight-lipped smile. 'You are involved, girl. You were on the spot and you might be the only person in the world who can say what happened.'

Two more customers came in and Stone had to stop listening to deal with them. A late rush, just what you needed when you were trying to eavesdrop a couple of women talking about a murder.

'She didn't like me,' Stone said when Katy had left the café. All the terminals but one were occupied by screenagers and a couple with two small children were sitting at a table in the window. Stone had been swilling the pavement outside and was carrying a bucket and a mop.

'True,' Eve confirmed. 'She was worried about the tattoos. Was it so obvious?'

'Bourgeois malice and resentment, thick as clotted cream.'

'You can detect that?'

'Eve, with your friend there, I could *taste* it.'

'You're as sharp as a cueball, Stone. Katy Madika would be shocked if you told her. She sees herself as objective, fair-minded.'

Stone shrugged. 'She was frostier than February.'

'She always wore her emotions like make-up. I think Katy is afraid of close feelings. That was why we all loved her so much when she was younger. You didn't run up to her and hug her. But you wanted to.'

'Not my kind,' Stone said. 'I didn't run out the door when she came in. But I wanted to.'

'She's married to a black doctor,' Eve said. 'Daniel. But they're not very good for each other. Too alike. They both see themselves as special people, something above the average, as though they share a destiny that involves the redemption of the world. But in reality they are like everyone else, and that's the one thing they can't stand.'

Eve watched him rinse out the bucket and put it in the cupboard under the stairs.'

'By the way,' he said, 'd'you have a copy of *Abbey Road*?'

'The Beatles? Yes, d'you want to borrow it?'

'Jus' for a couple of days. That OK?'

'Sure. I'll bring it in tomorrow.' She eyed him, her head on one side. 'Your eyes are bloodshot,' she said. 'You look as though you could do with a good night's sleep instead of running around like this.'

'No time for sleeping,' Stone said, grabbing a tray and making for the tables, collecting empty cups and plates. 'You finish writing your speech. I've got work to do here.'

6

About Feeling Good

The guy hadn't been in before. Not on Stone's shift. Might be Eve would recognize him but she wasn't around. You got them from time to time. Kind of guy that wears his identity like a badge. There were the Dorks for Jesus; couple of them came in on a Friday afternoon and trawled through the Christian sites, hoovering up snippets of spiritual info, spreading their own straight-laced version of love across the bulletin-boards. There was a trainspotter complete with anorak and a scent like the interior of a railway carriage, misted and dusty spectacles. Tuesdays, he'd get up a picture of one of the preserved Great Western locomotives and sit gazing at it for the whole hour, then leave with his eyes glazed over; a man seduced by a moment of technology.

This one was different. German Eagle stud above his eye, nervous manner, out of his depth at a keyboard but with enough savvy to find his way around. Logged on to a couple of right-wing sites, knew their addresses from memory. He ordered a strong cup of tea and Stone served it lukewarm, one of the privileges of waiting table.

All attitude. The guy saying, *This is me. You don't like it we can fight to the death. Your death.* Stone didn't stare. He looked at him from time to time, tried to go past the image, under his skin, inside his head. But there was a wall shielding him from the world.

It was tempting to demonize the guy, say anyone who pinned an anti-Semitic symbol to his head was insane. But that was too simplistic, it let everyone off the hook. Something incongruous about the Tesco carrier-bag between the man's legs, bulging with food;

what looked like biscuits and pork-pies, packet of custard-creams poking out the top and the neck of a bottle of Bell's.

Stone had a photograph at home. It was a picture of a lynching in Omaha around 1920. He took it out and looked at it occasionally, wondered about it. There were over forty white people in the picture, all gathered around the burning body of a young black man. The victim's hands were chained behind him and the spectators had lost interest in the proceedings while they had their photograph taken. They posed and smiled like they would in front of any trophy; their faces were the same as the faces of men who had won a golf tournament or caught a big fish. Not one of them betrayed feelings of guilt or an awareness that the deed in which they were participating could be construed as anything other than harmless fun.

And they were not special people. Not KKK. Not mad or insane. They were a normal cross-section of the local population. They didn't wear German Eagle studs or swastika armbands or have shaven heads. These were family men, some of them had brought their sons along to see the show. They were wearing shirts and ties and brimmed hats or flat caps. They were in their twenties and thirties and forties and fifties and if it was Christmas they'd be singing carols.

In that photograph there were no icons or symbols, only an obvious enjoyment of the sport of cruelty. They were doing what they were doing because it gave them pleasure. They didn't have to be there. The violence and insensitivity empowered them in some way, made them feel good.

Taking life is such an easy thing to do. That's why society makes it taboo. But if you dehumanize your victim, reduce him to the state of a thing, the rest is simple. You don't need specialized equipment or expertise. You only have to stir up the fury within yourself and unleash it onto the hated object.

Stone had done it. He knew how simple it was. And he wondered if the guy at the terminal had done it, or how long it would be before he got around to it. The man's life was ringed with images of hatred and he was driven to fill his mind with more. Each click of the mouse, each hesitant touch of the keyboard released another gush of odium to reinforce his already inflamed consciousness. He was burning with twisted ideals, his soul consumed by the flames of his own desires.

Stone turned back to the dishwasher and loaded it with cups and saucers. You do a long stretch inside and when you come out you think every young kid on the street is going down the same road you took yourself. There's something stuck in the back of your head that fancies itself as a teacher, a saviour. You look at someone's destiny, make it up out of moonlight and magnolias, and you think you can step in there and transform it.

But you can't alter the way someone wants to go. You can't change the world. All you can do is change yourself. Try to.

He took an order for cheese-on-toast off a woman wearing a bikini top with shorts and served it to her at the table by the window. She'd been in a few times and tempered her opinion of him. Now she regarded him as all right but odd. The day before yesterday he'd been simply odd. It was partly the tattoos but it was connected with the eye contact or lack of it, the way he occupied a servile position without a hint of servility. She had a pretty face. Oval-shaped with straw-coloured hair and freckles around her nose and on top of her chest.

The customers who knew Stone and considered him all right but odd and the new customers who regarded him as simply odd would all have been hard-pressed to verbalize their feelings about him. In using the term 'odd' they didn't mean that he was bizarre, deviant or weird. They identified a strangeness about him that was repressed, enigmatic, perplexing. There was a metaphoric haziness that went before him, obscuring the sight of him. But when you puzzled your way through the mist there was someone behind it who was recognizably human.

When he went back to the counter to get the woman's coffee, the guy with the German Eagle stud had split. Skipped without paying for his time at the terminal. His cup of tea was still by the monitor, untouched and cold.

7

Black Boy Burning

It was a warm night when Chaz left Ms Lumsden's house, his jacket slung over his shoulder. He fingered the cash in the pocket of his jeans, the proceeds of a night's babysitting, and he calculated how many more nights' work he'd have to put in before he could afford the new DVD player.

The baby had sprung awake while Ms Lumsden was out playing snooker with her friends, and Chaz had cradled the tiny thing in his arms and hummed the mocking bird song until she'd gone back to sleep. So pink against his black arms, hard to believe she was real. So soft and fragile and small. Made you think about the world when you held a tiny thing like that close to you.

Chaz had been thinking about the world anyway, over the last couple of years, since his thirteenth birthday. One of the things he'd been wondering was when he'd start to think about girls like the other boys at school. Because when Chaz listened to the way they talked it seemed to him that he thought about the other boys more or less in the same way that the boys were thinking about the girls.

Ms Lumsden had talked him through that one. She'd explained that some people preferred to be with their own sex. Not many people, they were a minority and sometimes felt isolated, depending on the state of the society in which they lived. But it was possible to lead a good and fulfilling life even if you were part of a minority. Nature was rich and threw up all kinds of combinations. It didn't help to think of everything in terms of right and wrong. There was something wonderful about everything in creation.

Chaz had always known that life was like that. Before he'd heard about the same sex thing, before he'd become aware that most people in the country were white and he was black. For as far back as he could remember, before he'd suspected any of those things, he'd known that his life was going to involve some kind of battle.

As he cut through Margaret Street a solitary car passed, travelling in the same direction. The white guys inside gazed at him as they passed and the one in the back gave him the finger. Their faces were ghoul-like in the streetlights, drained, their lips devoid of colour. Steroid enthusiasts? Whatever, they were not interested in the boy's prospects. The brake lights flickered and Chaz's heart sank, but the car picked up speed again and travelled on towards Beverley Road.

That was another thing in addition to being black in a white world and gay in a miserable one; Chaz was also tall. You'd think if there was something wonderful about creation it might have made him a tiny bit shorter. He adjusted his glasses on the bridge of his nose and walked on, hoping the car wouldn't come back.

The thing about being gay wasn't sorted yet. Oh, it was fairly certain that the other guys at school got a boner when they watched the girls in the playground and Chaz got hard when the guys were playing football. But sometimes he got a boner when he talked to Mercy Philips as well and she wasn't a guy. Nothing like a guy. Curly hair, breasts, soft, downy forearms, swollen lips and huge, innocent eyes. So how d'you explain that, then?

'Nigger boy, nigger boy.' The guys in the car were back. They'd been round the block and come up behind him. Chaz glanced across at them and looked away, keeping his eyes fixed on the lights of the main road 100 metres ahead. But he'd seen the guy in the back seat who was chanting at him; about twenty years old, maybe older, with a stud above his eye and long black hair that was stiff with grease.

Two things, Chaz thought. You have to be cool, keep walking, don't engage with them. That's the one thing. The other is that you have to stay alert, get ready to move fast towards the lights of Beverley Road. As soon as they make their move. Don't let them corner you in a dark street like this. If the car stops, you run for your life. You fly, boy. You better.

'Nigger boy, you come and clean this car?'

There were 50 metres to go. Chaz glanced at the tarmac then looked straight ahead. His head shaking.

'You wanna banana, monkey man? You wanna clean this car for a banana?'

The guy driving the car pushed down on the accelerator and the thing roared. Chaz relaxed for a fraction of a second, assuming, madly, that they were going away from him. But the car was up on the pavement now, its nose cutting off his access to the bright lights ahead of him. He turned to run back the way he'd come but two of them had him hauled over the boot of the car before he'd had time to blink. There were three of them suddenly, holding an arm or a leg each. One of them was huge, not tall but fat with a shaved head and missing front teeth, and he had his hand over Chaz's mouth. Chaz didn't want to think what the hand tasted of, some dark and musty bodily secretion.

All that worrying about sexuality and examinations and Mercy Philips and identity, and now he was going to die. Everything in his life had been a waste of time. It was going to end against the boot of a rusty car in Margaret Street.

The guy with the stud above his eye cupped his free hand around Chaz's crotch and squeezed. 'Big dick, monkey man,' he said, 'but real small brains. Hardly any brain at all, just as much as you need to swing from one tree to another.'

The fat man removed his hand from Chaz's mouth. The guy with the stud said, 'What's your name?'

Chaz told him.

'And when I talk to you, monkey man, next time I talk to you, you think you're just gonna pad along the street and ignore me? Treat me like I'm talking to myself? Like you're too high and mighty to answer my questions?'

'No.' Chaz shook his head.

''Cause I could easily dip your head in petrol and light a match. Y'know that?'

'Yes.'

'Watch a black boy burnin'?'

Chaz nodded, felt his eyes staring in their sockets.

The guy smiled. 'What're you doing on my street at night?'

'Going home.'

'Where've you been?'

'I've been babysitting.'

'Who for?'

'My teacher.'

'White teacher?'

'Yes.'

'You been fucking her?'

'No. I've been babysitting.'

The man with the stud said, 'If I thought you'd been fucking that white teacher I'd cut your balls off and feed them to the cats.'

'I haven't,' Chaz said. 'That's the truth.'

'Or any of the white women round here. 'Cause they're ours.'

'*And* the black women,' the fat one said. 'They're ours as well, Mort.'

Smiles all round. 'Yeah,' Mort said. 'The black womens's ours as well. It's all ours. Right, monkey man?'

Chaz nodded. 'It's all yours,' he said.

'What we gonna do with him?' Mort said.

'What would Omega do?' said the last one, a ginger-haired guy who hadn't spoken before. 'To keep the streets clean.'

'Let's have his tackle off,' the fat one said. 'Hang it in the back of the car.'

They unzipped him and pulled his jeans and jockeys down around his ankles.

'Ugh, look at that,' said Mort.

'Fuckin' black worm,' said the one with ginger hair.

'Chop it off, Mort,' the fat one said. 'The bollocks as well. That's what Omega would do.'

'Keep his mouth closed,' Mort said. He took a flick-knife from his back pocket and sprung it open. 'This'll save some poor cow being poked by a spook.'

'That teacher'll be grateful to us one of these days.'

The fat hand was clamped over Chaz's mouth and he bit down on it with as much strength as he could find, at the same time kicking out with hands and feet. The fat guy screamed and pulled his hand away. An arc of blood followed its trajectory.

At the same time a house door opened and an old woman in jeans and slippers came out. 'What's going on here?' she wanted to know. She banged with both hands on the door of the neighbouring house, which was opened by a tall white man in overalls.

'You trying to wake the kids up?' he said.

'I think you should ring the police,' the old woman told him.

'Time to go,' Mort said. They dropped Chaz and he felt himself slide down the boot and onto the tarmac. The car doors slammed and the vehicle moved away to the end of the street and disappeared round the corner.

'You should cover yourself up, boy,' the old woman said to Chaz. He rolled over onto his knees and spewed into the gutter.

'Christ,' the guy in the overalls said. 'He's showing us his ass now.'

8

The Missing Lodger

Nell and Heartbreak had been jiving at the Rock 'n' Roll Club on Spring Bank but they'd left early. They walked together in silence along Princes Avenue, Heartbreak with a strange shuffle step, as if his feet weren't designed to come into contact with the ground. Nell, a tiny leathery woman in her fifties, said, 'Why d'you wanna drink when you're dancing?'

'I was all right till the last pint,' Heartbreak said.

'And then you were all wrong. If you're swinging me round the floor you have to be there to catch me.'

'I did catch you, Nell. What are you saying?'

'Yeah, you caught me, just. You nearly missed me. I'd have been sat on my ass in the middle of the floor, probably broke a leg.'

'Jeez, Nell, you're walking as good as me. To hear you talking you'd think I was pissed out of my head. Look at this, I'm walking in a straight line.'

'Nearly. You're nearly walking in a straight line. You keep bumping into me.'

'OK, it was the last pint. I've admitted that.'

'You don't listen.'

'That's not true. I always listen to you. I always made it a point to listen to women unless they're after cheating you, which half of them're doing half of the time.'

'Thanks, Heartbreak. That makes me feel really good.'

'And you know that wasn't meant for you. You're different to those cheating broads. I'm not blaming you for anything.'

'That's because I haven't done anything. It was you who got pissed and dropped me on the dance floor. *I* was drinking orange juice.'

'I didn't drop you, Nell.'

'You nearly did.'

'I caught you.'

'Only just.'

'Jeez, what d'you want me to do?'

'Say you're sorry and promise you won't do it again.'

Heartbreak stopped under a street lamp and turned her towards him. On the other side of the street they could see the diners in the window of the Thai restaurant, their faces flushed with velvet colours imported from the Orient. 'Nell,' he said, 'I'm sorry I had that last pint. Next time we go dancing I'm not gonna drink so much. I might have a pint or two, but that'll be the limit. I won't have a last pint. I nearly dropped you back there during that Brenda Lee number and if I hadda done you could have broked a leg, which would have been terrible. And it would have been my fault. And I'd be mortified, coming to visit you in the hospital with a bunch of flowers and a bottle of Lucozade.'

'Thank you,' she said. 'I accept your apology. You are a gentleman.' She set off walking along the street, Heartbreak beside her.

'Give us a kiss, then,' Heartbreak said. 'So we can carry on with our lives.'

Nell went up on her toes and planted a kiss on his cheek. He tried to give her one back but it landed in her eye.

'What'd you think to the new guy?' Heartbreak asked as they turned into Newland Avenue.

'He's one of these guys doesn't listen to the music. You're dancing with him but he's doing some kind of gymnastics, into a rhythm that's got nothing to do with the music, like he's invented it in his head. He doesn't need a record to dance, he's got one built in, only if you're the one dancing with him you can't hear it, so every move he makes is a surprise.'

'I asked you that because I met him in the bar and we introduced ourselves – he's called Stanley something – and he stuck out his mitt, but there was nothing there. Know what I mean? You think you're gonna get hold of something because you can see it, but when you touch it there's nothing there.'

Heartbreak slowed down outside Pool's Corner, see if there was any second-hand gear in the window he might be able to use, but Nell didn't break her stride and he had to run to catch her up.

'Substantial.'

'How's that?'

'You can't say there's nothing there,' Nell said. 'If you take hold of the guy's hand then there's something. His hand isn't made out of air. He's not a ghost. What you mean is there's nothing substantial there.'

'I do?'

'Yeah, you do.' She paused, let Heartbreak assimilate the information. 'He's effeminate,' she said.

'No, that's not it. There's plenty of females you can get hold of and you know you've grabbed something. They're physical. They're moving, inside, there's some willpower or blood running through their veins. This Stanley guy, he's just limp. I dunno, I might've imagined it, we probably shook hands. But I couldn't be sure.'

'It's a gender thing.'

'I can hear what you're saying, Nell, but it doesn't square with my experience.'

'I'm saying he might be like that with you but he wasn't like that with me. And when I talked to Edna in the bog we both agreed that Stanley the new boy is not much of a dancer but he's got more hands'n a watch factory.'

Heartbreak laughed. 'So that's all I know, eh? I never could keep up with the news. There was a war once I missed completely. It was all over before I heard it'd started. People don't bother telling me things.'

'I don't wanna go through this again, Heartbreak. But you don't listen a lot of the time. You drift off and it's as if you aren't around. You're physically here but your mind's somewhere else. We're sitting together, or we're walking along side by side, and I think I'm by myself. Back there at Pool's Corner, we're in the middle of a conversation and suddenly you've gone. I'm walking home by myself.'

Heartbreak didn't reply. He had got his name because he'd had an

40

affair that ended badly way back when – sometime in the seventies, eighties – and he'd never got over it. Before he and Nell started seeing each other people would catch him talking to the ghost of this old girlfriend. It was all so long ago that nobody could remember her name or what she looked like. Except Heartbreak, of course, he probably had a fairly good picture of her in his head.

But then again, maybe not. Guys, in Nell's experience, were pretty good at making up a likeness in their heads that bore little or no resemblance to the actual person. Your average guy was a magician who could conjure up some impossibly beautiful woman to fill the space left by a lumpy girl who ran off with his best friend.

Sally Lewis, Nell's sister, was standing in the street with Mrs Robson, who was, as always, in an apron. She must have had a cupboard full of them, all the same pattern. Got lucky one day and come across a job-lot, fell off the back of a lorry.

'Has there been a burglary?' Nell asked.

'No,' Sally said. 'We've lost Mrs Robson's lodger.'

'It's not eleven o'clock yet,' Nell said. 'He'll still be drinking.'

'He doesn't speak English,' Mrs Robson said. 'And he's been missing all day. He asked specially when dinner would be ready. Doesn't like to miss his food. He was in a camp over there, half starved him, they did. I know he was coming back for dinner. He wouldn't've missed it.'

'Over where?' Heartbreak asked. 'What camp?'

'Kosovo,' Mrs Robson explained. 'They burned his house down and put him in a camp. Now he's something to do with the government. He's here to learn English.' She had a pair of squeaking earphones slung around her neck, the wire leading into the pocket of her apron.

'He'll have got himself a woman,' Nell said. 'Young bloke like that, far away from home. Good-looking, too. What's he called, Shaban?'

'That's right,' Mrs Robson said. 'Shaban Brovina.'

'That's exactly what I said; he'll have found a woman,' said Sally. 'But Mrs Robson's not convinced. I told her, I said I'd have had him myself if he'd asked.'

'He was so keen to get back for dinner,' Mrs Robson said. 'I hope he turns up soon or I won't be able to sleep.'

'I'll come and sit with you for a while,' Sally said. 'There's nothing on the telly. And I can help you give him a talking to when he turns up. Chastize the young fellow.'

'So, this Stanley guy,' Heartbreak said, 'he tried to feel you up?'

'It wasn't personal,' Nell said. 'He tried it with everybody.'

'So he's a prat, then?'

Nell shook her head. 'I wouldn't say that, no.'

Heartbreak looked at her.

'He was interesting,' she said. 'He talks about culture and art, and he's got pertinent things to say.'

'Pertinent. Culture and art?'

'Yeah, paintings and books. He said that when you try to interpret what a work of art is saying then you rob it of what it is and put an interpretation in its place.'

'Yeah?'

'Yeah. What d'you think to that?'

'Jeez, Nell. Sounds to me like the guy's a prat.'

'Can you answer the question without calling the man names?'

'I don't know,' Heartbreak said. 'It's fuckin' surrealism to me. One of them. Who cares?'

'Well, Stanley cares. He feels passionate about it. And I care as well; it was interesting to meet a man who isn't frightened of ideas.'

When they got to Nell's garden gate Heartbreak gave her a squeeze and a kiss. 'I don't know how to compete with a guy like that,' he said.

'I don't want to screw the guy,' she said. 'I just enjoyed talking to him.'

Heartbreak shook his head. 'In a way that's worse, Nell.'

'Just think about it,' she said. 'What art is and what life is. The guy isn't any brighter than you.'

Heartbreak headed for home wearing his just-been-shot-in-the-back face.

9

Blood on the Cannon

'Where's your camera?' Daniel had asked when Katy got home.

The lie was already formed on her tongue. She hadn't prepared it beforehand or even thought that he would ask about her camera. He was a man, her husband; he didn't notice little things, only issues affecting the world or his car.

'I took it back to the shop,' she said, marvelling at the hint of irritation in her voice. 'There's something wrong with the shutter mechanism.'

'So you didn't get any photographs?'

'God knows. There might be a few. I don't know what they'll be like, though. How was your day? Where's Chloe?'

'In the sitting room. I gave her a bottle.'

Katy went through, Daniel following. She knelt beside Chloe's wicker basket and looked at her daughter. Daniel had propped her bottle against the side of the basket and wedged it in position with a pillow. Chloe had turned on her side to get a better grip of it and when Katy loomed into view the child tried to smile through the feed, but didn't make a very good job of it.

'What are they going to do about the camera?'

'Fix it, I hope. I've got to ring them in a couple of days.'

'They should replace it. Tell them you don't want it repaired, you want a new camera.'

Katy shrugged. She collected Chloe in her arms and sank into the sofa with her, holding the bottle to the baby's mouth. 'I'll talk to them,' she said. 'They weren't being awkward or anything. I'm sure they'll do the right thing.' You tell one simple lie, she thought, and you have to invent a whole world to substantiate it.

There was a sense in which it was Daniel's fault that she had told the lie. She had told it to protect him from the truth, because the truth of what had happened to her was too much for him to take. Daniel would worry about the implications of the threat from the man with the Panama. He would want to uproot the family, take Chloe and Katy away, maybe back to Kinshasa. Everything they had built up here would be lost.

If Daniel had been a stronger man there would have been no need for the lie. She would have told him about the killing she had witnessed, about her camera being stolen, and a stronger Daniel would have dealt with it. He would have taken responsibility for it. She wouldn't have had to worry about it at all.

When she thought about it, Katy wouldn't have minded going back to Kinshasa for a while, until everything blew over. She would have enjoyed it for herself, but she didn't want to take Chloe there, not while she was so young. Maybe in a couple of years . . .

She watched the late news on the television but there was no mention of a killing in Hull. After lying awake for an hour she got out of bed and went downstairs. She tuned in to Radio 5 Live and waited through three news bulletins. But there was nothing.

On the morning edition of Radio Humberside there was not a word about the murder. Katy left Daniel in bed, bundled Chloe into her pram and walked into the town, feeling her pulse-rate increase as she passed the statue of Queen Victoria on her left and the Ferens Art Gallery on her right. Was it possible, after all, that she had imagined, somehow invented the whole incident? Katy didn't believe that, but here she was, approaching the scene again twenty-four hours after it had happened, and this time she was looking for evidence to corroborate her memory.

The Euro Café was open as usual, its tables spilling out onto the cobblestones of Prince's Dock Street. The table the hook-nosed young man had used was empty, as if the customers knowingly avoided sitting at it. Katy wondered if the ghost of the young man was still there, invisible, sipping gingerly at an everlasting cappuccino to save himself walking into the arms of death.

Katy pointed the pram along the street and retraced her steps of the day before. At the old Spurn lightship she hesitated for a moment, wondering if she should return to the scene so soon after the events she had witnessed. She might have gone home, she told herself later, if Stone Lewis had not walked up behind her and asked if she'd ever been inside.

'Inside?' she asked. She felt blood rush to her face, hating the fact that she had no control over it.

'The lightship. Have you been aboard?'

'Oh, no. I was just looking at it.'

'On your way to revisit the scene of the crime?'

'Well, yes, but I . . .'

'Eve told me what you said yesterday. About what happened. I was curious, thought I'd come and take a look. It's further along the street, isn't it?'

They walked together. Katy glanced at the teardrop tattoo under his left eye from time to time. Such a strange thing to do, she thought, to disfigure your face like that. It wasn't attractive, not at all. More like a scar. The other tattoo, the swallow in flight, was on the right side of his neck and Katy couldn't see it as they walked along. But it was there in her mind's eye, gaudy, with its forked tail, red throat and deep-blue back.

'How old is he?' he asked, nodding towards the pram.

'She. Chloe.'

'Whoops.'

He was wearing black cotton chinos and highly polished black shoes with white socks, a soft leather jacket over a white T. His dark hair was too long to be smart and he allowed it to hang in front of his eyes. His lips were soft and large, however, like a girl's, sensual, somehow insolent. The kind of man Katy's mother had warned her about. He would be attractive to some women, but not to Katy. He made her think about lust and copulation, but not in the way she liked to think about those things.

There was something else about him, too. He was wired, taking everything in, moving his head and eyes faster than normal people. He was clenching and unclenching his fists and he would put his hand in his pocket and then withdraw it again, recommence the clenching thing. It was as if he were drugged, on some kind of upper.

45

Katy couldn't think what they were called these days, but she'd used them at university, amphetamines. Maybe something stronger.

As they approached the cannon Katy slowed down and Stone Lewis strode on ahead. 'Here?' he asked, glancing behind him. 'Was it here?'

'Yes. I was on the bridge above the lock gates, but the man was slumped over the cannon. There was blood pouring from his head.' She took a couple of steps forward but didn't get as close as Stone.

He looked towards the lock gates. 'You were a long way away.'

'I know what I saw. I've got the photographs.'

'Yeah.' He crouched and examined the paving stones around the base of the gun. He rubbed at a dark stain with his index finger and brought it up to his nose.

'Blood?' she asked. 'It's blood, isn't it?'

'I don't know.' He looked at her, squinting against the light. 'This is clubland at night, the fruit market during the day. Look around, there's stains all over the place. And even if it is blood, it doesn't prove anything.'

'But I saw it happen. They shot him in the head.'

'Yeah. I believe you.'

But he didn't sound convinced or convincing. When he stood he was shaking his head. Those jerky movements. For a moment she thought he would shake his head for ever. Bloodshot eyes staring at her.

'What would it take to convince you?' Katy asked.

'A body.'

'Listen,' she said. 'Let's assume there was a body, and that the police have found it, but for some reason they don't want it to be generally known.'

'Doesn't work,' Stone said. 'If there'd been a murder like that in a public place, the area would be cordoned off, there'd be a manhunt going on. They couldn't keep it under wraps. Cops'd be running around everywhere.'

'Now, listen to me,' Katy said, getting an edge into her voice. 'I saw a man killed yesterday morning. There's no doubt about that. The man was shot in the head and he was dead, the blood was pumping out of him. There's no way he could have survived that.

46

And it happened here. On this spot. I witnessed it. I photographed it.'

'Only thing I can think of,' Stone said, 'is the body was moved. Maybe today or tomorrow we'll hear about a body being found somewhere else. In the meantime, if you're so sure about what you saw, you should go to the police.'

Katy shook her head. 'I'll give it another day,' she said.

10

St Vincent's

Strange, the tattoos. Katy hated them. There was something attractive about Stone Lewis but at the same time he repelled her in a hundred different ways. He was a back-street man; there were no trees in his landscape. He didn't try to be cool but he was anyway. A man with no ambition. How did you account for that? A man still under thirty and he didn't have a plan. Tattoos on his face and neck and working in a café. Something else strange about him, the way he appeared easy, laid-back one minute and the next he was twitching and nodding his head. At the same time there was a hesitancy about his responses, lizard-like, as though he measured everything before he moved.

His sexuality was the attraction, no getting away from that. Katy hadn't strayed in her marriage and she didn't plan to, but if there were to be a one-night-stand, then Stone Lewis was made for the job. It would be like a meal to him, a quick snack. He wouldn't come sniffing around the next day for another instalment. There would be little chance of complications. A respectable woman's infidelity would be merely something else he could add to a lifetime of half-remembered events.

Or would he surprise her?

No way of knowing. The man wasn't transparent enough. And his women would not be like Katy Madika. She imagined him with stereotypes, slinky women with blonde hair and cigarettes and skirts slit to the ceiling. Fishnet stockings and lips painted the colour of fresh blood. Designer sex bombs, always in their own minds fresh from the silver screen.

No, not stockings, too classy by far. His women would wear fishnet tights.

Walking along Beverley Road, so engrossed in speculation about the man she walked past the entrance to the park, decided to cut through Queens Road instead. A lad in a baseball cap wobbled on his mountain bike, turning to give her the look. Katy smiled; she could still get some things right. Pushing Chloe ahead of her in the Eichhorn Designer pram, keeping her back straight, taking long strides with her tanned legs in the short skirt from Calvin Klein.

The sky was iceberg blue, no clouds. High up, over to the north, a pilot in a silent plane was laying down some lines of frothy exhaust, twisting and signing like an ancient Akashic script, intelligible only to a handful of initiates.

The smell of hops and male secretions from the bar of the pub wafted across the road. A weasel of a man was standing in the doorway ogling her. Thin moustache and eyes with a bedroom in each pupil. Hands moving deep in his pockets. Katy marginalized him by picturing him on the lavatory with his trousers around his ankles.

This is the place to be, she told herself. An urban jungle on the banks of the Humber. My home town.

She took advantage of a break in the traffic and crossed the road. The sun was hot on her shoulders and the back of her calves. The shadow of the tall trees edging the park didn't reach this side of the road. When she licked her lips they tasted salty.

They'd move away before Chloe was old enough to go to school. North Ferriby or Swanland, somewhere on the outskirts where you didn't meet a predator on every corner. They'd have moved before now if it wasn't for Daniel. He liked Swanland well enough but he wasn't too keen on the people who lived there. Said they seemed a little whiter than most white folk, made him feel blacker than his relatives.

But he wasn't serious. If there was some place he couldn't go Daniel was the sort who set his heart on it. Eventually they'd settle for one of those detached houses with a double garage, fresh turf in the garden and Canadian maple floors in all the rooms. Most of the people in the village would be dead but there'd be other young

49

people like themselves. Upwardly mobile but inwardly stable, with solid values. Strong and uncompromised. Like Daniel.

At least, he used to be.

The car drove past her and stopped on the far side of the road, and the man with the Panama got out and waited at the kerb for the traffic to thin, his eyes fixed on her, the skirt of his white raincoat flaring in the breeze.

Katy ran.

If she'd been alone she might have taken a chance on outrunning him. The man was carrying more weight than he should and Katy was fit and lean. But Chloe's pram was designed to attract attention rather than speed and as soon as the Panama man got across the road he'd close them down.

St Vincent's loomed up beside her like a huge guardian angel. She manoeuvred the pram around the iron railings and through the tall oak door into the silent stone interior of the building. Centuries of awe and reverence hung in the dim light as the rays of the sun were filtered through the leaded windows. She looked for somewhere to hide but was drawn towards the main altar with its embroidered cloth and single candle, like one of God's warheads.

'Katy,' said Father York as he stepped from the door of the confessional. 'And you've brought the little one as well.'

'Father,' she said. The word itself took some of the pressure from her.

He was looking at her hair, concern in his eyes.

Katy took a small coverlet from the pram and placed it on her head. 'Sorry,' she said. 'I wasn't thinking.'

His eyes were back in twinkling mode, fired by the everlasting power of convention and tradition. 'Is something wrong?'

'There was a man,' she told him. 'I thought he was following me. I didn't know what to do.'

Father York nodded meaningfully. 'You did know what to do,' he said. 'Who was the man? A stranger?'

'Yes,' Katy said with a sidelong glance at the altar. Telling lies in God's own house. A part of her expected retribution in the form of a thunderbolt straight out of Heaven. 'I've never seen him before.'

'Well, he hasn't followed you in here,' the priest said. 'I'll have a look around outside.'

'No,' Katy said. 'I'll light a candle, and I want to say a prayer. But if you'll come out with me when I leave? To make sure?'

The priest pursed his lips and nodded his head, fabricating a look of reassurance. He was young, thirty-five or thereabouts but with prematurely greying hair. He had modelled himself on the priests in Hollywood movies, adding a tone of gravitas to his words and casting around for and uttering phrases that seemed to belong to an older man.

The church exploded with echoes when the outer door was pushed open. Katy and Father York turned simultaneously to face the source of the sound. Katy feeling her heart racing, ready to back into a corner now, to fight to protect her child. Her sense of the building as a sanctuary evaporated; suddenly it was a stone trap, a place from which there was only one, inaccessible exit.

Adrenaline flooded her body. She could feel it oiling the joints in her calves and thighs and as it rushed to her head she was aware of it prickling her scalp. She drew the pram closer to her and was ready to pluck Chloe from within it. An unwanted and useless image of a baby hidden in bulrushes came to mind.

Katy and Father York stood and watched the door of the church as it slowly swung back into its frame. The click of the latch ricocheted around the walls. And there was no man with a Panama or a white gabardine raincoat.

'Strange,' said the priest. 'Must be the wind.'

She shrugged and kept her eyes fixed on the door as her heart slowed and her bodily systems went back to something like normal. There was no wind out there. It was a calm, warm and sunny day. The man had pushed open the door and backed off when he saw the priest.

'I'll check,' Father York said. 'Make sure no one's loitering around outside.'

Katy lit a candle and went to the front pews and crossed herself in front of the altar. She asked God to care for her daughter and her husband and she asked to be left alone to get on with her life. She promised to be a good Catholic if she could be freed from the attentions of the man in the Panama. She said she was sorry to have lied to Father York and that she would never do it again. She tried to say the novena but couldn't remember the words without beads.

51

It was different now, very different to when she was a child. Even when she was at university this communion with God had held more meaning for her. Slowly, almost imperceptibly, her faith had ebbed away. She believed there was something up there, something like God, but she could no longer accept the trappings of the Church. The Church had too many words, too much pomp and theology. God was a silent presence. He wouldn't have thrown up all that doctrine. The priests of the world had cultivated creeds, encouraged them to grow so thick along the way that their branches hid the face of the Creator.

Father York walked with her to the top of her street. 'I can assure you that no one is following us,' he said when he left her. 'Whoever it was has given up and gone home.' He paused and looked at the sky. 'We are always safe, Katy, when we walk in God's footsteps.'

It was the best way to think, Katy agreed.

As she hurried along to the house she glanced behind her from time to time. But no one was visible.

11

Reincarnation

Mort helped Ginner with an article they were uploading to www.whiteprojekt.co.uk. Ginner could have written the article himself, he knew all the arguments about how jigaboos and Pakis were mixing with white women and diluting the culture and the blood. But Ginner's problem was that he wrote emotionally. Everything he had to say was charged with passion.

'That's fine,' Mort told him. 'There are times when passion is all you need. In a fight, or if you're having an argument in a pub, then passion'll see you through. But as soon as you take the argument out of the street and put it in print, in a 'zine, say, or on the web, then you have to play it down. Emotion is something, it works in the voice, but in print what you need, what makes people think, is science.'

Ginner nodded, unconvinced. Ginner was technical. Without him www.whiteprojekt.co.uk would never have got off the ground. This was a guy who could write html, could produce a page of code that looked as though a spook had written it on acid, but when it was uploaded the code was transformed into colour and proportion and image. Designer stuff, nailed your eyes to the page; sweeter than Rita.

'Science?' he said.

'Yeah. Technical jargon instead of emotional language. People wanna hear about ethnic cleansing. Everybody understands what that means. And this piece here about how thick your average black is, that's the kind of thing you can say on the street, but when it's in print it's not enough. If you say their IQs average around seventy-five, which is about the same as a white defective, everybody'll get the message. You're dealing with people who can read, here, Ginner, you know, fucking thinkers, intellectuals, so you have to hit them with something they can relate to.'

'Yeah.' Ginner went along with it. They altered the text, chopped bits out and added phrases that Mort dictated until the article was finished.

Later they walked along Anlaby Road to the Cod for a few beers, taking up the whole of the pavement. Old folk and women, Mort would move aside to let them pass, but guys under about forty and anyone with a hint of colour would have to move onto the road or cross over to the other side. 'They don't have to,' he'd say. 'They can fight if they like.'

'That article,' Ginner said. 'I wanted to put something in about reincarnation.'

'Stroll on,' Mort said, leaning on the bar of the Cod and eyeing the barmaid. 'Why'd you wanna do that?'

'I saw this programme on the telly, and they've proved it now, that it's a fact. They've got people who were born in France in the fourteenth century. This geezer, he's born in Watford, somewhere like that, he's never been out of the country, and they take him over to France and he knows exactly where it is, the place he lived six hundred years ago. Get this, though, he wasn't a guy then, he was a woman. This château place, he remembers all the details, pear trees, loose brick in the barn where he used to hide jewels. She, I mean; she used to hide rings and necklaces. Row of mountains in the distance and the moon rises up between two peaks. And it's all there, still there.'

'Jewels?'

'No, the jewels were gone. Somebody'd had them away. Six hundred years, it's a long time to leave your jewels behind a brick. But everything else was there.'

'And what's that got to do with the IQ of your average Paki?'

'It's evolution,' Ginner said. 'It's the same as we believe in. You start off as slime, something like a fish, and then you go through loads and loads of different incarnations, and finally you come back and you're a full-fledged white man, a complete Aryan.'

Mort liked that idea. It brought a smile to his face, but he couldn't see a way of incorporating it into the piece they'd written about race and intelligence. 'We'll have to write another article,' he said. 'Draft it out and we'll have a look at it next week.'

The Cod was a good pub. Mainly guys in there, although some of them brought women along, their wives or their girlfriends. Saturdays, before and after the match, the home fans would get tanked up in there, ready for the idiots from Darlington or Lincoln or Southend who thought they could stick it to the Tigers.

Gaz arrived with a woman. He didn't introduce her and she stood, framed by the bar for a while, then moved over to a straight-backed chair by the table. She moved Mort's carrier-bag of grub for his mother, placed it under the chair. Tried to look cool, as if she wasn't self-conscious, but she kept touching her face, crossing and uncrossing her legs. Mort glanced at her several times before he realized that she was a few years older than he'd first thought. She was a thin, wintry kind of woman who seemed not to belong to her body. Her legs were skinny and her clothes threadbare. She had dyed her hair black and her eyes were hollow and her mouth slack.

Gaz wore a green T-shirt, which was too small for his gut and which rode up and bared his belly-button. When he supped from his pint he left a foam moustache on his upper lip. He shaved his head and had front teeth missing, but this didn't seem to stop him pulling women. He wanted to explain about AH's stomach problems on the website, which was the main reason that Germany had lost the war, because the Führer had had to hand over control to incompetents. And the stomach problems explained why AH lost his rag from time to time, seemed a little harsh in some of his responses.

Ginner said it wasn't up to them to apologize for AH. Their job was to point up the truths about racial questions, explain how liberal and socialist governments were betraying their people through open-door immigration policies, and reply to the lies and fabrications of the Jewish-owned media.

Mort looked at the woman Gaz had brought with him. She was rolling herself a cigarette, nipping off the strands of tobacco that hung from each end, and placing it between her lips. She looked up with her hollow eyes and Mort averted his gaze. She had the look of a woman who had been imprisoned. Someone who had been beaten. She was like all the women that Gaz picked up; there was the same feeling about her as the women that sit in shop doorways with a tin whistle and a puppy. But alongside that there was a hard centre like the glass of a mirror. She didn't receive the world, she reflected it.

Mort wondered what Alice would say if he took something like that home. She was so thin she could've hid behind a lamp-post. 'Jesus,' Alice would say, 'she's out of *The Night of the Living Dead.*'

Gaz and Ginner had progressed to an analysis of why the government had allowed the trickle of Slovak Roma to reach tidal-wave proportions. Ginner was saying they ought to declare themselves affiliates of Omega, work directly on the streets for the revolution. 'Begin our own ethnic cleansing,' he said. 'One street at a time.'

'Yeah,' Gaz agreed. 'Hoist the Union Jack over every street that's white. If there's no flag flying the street still needs scouring.'

Mort moved over to the woman and sat on the chair next to her. She looked at him and exhaled a stream of smoke towards the ceiling.

'What do you want?' she asked.

'I was gonna ask you the same,' Mort said.

'I don't want anything. I'm with Gaz. When he's finished here we're going down the marina and get shitfaced.'

Mort smiled. There was something about her accent, the way she said *shitfaced* that didn't ring true. If you saw her and didn't hear her speak you'd place her on a housing estate, maybe one of the high-rises on Orchard Park. But when she said *shitfaced* you had to reassess because there was some education in there, a bit of class. Something like the accent old Dr Wilkinson had; gave her a kind of authority, allowed her to control her environment.

He wanted to tell her that when she was finished with Gaz she could go down the marina with him and get shitfaced all over again. Gaz wouldn't mind because Gaz made it a rule never to get involved with women. Gaz only wanted her body, and when he'd had that he wouldn't see her again. Mort wanted all of her, but he couldn't think of a way of telling her. And, anyway, she'd think he was coming on too soon. Hell, he *would* be coming on too soon.

He looked at her silently and she smoked her cigarette and gazed at Gaz and Ginner on the other side of the table. Mort wondered if they'd met before, in some previous life. Perhaps that was why he felt so drawn to her, because in a fourteenth-century French market they'd got shitfaced together on raw wine. And as the moon rose between two peaks in the distance, they'd fucked wildly in the endless orchards of her father's château.

12

The Kiss

Katy watched a late-night movie about a cheesy young American scientist on vacation with a wide-eyed wife and two small children. A normal family doing normal things until the scientist discovers that alien beings are enslaving the inhabitants of the small seaside town. The locals don't listen to him, of course, and most of them are turned into automatons by the end of the first half-hour.

Katy watched it through to the final credits. She watched the scientist take his family off to the State capital and explain his theories to the Governor, then to Washington where he met the President and his advisers. The weapons of mass destruction were brought out by the military but the aliens had already infiltrated central command and no one was sure who could be trusted.

In the end everything was resolved somehow. Katy lost the plot or couldn't stay with the logic of it. But the young scientist and his family were victorious and the aliens got back in their spaceship and went off to terrorize another planet.

This is what frightens us now, she thought. It used to be that people were frightened of the animal in themselves, that the latent beast would suddenly be let loose. We went in fear of reverting to bloodlust. But now we fear alienation, that we shall have no blood, that we will turn into machines, lose our humanity to cold reason.

And there was something else about the aliens. They were a threat because of their intelligence, their advanced technology. After all, it was they who had the power to come to Earth, not us humans who went to them. We were frightened of intelligence. We lauded it, rewarded those who showed any semblance of it, but underneath we distrusted it, feared it, worried that it might lead us to destruction, annihilation.

But that wasn't new either.

Daniel was up at six in the morning and Katy heard him leave the house twenty minutes later. In her mind's eye she could see him starting the car and reversing out of the garage with a piece of toast and Marmite in his hand, crumbs falling into the crevices of the leather upholstery.

She catnapped for another hour.

When Chloe awoke, Katy dragged herself from the bed and lifted her daughter clear of the cot. Smell of ammonia, a hint of warm dampness and a genuine smile of welcome. Chloe was at the stage where a smile involved every muscle in her body; her eyes shone, her tiny fists curled up tightly and she lashed out wildly with both legs.

After breakfast Katy bathed and oiled her. She opened a packet of Pampers and when Chloe was dressed they went to Katy's room and looked through the wardrobe. She chose a white cotton blouse, sleeveless, and black culottes, which she'd found in a charity shop in Windsor. Her sole visit to a charity shop and she didn't think she'd do it again. The culottes had the label cut out but Katy was fairly sure they were Klaus Steilmann. It was a pity about the label, but as the girl who sold them said, it did mean that she got them for half their real value. Still, there was the nagging doubt that they'd originated in Marks and Spencer.

From its hiding place under a corner of the rug by her dressing table, Katy took the Compact Flash card and slipped it into her pocket. She carried Chloe downstairs and tucked her into her pram, manoeuvred it carefully through the front door and down the step. At the garden gate she looked both ways along the avenue, still expecting to see a raincoated figure watching the house. There was a grey car by the side of the road with someone at the wheel, but too far away to see who it was. There was a blind man with a white stick on the opposite side of the avenue and the sound of a woman calling for a cat down near the fountain. Katy couldn't see the woman, only hear her voice, high-pitched, pulling out the vowel sounds longer than necessary. T-i-i-i-i-i-imbo-o-o-o-o. Repeating it, phonetically perfect every time. T-i-i-i-i-i-imbo-o-o-o-o. Katy imagined Timbo listening to that, sitting immovably behind long whiskers, a dead thrush between his paws, forever on the brink of philosophy.

She dropped Chloe at the nursery in the park and noticed, as she always did, a vacant area in the pit of her stomach. There is a deserted plain, she thought, something like the landscape of a distant planet where a mother and child merge; where they are so close that it is almost impossible to tell the difference between them. At every separation from her daughter, Katy was faced with a dull ache, a non-specific physical symptom that left her incomplete.

As she left the park, a grey Maestro came from behind and pulled into the stream of traffic. Katy looked at it hard as it sped away, but couldn't decide if it was the same car that had been in her street earlier. Paranoia doesn't help you think straight. How many grey cars must there be in this city?

As she turned into the street where System.ini was located, Eve Caldwell was coming from the opposite direction. Katy got to the café first and stood by the door until Eve joined her. Stone Lewis was already inside, the warm aroma of freshly brewed coffee percolating through the building.

'Give us a few minutes,' Eve said to Katy. She handed Stone a CD and he smiled at her and put it in his jacket pocket. Eve grinned back at him and set about emptying the dishwasher. Katy took a chair at one of the terminals and looked at the blank screen. To her left she was aware of Stone getting three mugs from under the counter, pouring milk into a jug from a large plastic container.

'D'you want to turn that on?' he asked. Katy had to think for a moment, wondering what he was talking about. 'The terminal,' he said. 'D'you want to use it?'

Katy took the Compact Flash card from her pocket and held it between thumb and forefinger. 'Do you have anything that can read this?'

'Not here,' Stone said. 'Ginny's got a photo-reader on the machine at home.'

'But you must be able to do it yourself,' Eve said. 'You're a professional. Why have a digital camera if you can't read the cards?'

'I could do it at home,' Katy said. 'But I want someone with me when I look at them.'

'And Daniel couldn't be that someone?'

Katy shook her head.

'Daniel?' asked Stone.

'Katy's husband,' Eve told him.

'These are the pictures you took from the bridge, right?'

Katy fixed her eyes on Stone. 'Yes.'

'And you can't show them to your husband? Why is that? He's too sensitive?'

'He doesn't know anything about this,' Katy said. 'I don't want him involved.'

'You don't wanna involve Daniel, you don't wanna involve the police but it's OK to involve me and Eve,' Stone said, handing her a mug of coffee. 'I don't get it. What's on these pictures? What are they going to show us?'

'I'm not sure. I took a lot of shots of the man who was killed. I mean, before he was killed. Maybe there's a shot or two of the other man. The one with the Panama.'

'And the killing?' Stone asked. 'Did you get that?'

'I'm not sure. I can't remember. I saw everything, but it's difficult to separate what I saw through the lens and what I saw without it.' She sipped from the mug and put it on the desk in front of her. She looked from Stone to Eve, and then back to Stone. 'I don't know where else to turn,' she said. 'You're the only people I've told about this. If you see the photographs maybe you won't think I'm unhinged.'

Stone and Eve looked at each other. 'We don't think that,' said Eve. 'But you have to admit it's a pretty unlikely story. I think you saw something, Katy, I'm just not convinced it was a murder. Nothing's been reported.'

They both looked towards Stone. He shook his head. As if to say that from his point of view a murder in this city wasn't as unlikely as Eve seemed to think. 'Let's look at the photographs before we come to a conclusion,' he said.

Eve stayed behind to run the café and Stone borrowed her car to ferry Katy back to his flat on Spring Bank West.

This was a strange man, Katy thought in the car. She found herself again taking in the teardrop tattoo under his eye. Strange because the teardrop was not a work of art in any way. It was a teardrop by accident. The colour and texture were wrong and yet it remained a teardrop, couldn't have been anything else. An abstract or modernist teardrop. And in contrast the swallow on the side of his neck was a lifelike presentation; a miniature but proportionally correct representation of a bird.

Maybe they're not so bad, Katy thought, surprising herself, lingering in the trap between revulsion and fascination.

His flat – *their* flat, because it was here he lived with his Vietnamese girlfriend – was revealing without offering much comfort about the man. The walls were strewn with drawings and paintings, most of them unframed. Studies of birds and insects, representational but stylized. A huge green dragonfly with human eyes, a woodpecker clinging to the bark of a tree, a red ladybird with six spots on its back and the original of the swallow transferred to Stone Lewis's neck.

'These aren't yours?' she asked.

'No, they're Ginny's. I can't draw.'

'They're wonderful.'

He smiled, nodding his head, pleased on Ginny's behalf. The recognition of her talent was praise for him as well. Lost all his cool when he smiled. Became like a child.

The flat was immaculate. It looked as though no one lived there. Every surface was polished and there was nothing out of place. Was this him? Or the girlfriend? It was more like a room in a small institution than a place where someone lived.

He took the CD that Eve had given him and positioned it precisely on the shelf next to the stereo equipment. He placed it squarely, lining up the front of the CD cover exactly with the front edge of the shelf. *Abbey Road*, she noticed, the Fab Four on a zebra-crossing, Macca without shoes. Ancient music. Katy couldn't think of one song on the album. Her father would be able to recite them in order.

On the same shelf was a framed photograph of the girlfriend. Gorgeous. Young and lovely. Like God had spent an extra day on her.

Stone booted the computer and brought up another chair while the operating system loaded. 'You've got the card?' he asked.

Katy handed over the Compact Flash card and watched him slip it into the photoreader. He loaded a simple PD viewer program and glanced at her as the first slide came on the screen. She put her hand on the desk and moved into the chair. 'That's him,' she said. 'That's the man, just as I first saw him.'

The image on the computer screen showed a man sitting at a table outside the Euro Café. In the background was the Quayside pub with its Holsten sign on the corner of Posterngate. The man was thin, in his early twenties, and had a prominent nose with a hook. He wore a light-blue linen suit. The camera had caught him in the act of lifting the cup to his lip.

There were various shots of the man as he walked along Prince's Dock Street, past the Java restaurant and at the junction of Castle Street. In one of the photographs, taken from Humber Dock Street, the man was standing on the quay with his legs apart. Katy had caught a blue iron drifter called the *Daisy Patricia* in the gap between his legs. And further along the street there he was again, by the Green Bricks, glancing sideways at the shoulder-length auburn hair and backless blue dress of the mother of a toddler.

'D'you make a habit of this?' Stone asked. 'Following strange men around, taking their photographs?'

She shook her head. 'It was a new camera. I'd never used it before. I don't know what it was about him. He was different, out of the ordinary. There was something exotic about him.'

'Why do you say that? Did you hear him speak? Was he foreign?'

'No,' Katy said. 'I don't know.'

Stone clicked the mouse and the next frame came on the screen. 'That's the man in the Panama,' she said. 'I told you. The white raincoat, the hat, everything.'

'Except his face,' Stone pointed out. 'We can see what he's wearing, but he's facing away from us.'

There were more shots of the same scene but in each of them the man in the Panama was leaning on the cannon, facing away from the camera.

Stone clicked his way to the end of the slides, the last ones showing what appeared to be the hook-nosed young man slumped over the cannon. But there was nothing to indicate he was dead. The pictures looked harmless, could've been someone larking around. No matter how long you looked there was no evidence of gore hanging in threads from his head. Stone clicked back again to the picture that showed the rear view of the man in the Panama.

63

He zoomed in on his profile. The picture quality dwindled rapidly as the man's head and shoulders filled the screen. It was not possible to get a real likeness of him as individual pixels obscured his features.

Stone pushed his chair back and slowly zoomed out of the close-up, back to the original picture.

'What do you think?' Katy asked.

'There's been no reports of a body.'

'There was a body there, on the screen,' she said. 'You saw it.'

'Yes, I saw it, and your man in the Panama.'

She wanted to lean forward and kiss him. She'd lived with the knowledge of a murder and the possibility that she'd invented it. She'd seen the doubt on Eve's face the first time she'd mentioned it, and she'd entertained the idea that her sanity might be slipping away. And then in the breath that it took to utter one sentence Stone Lewis had colluded in her experience. Katy felt empowered. She wanted to get hold of the guy and crush him to her breast.

He was looking at her strangely.

'What?' he said.

She shook her head. 'Nothing.'

'You were going to say something.'

'I want to kiss you,' she said, leaning forward and kissing him full on the lips. 'Thanks for seeing it my way.'

Stone Lewis turned round on the spot. He put his hands in his trouser pockets and took them out again. He smiled and then stopped himself smiling. 'Shit,' he said. Then he laughed. His laugh echoed round the room, a touch of mania in it, somehow way over the edge of humour.

13

Adapt and Survive

Aunt Nell was standing by the Lump, the pet name for her Mitsubishi Shôgun, with Mrs Robson, her neighbour, and a couple in their early twenties. The young woman was nervous, her arms held closely to her body and her tongue flicking between her lips. The man was dressed in a light overcoat with an unusual check. He touched the woman from time to time, held her arm or smoothed her hair.

Stone listened to their accents, trying to place their origin, guessed somewhere in the Balkans, but couldn't be sure. He remembered that Mrs Robson's lodger had gone missing and thought this must be him, newly returned. With a woman.

'No,' Nell told him. 'This is Shaban's cousin and his sister. They're here to look for him.'

'You know Shaban?' the man asked. He spoke with a rough Slav accent, his black eyes scrutinizing Stone's face. Confrontational. The woman said something as well, but Stone couldn't make out what it was, a series of sounds, perhaps echoing her cousin.

'I didn't know him,' Stone said. 'I knew he was missing.'

'We have to go to the police,' the man said.

'I said I'd go with them,' Nell said. 'They're a little reluctant.'

'You don't like the police?' Stone asked.

'Police are no good,' he said. 'Serbian, English, police all over the world.' He drew a line across his throat with the index finger of his right hand. 'Police work for government, not for people.'

'Shaban is dead,' the girl said.

The man put his arm around her and held her close. 'All her family are dead,' he said. 'Shaban is all she has left.'

'We don't know that,' Nell said. 'Why would he be dead? Does he have enemies?'

'Serbs kill him,' the girl said, her voice muffled by the shoulder of her cousin. 'They kill all of us.'

'We are Albanian Kosovans,' the man said. 'Serb Nationals take our villages and our homes; now they want our blood.'

'We don't know he's dead,' Nell said, ushering them into the Lump. 'There could be a perfectly reasonable explanation. People do go missing from time to time, but they don't all turn up dead.'

She gave Stone and Mrs Robson a smile and closed the Shôgun's door. The Lump roared into life and Nell kept her foot hard down on the accelerator as it began to move forward in a series of lurches.

They watched it drive to the end of the street and turn the corner. Mrs Robson plugged her earphones in and hit the start button on her Walkman. 'Sorry,' she said to Stone, taking the earphones off and leaving them around her neck. 'Habit.'

'When did they arrive?' he asked, motioning towards the empty street as though the Kosovans were still there.

'Yesterday afternoon. They stayed in Shaban's room last night. She was crying all the time. I'd just drop off to sleep and she'd be at it again. Poor soul, having nobody left in the world.'

'Can't be easy.'

'No, it's terrible. Everything that happened to them. The soldiers walked into their house and fired bullets into the ceiling. Said they had to be out in five minutes. They all ran in different directions. Then they arrested the men; Shaban's grandfather was over eighty and they arrested him as well, said he was a terrorist. His sisters and his mother were raped.'

Stone sighed. 'Ethnic cleansing,' he said.

'Yes, that's what they call it. It sounds so harmless, like it might be beneficial. Spring cleaning. I thought it was a good thing for ages, until Nell, I think it was, explained it to me.'

'They don't want to give it a name that explains what they're doing,' Stone said. 'They'd have to call it "killing people from different races or cultures".'

'Is it about prejudice, then?' Mrs Robson said. 'They cause all that misery just because of prejudice?'

'It's the main reason,' Stone said.

'I don't understand it. Shaban is a nice man, his cousin and his sister are the same. Why do people want to cause them so much grief?'

They had walked to Mrs Robson's house and Stone would, unthinkingly, have followed her inside, but she stopped with her hand on the door handle.

'Race isn't a thing,' he said. 'It's an idea. It's always changing. It's an idea that happens at specific times and specific places. It happened in Kosovo and it comes here, to Hull, from time to time when an asylum-seeker is beaten up or a young black kid gets a kicking on his way home from school.

'It's taking place in government policy over immigration. It's an idea that arises out of political ideology or psychological patterning, out of economic recession or a naïve reading of history. It's an idea that sells newspapers and can be used profitably, and it has been used for millennia to make little people feel bigger than they are.'

Mrs Robson looked into his eyes. She waited to see if he was going to say anything else. 'Goodnight,' he said. 'I'll keep a look-out for your lodger. I hope he's still alive.'

'Thanks.' When she opened the door the scrubbed smell of an old marriage wafted through. She slipped inside and Stone walked back along the street, heading for home.

Masturbation is the main activity in prison. Everyone does it all the time. There is more semen produced behind the walls of Her Majesty's penal institutions than in all the brothels of the nation. One of the philosophers in Gartree maintained there was more of the stuff produced in that nick alone than in the legal marriages throughout the land.

But prison was a cage. From time to time during his eleven-year incarceration someone would lean forward and kiss him like Katy had done. It was never a woman and there was rarely a feeling that it was an act done in freedom. Usually it would be one of the older cons, probably out of his head on smack, hallucinating a universe of violent sexuality where blood and sweat and torn flesh took the place of tenderness.

It would happen without warning, in the stage-rooms or the khazi. A flash of movement out of the corner of your eye and suddenly you'd be pinned to the wall. A soapy con, stinking of snout, slobbering his north and south all over your face, his hands grappling at your balls and his fingers already climbing up your ass. If he had a tool or a friend you were fucked.

Stone remembered their eyes, the men who were hungry for any kind of sexual contact. After years of imprisonment and enforced celibacy the body's chemistry tends towards chaos. Dreams become a succession of carnal rite and orgiastic frenzy that leaves the waking man like a slavering beast. His eyes flit from object to object, from man to man, he is incapable of a panoramic view. His thoughts centre on his sex and the others around him become vehicles for sensation. He'll obsess at the lick of hair on a neck or the curvature of a spine. His mouth is dry and he walks the gangways hugging the edge. At that point the con's eyes say it all; for the touch of another's flesh or the illusion of sexual love he will not hesitate to take your life.

There was always Rule 43, of course, where a con could ask for separation because of vulnerability. When Stone had first been banged away, Rule 43 accommodation was reserved for nonces and baby-rapers. But during his term in the joint this had changed. Now the majority of Rule 43 prisoners were permanent check-ins because they were in debt to a face or a firm of smack dealers, and they may already have been glassed, or were waiting for a blade in the belly.

Stone didn't get protective status because he never applied for it. Whatever came at him he took in his stride. He had to adapt and survive, walk slowly, do his own time. He listened and learned. He had two blankets, one sheet, one pillow-case, two T-shirts, two pairs of jeans, two jumpers, two pairs of underpants, two pairs of socks, one pair of shoes, a toothbrush, shaving brush and a comb. And he listened all day and all night. His feet echoed on the long corridors of the wings he inhabited, and the walls of his cell whispered back to him every sound he made.

Listening was important. Like everyone else in the world Stone had begun listening in the womb. There had been the peripheral gurgling and sucking sounds as blood and lymph and other liquids and foodstuffs had travelled around his mother's body, but there had been the more reliable and soothing sounds of her body's rhythms, her breathing and heartbeat, her regular periods of waking and sleeping and eating and fasting, which in turn had reflected the movement of the earth around the sun. But after his birth Stone had forgotten about listening until the day they decided to put him away.

For most of his life he had paid lip-service to listening. He had listened but without hearing and the lessons that most people learned through their ears had passed him by.

But that was then. Now he was on the out and he was keeping his ears open and his nose clean. He had a job at System.ini, and a relationship with Ginny, and his mother and Aunt Nell were close by. He would never shake off the cage, the shades of the prison that had embedded themselves into the crevices of his consciousness. He would carry that around with him for the rest of his life. But he'd never go back there, not while there was breath in his body.

And then Ginny decides she has to go back to LA to see her ex-husband, Sherab, because she thinks he's liable to top himself.

OK, Stone can understand that. Ginny wants to avoid the guilt-trip. She does what she can. She gets on a plane and travels to the other side of the world, stays in the guy's house with him, which is the same house they lived in when they were married.

And Stone doesn't worry about these things? Yeah, he does. Stone would worry if she were going to visit her mother in Dewsbury – if she had a mother in Dewsbury, which she doesn't. He'd worry if she were going anywhere and not coming back the same day.

But she's going to the US of A on her own and staying with who she's staying with, and all that might imply, and the word 'worry' seems inadequate to describe how he feels. He knows he's begun the retreat into a cold consciousness, which is why he's resurrecting the time he was stashed away in the system. He adapts and survives. He knows how to do it; you see life through blinkers. You refuse to be side-tracked this way or that. You have time to do, time to get through until Ginny returns.

The last thing you want is some voluptuous, accident-prone blonde to start kissing your face.

Now Katy had gone he played it back as objectively as he could. It was a simple kiss, he told himself. It was connected to her relief in seeing the photographs, in having her memory of the man in the Panama confirmed. It wasn't specific, a kiss for him. Whoever had been there with her, when she went through that particular wave of emotion, would have got the kiss.

Good, so it wasn't a come-on to Stone Lewis. It wasn't a promise. It wasn't sexual.

Still, it was a kind of beacon. It's not an everyday occurrence that a woman like Katy Madika comes along and plants one on your face. A woman with a husband and baby.

One of the other things Stone had to remember was that he was free, on the out, but only on licence. If he got into trouble he could be locked away again, if the authorities felt like it, for the rest of his days.

The fact that he had some knowledge of a murder and hadn't gone to the police would be enough. His first reaction to Katy had been to keep her at arm's length, but in a couple of days she'd somehow wormed her way into his life. Now he had evidence of a crime on his computer, which, in the eyes of the law, made him complicit in it.

And the kiss. He couldn't shake it off. He couldn't convince himself that it was innocent. He couldn't be sure that he wanted it to be innocent.

Stone got a plastic bag and walked around the flat finding things he didn't need. He put a copy of *Happiness is a Warm Puppy* in there, 1962 edition. A paperback of Ted Lewis's *GBH*. A pair of scissors and a tall pale-blue bottle that had once been filled with liqueur and was never going to be made into a table-lamp. In the kitchen he found an RSPB knife with a corkscrew and put that in the bag. He added a spare computer mouse and a pair of Chinese acupuncture balls.

Then he put the bag by the door so he wouldn't forget to take it to the charity shop when he went out.

He flicked through the images saved on his hard disk. It was more or less how she'd described it. They were both there, the hook-nosed guy and the other one in the Panama hat. There was the cannon and the body slumped over it, and Stone had found something like blood on the cobbles at exactly the same spot.

The people she had described did exist. There was nothing conclusive in the photographs to say that one of them had killed the other. There had been no reports in the press to suggest that there had been a killing.

It was possible that Katy Madika was only half right. That she had seen what the photographs showed, plus the blood pouring from the hook-nosed man's broken head, but she had assumed he was dead when he was maimed. She hadn't stayed around long enough to see the guy get up and stagger off home to bed.

Stone didn't believe that, mainly because the man in the Panama had pursued her and stolen her camera. Anyone can imagine they are seeing a dead body, but it is not so easy to imagine your camera has been stolen. Either you have it or you don't. And Katy Madika had started that day with an expensive piece of equipment she no longer possessed.

Stone didn't intend to go anywhere with this. He'd told Katy she should go to the police, take the photographs with her and tell them the whole story. She'd nodded and focused somewhere in the middle distance, agreed that that was the only thing she could do.

She hadn't promised to do it, though, only to think about it again.

He flicked the radio on, tuned in to Viking FM and it was as if the news had been stored up in there waiting for him. A surgeon had been beaten outside his house in Cottingham. The man had lost several teeth, two of his ribs had been broken and there was a question about whether he would lose the sight in his left eye. The attack, which was unprovoked, was carried out by a man who had, apparently, been waiting for the surgeon to arrive home and park his car. Police said the incident had racist overtones as the attacker made repeated references to the white surgeon's Bolivian partner.

Stone Lewis listened to the broadcast and thought about Ginny, imagined her retreating into a dark cave of fear and anger. Racist violence was the only thing he knew that could reduce her to the condition of a small child.

She couldn't comprehend that there were people out there who found her union with Stone so disgusting, so unnatural that they were prepared to maim or kill. Mad people, sick people, ignorant or politicized thugs, it didn't really matter how you described them. The fact was that they were there. They existed in the world.

He took the *Abbey Road* CD and checked for 'I Want You'. He placed it in the player, selected track six and stood back to absorb the sound. That guitar opening you think is just dramatic, something to grab you for starters, is going to dominate the whole song. When Lennon's plaintive voice breaks through with those three words the spell is hypnotic. Three beats from Ringo and the guitar's there again. It was like hearing it for the first time. You know you're hooked and that there's no way out of the tautology of the sound unless you switch it off. But that would be ironic because Lennon's going to do that anyway sooner or later. Later. He has to, because he's trapped in there as well. A prisoner. This is not 'Hey Jude', there's no way you can fade it out. You have to kill it.

Stone played it another three times. He stretched out in the empty bed and let himself think he might never see Ginny again, imagining that she'd opt to stay with Sherab in Los Angeles. He hauled himself to the side of the bed and switched on the light. He got up and dressed and booted his computer. Spent the whole night long trawling through newsgroups and chat-groups, talking to people with names like Sergeant Walt, Black Mambo and Slicklipsbaby.

14

Casanova

Nell had been to Tesco in the Lump. When she returned, Heartbreak was on the doorstep. He came loping down the path and helped her unload the week's groceries, bread under one arm, potatoes and baby carrots under the other. On the second journey he carried a cardboard box of cans and frozen dinners for Sally. When he'd finished he slumped on the couch, his face slick with sweat. The sun was blazing, a brilliant arc over the sky, and Nell went next door to Sally's house to check she'd got the right things from the supermarket and to borrow a pair of shorts for Heartbreak. Sally, in face cream and curlers, a black satin slip and high-heeled mules, found a pair of shorts but couldn't remember who they belonged to, some guy, one of the never-ending retinue of wooers that, inexplicably, beat their way to her door.

Sally was on a new high protein diet, which seemed to Nell to defy the laws of nutritional science. She ate egg and bacon for breakfast with a couple of pork sausages, paid no heed to fat content for the rest of the day, and cut out carbohydrates. 'I've lost another four kilos this month,' she said, smoothing a hand over her flat tummy. 'I never felt so good in my life.'

Nell smiled and nodded. It wouldn't last. Her sister's problem was a bipolar disorder that had her beaming or screaming but left little time for the in-between stage most people spent their lives perfecting. Sally was normality-challenged. She'd lived in the shaded areas of existence for most of her life and she could tell stories about those realms like an old sailor.

One day she'd wake up and it'd be like the sky was full of stars, everything in the universe had a sheen to it, a sparkle. Every word she needed, it was instantly there and she heard poetry where everyone else was deaf. She didn't walk; she ran and skipped from one wonder to another. She lived in a magical landscape, which her sister imagined was like Disneyland, but real. Then the next day Sally would wake up and it had all gone. There would be nothing but gloom. The world was flat, without dimension, and the colours had washed out. There was no poetry or music apart from an atonal succession of high-pitched pipes, which made her screw up her eyes and place the flat of her hands against her temples. And she didn't skip, she didn't get out of bed because her legs were like lead.

Heartbreak looked ridiculous in the shorts. They somehow contrived to point up the fact that he hardly had a hair on his head. His thigh and calf muscles were reduced to string and his legs were so white they were almost transparent. Each of them held purple varicose veins and pink striations like the vapour-trails left by aircraft in the sky. It was something of a victory, though, because Nell had never got him into shorts before. She wondered if he'd worn them since he was a schoolboy. If he had been a schoolboy. Somehow she couldn't imagine that.

'I've been thinking,' he said. 'You know that thing we talked about, art and life. What art is and what life is and that Stanley guy who was feeling you up.'

'What about it?' she asked.

'Life,' he said, 'that's living from day-to-day. You get up in the morning and go to bed at night. You eat and talk and do your work. You have kids or you don't and get punched in the hooter and fall in and out of love and see some football matches. Then with art there's some extra added on. You put all those things together that make up life and you get something else that isn't life at all but maybe it makes life look as though there's meaning in it. Can be in a book or music or something like that, or it can be like a daydream.'

'Films?' Nell said.

'Oh, yeah, sure. Films, opera, all that stuff can be art. So they say, not that I go a bundle on opera myself, apart from Pavarotti. But there's smaller stuff as well, which is also art, because you hear people say, "He makes an art out of it". It could be a teacher, say, who makes an art out of teaching kids, or a cook who makes an art out of cooking sausage. I dunno about teachers. Maybe it's anything in the world, if you polish it enough so you can see your face in it, then it becomes art. Yeah, maybe teachers as well.'

'What about you?' Nell asked. 'What's your art?'

'I knew you'd ask that. I dunno about me, Nell. I've been busy doing other things. I've been dancing rock 'n' roll all my life. That should count.'

'What about women?' Nell said. 'You've always been a success with the ladies.'

'Leave it out, Nell. I went for half my life without a girlfriend.'

'And the other half?'

'There's been one or two, I suppose.'

'I'll bet there has.'

He went quiet. Picked up the morning paper and turned to the back page. Moved his lips silently as he read a story about a man who cost thirty million pounds and nearly scored a goal.

Nell went upstairs and changed into sandals and a pair of shorts of her own. She wondered how creative she had been since giving up her job as a promoter of rock 'n' roll and country bands. She hadn't thought about creativity or art at the time, just been glad of the chance of some time to herself. When she came back down she made a jug of orange juice and put a tray of ice cubes in it. He was still reading the newspaper, or at least looking at the pictures.

'Heartbreak,' she said playfully, 'how do you account for your success with women?'

'How d'you mean, Nell? Somebody been saying something?'

'No, not specially. But you've been around a while. The women at the rock 'n' roll club like you. You've had your fair share of girlfriends in the past.'

'Yeah? So?'

'Don't be defensive. I'm not getting at you. I find it interesting.'

Heartbreak gave her a silent stare. Then he looked away, got to his feet and walked to the back door where he leaned against the wall looking out at the garden. Red hot pokers and sunflowers, a beech hedge that needed pruning.

Nell waited. She reached for her sewing basket and picked up a cotton skirt that she'd found in a Scope shop, began unpicking the hem.

'First thing,' he said, speaking quietly, almost to himself, 'the number one rule is not to talk too much. That's where a lot of guys go wrong, they think you can do it with words, but you can't. It seems like it's working if you talk a lot, because most women like to talk, and they'll give you all the jaw back and you can be fooled into thinking you're on a winner. But women understand that talking isn't the same thing as seduction. Talking's what they do with their mates. Seduction's something else. You have to do it with your eyes.

'If you're going to entice someone you have to show her you can see her. The best thing is to try to see right through her, deep into her soul. You have to go down somewhere inside her that she is only half-conscious of herself. Try to see the person she suspects she might be, the person she could be if she could develop it.

'Number two is, you don't talk about yourself. That's the other place men get it wrong. They think they're so important, so fabulous that women are dying to hear about them, how great they are, all the things they've done, the money they're making, all the famous people they've met. But women aren't interested in that at all. Women are interested in themselves.

'So you talk about them. They love that, to hear what you think about them. And they love you to talk about their hopes, what they want to do with their lives. Their problems, they like that too, talking about their problems. Their kids if they're young women, or their ex-husbands if they're a bit older. What they've learned through rubbing up against life. They don't want advice about problems, though, just to get them out in the open.'

Nell poured two glasses of orange and brought one over to him. 'Do you tell the truth?' she asked. 'Or do you make it up, tell them what they want to hear?'

'The truth,' he said, smiling. 'Now we're getting to the nitty-gritty. You always tell them the truth. Except in two cases. If the woman is beautiful or if she's intelligent. Because with those two, if you're going to seduce them you have to make them feel insecure, uncertain. A beautiful woman, the last thing you do is tell her she's beautiful. You do that and she'll walk away. You'll've blown it before you start. They're sick of hearing people tell them they're beautiful, and the clever ones are sick of people telling them they're intelligent, so that's not going to get you anywhere. What you have to do is, if she's beautiful you tell her she's intelligent, and if she's intelligent you tell her she's beautiful.'

Nell snorted. 'That might work with a beautiful woman,' she said, 'but it'd never work with someone who was intelligent.'

Heartbreak shrugged. 'Works every time,' he said. 'I've never known it fail.'

'Men are such bastards.'

'That's the third rule,' Heartbreak said. 'If you're gonna pull women you don't have to be too nice. You don't have to go over-the-top nasty, but there's gotta be something about you that's on the edge. That's the case with most of the women I've met, Nell, they don't want nice, they want somebody who's a bit of a challenge, somebody they have to run to keep up with.'

'When you started I thought you might have something,' she said. 'But you're talking bollocks, now.'

'Hang on,' Heartbreak said. 'I haven't finished yet. You know who was the greatest lover in history?'

'Romeo?'

'No, Casanova. And you know what he said about this stuff? About pulling women? He said, if you want to seduce a woman the most important thing is to make her dream.'

'He told you that, did he?'

'I'm not that old, Nell. He wrote it in a book. His life story, about how he was a spy and he travelled round Europe and everywhere he went there was another woman. Eighteenth century, way back.'

'And you read the book?'

'I know a man who did. And another thing he said, Casanova. That it's always the guy who takes the lead in a seduction, but it has to be done in the right way. You have to be authoritative without being authoritarian.'

'That's difficult for most men,' Nell said. 'In my experience they're usually good at being authoritarian without being particularly authoritative.'

'I hear what you're saying,' Heartbreak said. 'But I'm going to ignore it. Something else, though. And this wasn't in Casanova's book. Most guys think if you're seducing a woman it helps if you've got a fat wallet, or if you can flash a bit of the green stuff about. They think if they can arrange to arrive in a little sports car, one of those two-seater jobs, open-top, they'll be sorted.

'But it's not true. I know everyone likes money, but in this area we're talking about now, it doesn't go very far. I know a bloke lives on Anlaby Road, down by the bridge there, hasn't worked since Harold Wilson's government and he never has a sou. But he pulls different women week after week. D'you know why?'

'Because he's sex mad?' Nell ventured.

'It's because he loves women,' Heartbreak said. 'That's the key. The main thing. To succeed you have to have a passion for women. These guys who are passionate about cars or football, whatever it might be, they're never successful with women. Women want to be loved first, they want to be number one, above everything else. That's what it's all about.'

'And men?' Nell asked. 'What do they want?'

'Hell, I don't know about men, Nell. You asked me about women and I've told you what I know, what I've learned over the years. Some of it might be right and some of it might be wrong. But I don't know nothing about guys. You'd have to ask a woman.'

'I'm asking you,' she said. 'What do men want?'

Heartbreak raised his eyebrows. Thought for a couple of seconds too long and messed up the timing. 'Gentlemen prefer blondes,' he said. 'But they'll take whatever they can get.'

'Look at you,' Nell said when Stone walked into the garden. 'Ginny's been gone, what, two days, and you've stopped shaving. You look as though you've been dragged through a hedge.'

Stone passed his hand over his chin. He nodded at Heartbreak and went to Nell, put his arms round her and gave her a hug, rubbing his face into her neck. She yelled and pulled away, holding him at arm's length. 'Keep your distance,' she said. 'You've got bristles like nails.'

Stone laughed and lunged for her again as she dodged out of the way. 'Go next door to your mother,' she said. 'Sally likes all that stubble and stuff. Wild men with whisky on their breath. I like 'em clean and smelling of aftershave.'

'I'll go home and scrape my face,' he said. 'Be back in about an hour.'

'No, you won't,' she said. 'Now you're here you'll stay for

something to eat. I'll bet you haven't had a cooked meal since she went.'

'How much? A tenner?'

Nell nodded. 'I'm not counting chips and beans,' she said. 'Or anything out of a tin.'

'No bet, then. I don't take money off old ladies.'

'Nell isn't old,' Heartbreak said, getting to his feet. 'She's not much more'n a girl.'

'I'm fifty-seven,' Nell said. 'It's old enough to manage you two and young enough to take on another one if I've a mind.' She walked towards the kitchen but stopped and turned at the door. 'And another thing,' she said to Stone. 'Your eyes are bloodshot and staring. If you don't eat and you don't sleep there'll be nothing left of you when Ginny gets back.'

'She's right,' Heartbreak said when Nell had disappeared into the kitchen.

'Shelve it,' Stone said. 'I'm trying to unload at the moment. I don't want people nagging at me.'

'You want some orange juice?'

'Yeah, that'll do for starters.' He waited for Heartbreak to pour the juice into a glass, then took a long swallow of it. 'Good,' he said. 'Just hit the spot. What d'you know? Anything new?'

Heartbreak put his thinking face back on. 'There's this guy gone missing, lodger of old Mrs Robson. Did you hear about that?'

'Yeah. He hasn't turned up yet?'

'He's disappeared. One day he was here, talking about coming home to dinner. The same day he doesn't turn up for dinner and she's seen neither hide nor hair of him since. His relatives think he's been bumped off.'

'I met them. Kosovans.'

'What's strange about it,' Heartbreak said, 'the guy had paid up front for a fortnight. He was some kind of civil servant over there, Kosovo, here on a language course, learning English. All his gear's in the house, his cash, his passport, photographs of his wife and kids. Didn't look like he was thinking of doing a bunk when he went out in the morning, so everyone's worried about him. I thought maybe he got a knock on the head, lost his memory. But they're convinced it was a Serbian plot.'

Stone looked at his glass. 'You got any more juice?'

Heartbreak showed him the empty jug. 'Nell'll make more if you ask her.'

'In a minute. I don't wanna get another earful.'

'So, what's happening in your life?' Heartbreak asked.

'Ginny's away. I got an e-mail saying she'd arrived, but I haven't heard anything since. She's staying with her ex-husband, so I'm jealous as hell. I expect she'll ring and tell me she's not coming back, then I feel guilty for not trusting her. Same time I've got this other woman, Katy, breathing down my neck, says she's seen somebody being murdered down by the marina. But Eve, you know, my boss at System.ini, she reckons Katy's unhinged, so I don't know who to believe.'

'Murdered? What, recently?'

'Couple of days ago.'

'First I've heard about it,' Heartbreak said.

'Yeah, that's the trouble,' Stone said. 'Nothing in the local press, no body in the river.'

Heartbreak shook his head. 'Stay away from mad women, Stone. Don't get involved.'

'I'm not. I want out. But she's a friend of Eve's, then I bumped into her by accident. It's a long story.'

Nell appeared in the doorway to the kitchen. 'There isn't any kind of romantic aspect to it, is there?' she said. She spoke quietly, her eyes fixed on Stone's face.

'Not on my part,' he said. 'She's interested, I think. Maybe not. Maybe I'm imagining it.'

Nell narrowed her eyes. 'Don't do anything you'll regret,' she said. 'Ginny'll be back soon, and she's expecting you to keep your zip up.'

Heartbreak said, 'The whisper of a beautiful woman can be heard further than the loudest call of duty.'

'Shut up,' Nell said. 'Nobody's talking to you.'

'It's not like that,' Stone said. 'I probably won't see her again.'

'Good. There's a fry-up on the table. Should be enough for both of you. I've made more juice as well. I'm going next door to see Sally; shall I tell her you're here?'

'Yeah. I'll call round before I go. How is she?'

'Weepy. Nobody loves her; the world's not on her side. It would have been better if she'd died when she was a teenager. Oh, yeah, and will I buy some poison for her.'

'Jesus,' Stone said. 'No change there, then.'

15

I Want You

When Nell returned, Heartbreak was sitting at the kitchen table with his head in his hands. Stone had washed the plates and left them to drain by the sink. He was standing at the end of the table singing 'I Want You (She's So Heavy)', the first part where the three words are repeated, pulling out the vowel sound in imitation of Lennon: *I want you-oo. I want you-oo-oo.*

He stopped and smiled when Nell entered the room. 'It reminds me of Sylvia Plath,' she said. 'Remember "Daddy"? The way she pulls out the oos?'

'Yeah,' said Stone. 'I remember you reading it to us. But I'd never've put the two together.'

'Lennon knew what he was doing.'

Heartbreak pushed himself back from the table. 'The Beatles is our generation,' he said. 'Me and Nell's. We all came from the same places, lived in the same world. We understood each other.'

'Lennon was dead before I really heard him,' Stone said. 'But there was a couple of years when I was about twelve, thirteen, me and Aunt Nell used to sing the songs. She'd play the piano and I'd try to get all those weird chords on the guitar.'

'Good days,' Nell said. 'But that song refers back to something by Dylan. Did you know that?'

'Yeah, "I Want You" from *Blonde on Blonde*. Very different. It's as if Lennon drags his song into the future, up through all the years he wasn't going to be alive. It goes through Punk and Hip Hop, all those fads and fashions, and settles down somewhere where hope and despair are too much for each other.'

'You're thinking about that scream halfway through?' Nell said.

Stone nodded. 'It's the only scream I know, recorded scream, that isn't faked. It comes out of every pore in his body.'

'Rock 'n' roll,' said Heartbreak. 'That's what rock 'n' roll is, a scream.'

'But Dylan had a rock 'n' roll band,' Nell said.

'No,' Stone told her. 'Not the same. Dylan is a lyricist, a poet, he's a musician who follows musical trends. Essentially he's a bluesman. Lennon comes from somewhere else; he's damaged, an abandoned child. When Dylan sings "I Want You" he's talking to a woman, he's singing a love song. But the *you* that Lennon wants is himself. It's himself and the Universe, it's justice and God. It's as if Lennon has reached out for the face of God and touched the hand of the Devil. He wants too much; the world he's inherited can never provide it. He wants his mother and his father and he can't have either of them so he wants to jerk-off the universe.'

'I sometimes used to think Stone had inherited the family gene,' Nell said to Heartbreak later.

'I thought that was the point of families,' Heartbreak said. 'Genes are what makes families in the first place.'

'Doesn't make them all good, though, does it? This manic depression that cripples his mother, he avoided that but it didn't stop him catching something else.'

'You think he's gonna end up like Sally?'

'No. He's got a different temperament. He'll never be like her. But I can sense it in him, the same kind of despair that she feels and the same kind of mad high. What Stone has is different. There's a dash of autism in it.'

Heartbreak went to her and put his hand on her arm. 'Sometimes you see things because you're looking for them,' he said. 'You know what I mean, Nell?'

She shook her head. 'I'm not telling you something I fear, Heartbreak. Stone has a special way of seeing the world.'

'It might not be as bad as you think, Nell. These things, they're not all the same. It doesn't mean he's gonna be like Sally.'

'I know, Heartbreak, but it does mean he's got to be strong. When you experience the world differently to other people it builds up

83

inside. Keeps everyone at arm's length. Sometimes seems like you're gonna burst.'

Heartbreak put his arms around her and crushed her to his chest. She looked up into his eyes. Old Father Time had left a footprint or two on his face. 'You trying to cheer me up?'

'Yeah,' he said. 'I don't want your jam pies to start leaking.'

Nell laughed.

Heartbreak said, 'Funny, eh?'

'A scream,' she told him.

16

Talking About Women

She was called Joolz. She had a bedsit on Beverley Road and she'd taken Mort back there and introduced him to her cat called Tilley and given him a cup of coffee with powdered milk, because the real stuff was for the cat, and asked him what was the most exciting thing he'd done in his life. Mort told her he hadn't done it yet. He told her when he'd done the most exciting thing in his life he'd have nothing left to live for and he'd top himself. Either that or he'd get to be thirty-five and then he'd top himself anyway, because he didn't want to get old and walk around with his mouth open and look like a berk.

She thought about it. She looked off into a space where there was nothing to see and nodded her head and fingered the hem of her skirt and a spot on her cheek twitched as if there was a beetle under her skin. But she didn't say anything.

It was as though she was waiting for something to happen to her. It could be that she expected Mort to come on to her, make his move, and she was waiting for that. But he wasn't sure. It seemed to him she was waiting for anything. Whatever happened next she'd be ready for it. Even if it was something she hadn't thought about, something unexpected, she'd readjust herself and turn to face it. She'd take it on.

This thing, this event she was waiting for. It didn't have to be something good or pleasant. But something, good or bad, something insignificant or memorable was going to happen next and Joolz was like a coil sitting there waiting for it.

'Nice place,' Mort said, looking around the room.

She smiled briefly. It was a bigger room that had been divided to make more money for the landlord. There was a plaster rose on the ceiling and the dividing wall went through the middle of it. A lethal-looking electric cooker stood alongside the sink and Tilley's feeding bowl was on the floor next to it. Water and sewage pipes ran around the base of the room and surface-fixed electric wires were loosely tacked to the wall up close to the ceiling.

There was a couch, which the cat had all but shredded, and a single dining chair neatly tucked under a bare wooden table. The bed was on the inside wall. It was unmade, the sheet wrinkled and grey, and there was a single dent in it where her body had been the night before. A large television stood at the base of the bed. Where the on/off switch had been there was a hole in the plastic casing.

No books. A single picture on the wall, of a Cossack in high leather boots. She had hooked up a line to dry her washing over the sink, one end tied to the window and the other connected to a bunch of electric wires. There were two pairs of knickers hanging there, one black and the other red.

'It's a room,' she said.

Mort thought she would ask him where he lived and he gave her a lengthy silence to let her get her mind around it. But she didn't come up with anything, carried on fiddling with the hem of her skirt. Gave a couple of sighs.

He couldn't take his eyes off her.

There was no Tesco store near her flat but she showed him where she shopped for herself and the cat. She followed him along the dusty aisles while he found bread and jam, biscuits and a reduced packet of doughtnuts. He put some dubious-looking pork-pies into the trolley but added two large chicken-and-mushroom pies as an extra treat. Ready sliced ham, individual cheese portions, and eggs, bacon, sausages and beans for breakfast. Two bottles of Bell's. A chicken, an onion, butter and double cream.

'I've never shopped that much in my life,' Joolz said.

'You haven't got a hungry mum at home,' he told her.

Gaz said, 'It was on the news this morning.'

Ginner said, 'A surgeon. He's in the hospital. He's lost an eye, had his teeth kicked out.'

'Broken ribs,' added Gaz.

'White?' Mort asked. He glanced over at Joolz who was sitting in a straight-backed chair by the wall in Ginner's room. He couldn't grasp what it was they were telling him.

'Christ,' Ginner said. 'The guy's married to a Bolivian woman. It was a warning. They told him he was diluting the blood of the race.'

'Oh,' said Mort, and he heard himself say it, a late dawning, as if he'd noticed it was daylight at midday. 'But who'd do that?' he asked. 'That's our job.'

Ginner shrugged. 'Somebody out there understands morality.'

Something cold ran up Mort's spine. Ginner could do that. It was the same when he'd been talking about reincarnation the other day. *Somebody out there understands morality.* It was the kind of thing you might expect to hear on BBC2 or Channel 4. You'd never expect to hear it in a guy's flat in Linnaeus Street.

He shouldn't have been surprised because of the three of them it was often Ginner who carried authority when it came to grey areas. Mort had the willpower and he was decisive and prepared to make things happen, but it was Ginner who could place them in the stream of history, who could explain how the prevailing political situation made their existence as a group inevitable.

Gaz was a storm-trooper; you wouldn't give him too much responsibility, and you'd always have to watch him. He was useful to have around but at the end of the day there was a part of him that remained uncommitted. There was a sense in which he would always be playing at it. Gaz was intelligent, though, there was no doubt about that. You had to be fairly bright to understand the arguments.

But it was Ginner who was the brains. Ginner could read books that'd put your average mind to sleep in about ten minutes. Fuckin' Homer, he'd read him, and Machiavelli and even David Irving. Ginner had a leather-bound copy of *Mein Kampf* that he read from beginning to end every year.

AH and his friends grew their own vegetables, Ginner had told them not long ago. They'd employed a gardener who planted and cultivated according to the positions and movements of the planets. The National Socialists in AH's Germany lived on food that incorporated cosmic powers. The ancient gods looked down on a race that was unadulterated and that was constantly renewed by the purifying powers of the universe.

Mort and Ginner and Gaz had agreed to get an allotment so they could experiment with growing 'revolutionary' food, but Mort, who had been nominated for the job, had not yet got around to filling in the council's application form.

'Get rid of the slag,' Gaz said, glancing at Joolz.

'Why?' Mort asked defensively. He didn't like Gaz calling her a slag. The slur went beyond her somehow, included Mort himself. But for Mort to take on a defensive tone against Gaz and in favour of an outsider, a woman at that, was unthinkable.

Gaz and Ginner looked at him. Neither of them spoke. For a while it was as if all the frozen spaces of the universe had invaded the room. Mort fancied he could hear the chink of ice forming in the breach between his friends and himself.

'Business,' Ginner said, his voice almost a whisper.

'Yeah,' Gaz echoed. The tremendous violence that was always present with Gaz expressed itself in a monotone, which faded to the murmur of a breeze. When this was past he would erupt into uncontrollable rage.

Mort looked at Joolz and tossed his head in the direction of the door. 'I'll see you later,' he said.

'What time?' She got to her feet. 'Where? What's going on?'

He bundled her out of the door. 'Save the questions,' he said. 'It's nothing to do with you.'

He closed the door in her face and she kicked against the wood. 'Christ sakes,' she shouted.

Mort stood with his back to the door, facing Ginner and Gaz. Gaz had his eyes closed and Mort prayed that Joolz would not kick the door again, not shout anything else. *Be quiet*, he said inside his head. *Don't make another sound.* He could envisage Joolz hammering at the door with her fists and Gaz striding across the room, opening the door and slamming his massive knuckles into her face. Joolz tipple-tailing down the stairs, the bones of her legs and spine cracking as they encountered the edge of each tread.

But Joolz wasn't stupid. She knew how far she could go. She'd had a lifetime of men like Gaz, years and years of experience, and even if she hadn't, if she'd never encountered a Gaz before, she'd still know not to push it. That was the class she had, the part of her that made her different to other women.

Mort exhaled as he listened to her steps on the thin carpet of the stairs. He waited for the outer door to slam, but it closed quietly behind her, an almost imperceptible click as the tongue of the Yale slid into place. Gaz shook his head and Mort remembered what it was about him; Gaz had far too much to prove and not enough time to do it. If he lived for a hundred years it wouldn't be long enough to justify his existence.

Ginner said, 'Women: you can't live with 'em and you can't live with 'em.' It was enough to break through the crust of hostility between Gaz and Mort, bring all three of them back together again. The three musketeers they'd been at school, and still were in a way, all for one and one for all, even though adulthood had brought a different face to their union. The fissures that separated them, one from the other, were now more apparent, each in his way driving the others to the extremes of their character. What had once been the bond of similarity between them now revealed itself as a series of complementary distinctions.

'What's the business?' Mort asked as they sat at the table.

Ginner tapped the side of his nose with his index finger. 'We've been approached by Omega,' he said.

'Who?' asked Gaz.

'No name, just a phone call. They want to meet.'

'When?' Mort asked.

'Soon as possible.'

Mort and Gaz exchanged a glance. 'Set it up,' Gaz said. 'We could use some excitement round here.'

'Tonight,' Ginner said. 'Here; eight o'clock?'

Mort nodded agreement. He wanted to meet with Omega as much as Ginner and Gaz, he only wished it was another night. There might be time to get to Joolz's flat before the meeting, straighten things out with her. But to fit it in he'd have to rush through his time with Alice, piss her off. Still, that was life. Somebody had to suffer.

He wasn't too sure about Omega contacting Ginner either. Gaz was the weak link of the group, so it would've been worse if they'd contacted him. When he thought about it he couldn't remember any of the rightist groups contacting them through Gaz. But approaches from outside usually came through Mort. They'd contacted Ginner because of the website.

Maybe it was a set-up? Special Branch trying to infiltrate? But Gaz and Ginner would be aware of that possibility. Nothing incriminating would be said at the first meeting.

Gaz came over and put an arm around his shoulder, crushed hard. 'She's a waste of time,' he said. 'Shit for brains.'

Mort grinned. That was what you said about women. It was a joke but it was serious as well. He kept the grin going as he wondered how some people could put words together that didn't have an answer. And it wasn't because the words were true, that they expressed something that was unanswerable; it was more that the words were a trap, if you disagreed with them you'd be exposed as a fuckwit.

17

Omega II

Ginner had hung the Union Jack in his room. Took up the whole wall, made you blink when you came in. And he'd swept the carpet, given it a good going over, so all the dust that had been trapped in there was now hanging in the air of the room. You couldn't see it, but you breathed it in, made you feel like an idiot with asthma. Mort found himself coming with tiny wuss-like coughs until his lungs got used to it.

The PC was switched on and the opening page of the whiteprojekt website with the Union Jack and a pair of boots was facing out into the room. Ginner's crash helmet was standing on top of the monitor, the goggles propped on the front like huge eyes. Ginner had combed his hair and put on a clean T and a new pair of black jeans. He'd cut his top lip shaving and had a piece of bog-roll stuck to it, a tiny speck of blood showing through. 'What d'you think?' he asked, gesturing at the room. 'Clean, eh?'

''Peccable,' Mort told him. 'Looks like you've had a woman in.'

Ginner reddened a little, smothered a smile of pride.

Gaz sat stiffly by the side of the computer. He was wearing a black shirt and a sleeveless black leather jacket with a sheepskin lining. Streams of sweat were oozing from his shaven head, converging around his nose and mouth. 'Fucking hot, though,' he said when Mort caught his eye.

'You could take the jacket off,' Mort told him. 'It's a warm night.'

Gaz snorted but didn't move.

Mort looked in the mirror above the mantelpiece. He hadn't thought to change his clothes, do anything about his appearance. He didn't look too bad, though. He'd had a shower a couple of days ago, so at least he was clean. The swastika stud above his eye was slightly understated, better than the eagle for a meeting like this. When the Omega people arrived they'd see somebody who was at home on the street, a man unafraid to make a statement and defend it.

'Got a comb?' he asked. He took it from Ginner's outstretched hand and pulled it through his mop. Didn't make much difference, though, so he ran it under the tap, wetting the front of his hair and plastering it down to the side. Made him look like a young AH without the moustache and with a swastika stud above his eye. Mort and Gaz both believed AH would have gone in for piercing if it had been fashionable back then.

He wouldn't have used television, though, no matter how good the technology. Kennedy, Clinton, guys like that came over well on television; modern politicians knew how to use it to pull the wool over everyone's eyes. But AH needed to be seen in the flesh. He would still use the big rallies, somewhere he could project his voice and his body, his charisma. Ginner didn't agree with that, he thought modern technology should be used by the revolution. All the little people used it to their advantage. 'If we don't use it, we'll be left behind,' he'd said. 'Look at Haider's Freedom Party. It worked for them. And for Jean-Marie Le Pen in France.'

This discussion had led to the establishment of www.white-projekt.co.uk.

'Time is it?' Mort asked.

'Ten to,' Ginner said, glancing at his watch. 'They'll be here soon.'

Mort looked at Gaz, the sweat now pouring down his face. 'Christ sake,' he said, 'Gaz, you're not gonna make it through the night dressed like that.'

Gaz looked down at himself. 'What's wrong? My best shirt?'

'You're dripping, man. That jacket's for winter. You look like you're going on a Polar expedition, Scott of the Antarctic, something like that.'

Gaz looked at Ginner for help, but Ginner shook his head. 'He's right, man, you look like you're melting.'

'Fuck,' Gaz said, getting to his feet and pulling his jacket off, throwing it on the floor. He unbuttoned his shirt and tried to slip out of it, but it was stuck to his arms with sweat. He peeled it off and hung it over the back of a chair. 'Two minutes till they get here and now you tell me.' He went to the sink and ran the cold tap, stuck his head under it.

There was a knock on the door and Ginner got to his feet. He smoothed down his T and went to answer the door as Gaz surfaced, his eyes closed, groping for a towel.

The guy who came into the flat was about fifteen years older than Mort. There were two things about him. The first was that he was alone. Ginner let him into the flat and poked his head around the door, see if there were more of them, then drew his head back inside and closed the door after him. Ginner's leathers were on the back of the door and they looked like a guy for a moment, swinging back and forth. The second thing about him, the stranger, was that he had two vertical scars, one on each cheek, which looked for all the world like the scars you see on some coons, the ones fresh out of the jungle. Their mothers or the witchdoctor do it to them, God knows why, keep evil spirits away or some such mumbo-jumbo.

The guy was solidly built, not big, but what there was of him was muscle and bone. He was one of those guys you could be taken in by at first, imagine he was a bantam-weight. But when you looked again you'd see he was light-heavy, might even go into the top rank if he dieted on organ meats and protein. Plus he wasn't just well-built, this was someone who worked at it, kept himself toned. His body was important to him; strong legs to take him away from trouble and sinewy, muscular arms to dish it out.

He was sharp, too. Eyes as skinned as a bird of prey. He took in the room, compartmentalized everything with a couple of glances. He assessed the weight and intentions of Mort and Ginner and Gaz, and placed himself in a position where he could see them all. Within a few seconds, before anyone spoke, he dropped his shoulders and smiled, relaxed into the environment, and he did it with such charm and presence of mind that you forgot he'd been on guard when he entered.

'Warm night,' he said as he watched Gaz struggle into his leather jacket. Gaz had left his shirt on the back of the chair, so his arms were bare and he looked cooler, though a couple of drops of water still clung to his chin.

'Yeah, I'm Ginner,' said Ginner, offering his hand. 'This is Gaz, and this is Mort.' The guy shook their hands, though Mort felt it would have been better to give him a high-five. Looked like the kind of man who would appreciate that. Someone who understood and appreciated convention, but who would side-step it with an easy nonchalance.

He looked into Mort's eyes but spoke to them all. 'Call me Omega,' he said. 'The less we know about each other the less we can tell.'

You listened to every word. There was some kind of accent there, but it wasn't easy to place. Not a million miles from Australian, but you wouldn't put money on it. What was compulsive wasn't the accent or the tone or timbre of the voice, it was more the way he put the words together, the spaces between them, which were longer, more jagged than normal speech. It was as if he had a thought between every word, like he was chewing the next one, thinking maybe he'd send the sense of it in a different direction. If you didn't pay attention, concentrate on what he was saying, you might lose it altogether. And you didn't want to do that.

'We expected a group,' Mort told him. 'We thought it was a meeting.'

'Just me this time,' said Omega with a voice like bitter coffee. 'If we come to a working arrangement you'll meet the others.' If you'd been able to touch the sound it would have been like that shirt of Alice's, the material so close you couldn't imagine it ever being woven. Mort used to have a shirt, couple of years back, chestnut brown, warm as soon as it touched your skin. That's how the voice got you, like a day in autumn when the sun thinks it's still summer.

Absurdly, Mort wished that Joolz could be here to share this time. Alice, too. Without being able to put his finger on it, there was a glut of meaning; as though the event needed more people around it than Ginner and Gaz. It was lonely, like Bethlehem without Jesus.

They arranged themselves around the table. 'The surgeon in Cottingham?' Ginner said. 'Was that you?'

Omega touched his nose with the forefinger of his right hand. 'We have been active in the area for a few days,' he said. 'Now we are looking to recruit local groups and individual lieutenants. We need people with a developed consciousness who are, at the same time, willing and prepared to take direct action.'

94

'That's us,' said Gaz.

Omega looked across the room at him. 'We're not concerned with bricking the windows of a few Pakistani families,' he said. 'Casual harassment like that has been tried for years, to no or little effect. We were involved, some of us, in the fire bombing of Turkish hostels in Germany, and it is more this kind of direct action that we have in mind.'

He used the whole word, *Pakistani*, short first vowel, the penultimate one long and drawn out, the word transforming itself into a term of abuse as each syllable freed itself from his lips, relegating the diminutive and well-used *Paki* into a form, almost, of endearment.

'In the short-term we're targeting mixed-race couples, either partner, sometimes both. Leave the black and Asian communities alone for now. We can take them anytime. For the moment we concentrate on the single issue.'

'There's a black kid we're on to,' Ginner said, 'been fucking his teacher.'

Mort looked at Gaz but Gaz had already assimilated the fabrication. The black kid had been accused of fucking his teacher and was, therefore, guilty. He was guilty because he might be fucking his teacher, and he was guilty because you could bet all the money in the world that there would be a black kid just like him somewhere who was actually fucking his teacher.

Mort wasn't shocked or outraged on behalf of the black kid, or on behalf of any half-baked liberal ideals of truth or justice. He simply noted that Ginner had moved the argument on. Instead of saying that the black kid *might be* fucking his teacher, he had taken away the doubt. What Mort noted was a trick; how if you take something away from or add to a collection of sounds you affect what happens next. If Ginner had said the black kid *might* be fucking his teacher they'd have had to find out if it was true, but as it stood he was damned.

'Interesting situation,' said Omega. 'We take the kid or the teacher; it really doesn't matter. The final decision will depend on which one of them is easiest to get at.'

'When you say we take the kid or the teacher,' Ginner asked, 'what do you mean?'

Omega's smile came into play again. 'Nothing complicated,' he said. 'We keep it as simple as possible. We break bones, we crack heads. We draw blood.' He fingered the scar on his left cheek. 'We disfigure. It's an old recipe but it works surprisingly well.'

Ginner laughed and Mort joined him, both of them tickled by the simplicity of it. It was Gaz who asked the question that neither of them would have got around to. 'That what happened to you?' he said. 'The scars on your face?'

Omega turned in his seat so he was sitting squarely in front of Gaz. He shook his head from side to side. 'These are not battle-scars,' he said. 'They are more in the way of an education. You could call them the scars of a past life.'

'Reincarnation?' said Ginner.

'No,' Omega said. 'More to do with youthful enthusiasm. Idealism. It's a long story, but I'll tell it if you like?'

Ginner nodded. The others didn't say anything but Gaz shuffled forward in his chair and Mort had a vision of a campfire, everyone gathering round to listen to an elder or a storyteller. Someone who carried the collective consciousness of the tribe, the racial memories of a people.

'He saw that those people, the natives in Africa, were shaped by primary and irreducible forces,' Mort told Joolz later.

'What does that mean?'

'Primary forces, it's the landscape, the weather. And he saw that they could only handle one thing at a time. Europeans take it for granted that we multi-task. That's the difference between us and kids. Kids just do one thing at a time, but grown-ups handle lots of different things at the same time.'

'Women are multi-tasking,' Joolz said. 'That's what I've heard.'

Mort looked at her. She'd been drinking, that's why she had so much to say. 'D'you wanna hear about this guy or not?' he said. 'If you want to interrupt all the time that's great, we'll talk about something else.'

'I was just saying,' she said. 'I thought it was a discussion.'

They were in Joolz's flat and they could hear the traffic in the street below, the occasional late drunk trying to stay with the melodies in his head. There was some kind of scent in the air, turned you on, made you feel like there could be something else in life that you'd never really suspected.

The chicken had been cooked and left to go cold. Mort had chopped it into tiny pieces and removed the bone, left it piled up on a breadboard on top of the cooker. Joolz's cat was interested but too frightened of Joolz to get close to it.

Mort took a breath. 'They develop until they're about twelve,' he said. 'Then they stop. So they're always like children. If it wasn't for us going out there, showing them how to live they'd probably've died out.'

'So how did he get the scars?'

'I was coming to that. It was an initiation. This is before he realized they were a dead culture, that they didn't have any future. He volunteered. He wanted to be like everybody else in the village, so he asked them to cut his face.'

'Sounds like a nut.'

'Something he had to go through, he reckons. Without the scars he might never've found his way to the movement. That's how destiny works. It's like with Nietzsche.'

Joolz got off the bed; she took the pink bogroll off the top of the television and left the room. Tilley followed her. Mort moved over to the cooker and removed the breadboard with the chopped chicken. He put a sliced onion in a pan with the butter and slowly added the chicken.

It was true what the guy had said. Scars were what education was about. Real education left scars behind. You couldn't always see them, they weren't necessarily on the surface. But if you'd been through the mill, if you'd learned something in life, there would be scars there, maybe just under the skin, or deep down inside where nobody else could see them but yourself. A scar was a kind of decoration, like a medal. It showed that you had faced the enemy and come out alive.

Until today Mort had been unable to see the future. He had suspected that he would be involved with greatness, but his suspicions were tinged with uncertainty. Now there was no doubt; the road ahead, with Omega in the driving seat, led all the way to Glory.

When she came back Joolz returned the roll of paper to the top of

97

the television and slumped in a chair. She said, 'I wouldn't let no natives go to work on my face.'

When everything in the pan was cooked Mort turned the heat down and added the double cream. 'I used to make this with chicken livers,' he said. 'But there was never enough for Alice, so now I use the whole chicken.'

He removed the pan from the cooker and brought it over to her on the bed. 'Smell that,' he said. 'Good, eh?'

'It's a lot of dip,' she said.

'Alice is a big woman,' Mort said. He smiled. 'This is one small dip for my mam, but one giant dip for mankind.'

18

The Full Breakfast

Phineus Marman opened the door of the British Breakfast Café and stepped inside. He paused there, waited until everyone in the place had a good look at him. As he glanced from table to table, the eyes that had registered surprise looked away. They got used to it, adjusted quickly. It was only an old black man coming in. Not a threat.

Heartbreak waved from his table by the window and Phineus squeezed his way between tables and chairs. Madonna's 'Crazy for You' was coming out of two speakers above the counter. A couple of people edged their chairs in so Phineus could get past. Heartbreak was on his feet, extending his hand as Phineus arrived at the table. 'Hi, man,' he said. 'How you doing?'

'Bearing up,' Phineus told him. 'Keeping on, keeping on.' He grinned.

'How's Palesa?'

'She's never gonna get better,' Phineus said. 'I dunno if she knows who I am some days. It's like visiting another planet.'

Heartbreak shook his head. 'That's hard. Give her my love when you see her.'

'I'll mention your name. She likes you.'

'She's a good-looking woman, Phineus. I miss seeing her around. How's young Chaz? What's he up to?'

A waitress with steamed-up spectacles arrived at the table and brushed a wisp of hay-coloured hair from her eyes. She was sixteen trying to look twenty-four and getting more than halfway there. She glanced from Phineus to Heartbreak but didn't say a word. She placed her pad on the table and hovered over it with a stub of pencil.

'Yeah, I'm here for the full breakfast,' Heartbreak said. He looked at his friend. 'What about you?'

Phineus hesitated, glanced around as if his mother might be watching, though she'd been dead for twenty years. 'Make it two,' he said. 'Toast and fried bread on the side. Big pot of tea.' He looked at Heartbreak and grinned. 'Hey, why not?'

The waitress drew some Egyptian hieroglyphs on the pad and slipped away.

The two men looked at each other.

'Chaz?' Heartbreak prompted.

'He's fifteen. A good kid. You remember what it's like when you're fifteen? You're a scab on the face of the earth. But he's dealing with it. He'll be OK if he gets a couple a chances.'

They both fell quiet. Phineus closed his eyes and tapped his fingers on the tabletop as Janis Joplin's 'Summertime' eased itself out of the speakers. Heartbreak watched him for a moment then took a breath. 'On the phone you said the kid was having trouble.'

Phineus opened his eyes. He said, 'Racists.' The word was half whispered.

'At school?'

Phineus shook his head. 'On the street. Beverley Road.'

'When?'

'Couple'a nights back. He wasn't hurt. Somebody disturbed them. But it was ugly, could've got bad. They was prowling the streets. They mentioned Omega.'

'That a fascist group?'

'Terrorists,' Phineus said. 'They want to kill a few black people, so the rest of us get the message.'

'Killing doesn't work like that,' Heartbreak said. 'You get a taste for it. After the first couple of times you can't stop.'

'They're scum,' Phineus said. 'They frightened the boy bad.'

'How's he taking it?'

'I can't let him out until we've stopped them.'

'How many?'

'Three, maybe four.'

'We know where they live?'

Phineus shook his head. 'I'm working on it.'

'Your brother Mike up for this?' Heartbreak asked.

'Yeah, and the brother-in-law, Little John.'

Heartbreak nodded. 'Count me in, and I'll bring Deke along. Maybe Stone. I'll see, he's under the weather at the moment.'

'Deke?' Phineus said. 'Does he still get about? How old is he?'

'Sixty-five,' Heartbreak said. 'Few years older than me. But he's always game for a rough-and-tumble, you know that.'

'Five of us should be enough,' Phineus said. 'Better if it was six; these guys are young, big strong 'uns according to Chaz.'

Heartbreak sighed. 'I'll have to bring me baseball bat,' he said.

Heartbreak tucked in as soon as it arrived but Phineus gazed down at his plate as if it had fallen from the sky.

'Something wrong?' Heartbreak asked through a mouthful of sausage and fried bread.

Phineus shook his head but continued looking at the plate piled with sausage, bacon, mushrooms, eggs, beans, tomatoes, black pudding, buttered toast and fried bread. 'I don't remember the last time I had a breakfast like this,' he said. 'Must've been before I got married.'

Heartbreak raised his eyebrows. 'A man needs to eat,' he said, ripping a slice of bacon apart with the urgent pleasure of a wildcat at a kill.

Phineus sliced the end off a sausage and tentatively dipped it in the yolk of an egg. 'We've always avoided fatty foods,' he said. 'Palesa reckoned the best way to eat was to chew each mouthful fifty times. You drink your food and eat your drink, that's what she told us. Eating meat was an attempt at suicide.'

Heartbreak reached for another slice of bread. 'Y'know what gusto is?'

'Yeah, watching you go at that lot I know exactly what it is.'

'There's no health police in here,' Heartbreak said. 'You can relax and enjoy yourself. If you eat what you like and don't worry about it your body'll digest everything like it's supposed to.'

'You a dietician or something? Nutritionist?'

Heartbreak shook his head. 'Naw, they're all fascists,' he said, 'people who tell you you can't digest sausage meat. I've lived for sixty-two years and I never listened to one of them. All my mates've been dropping dead the last twenty years, or they've got diabetes or cancer or something and can't come out to play. They've been living on yoghurt and fucking sprouts and squealing every time they seen a steak, and where's it got them?'

Phineus shook his head. He said, 'Feels like you're gonna tell me.'

Heartbreak went back to his plate. He demolished a tomato and scooped up some of the mushrooms on a piece of toast. Phineus waited. Heartbreak took a mouthful of bacon and a glistening sliver of egg-white. He reached for his cup and took a mouthful of tea.

'Listen,' he said. 'These people who tell the rest of us what to eat, they change their minds every year. As soon as they've got us convinced something is bad and killing us they do more research and find it's got wonderful healing qualities and we can't live without it. Then they pick on something else. That's the one thing. The other thing is they act as if we're not omnivores – you know what that is?'

'Omnivore?' Phineus said. 'Somebody who eats everything.'

'This is our species,' Heartbreak said. 'This is how we've evolved. We eat everything that's available. This is one of the advantages of being human. Our bodies choose what to reject and what to use. All we have to do is eat as wide a variety of things as possible and our bodies do the rest. If you need vitamins and not so much protein today your digestive system'll get rid of the protein and hang on to the vitamins. Tomorrow you'll need a different mix, but you don't have to worry about it. Your body knows.

'If you sit on the edge of a chair nibbling at a fat-free biscuit and wondering if it's doing you any good, your body thinks you've gone crazy. Y'know what it is, eating like that? It's nervous tension, and y'know where that leads?'

'Where?'

'Cancer.'

'So what you're telling me,' Phineus said, glancing round the café, 'is this is the healthiest joint in town.'

Heartbreak nodded, his mouth full of protein. When he'd cleared a little of it he held up a finger and said, 'One proviso. You need exercise. You can eat here every day if you like, but you have to walk here and walk back home again. And then take some more exercise.

Me and Nell, we go dancing twice a week. If you eat and don't have exercise you'll blow up like a balloon.'

'No,' Phineus said with a twinkle in his eye. 'Well, I'll be damned.'

'Most of us are,' Heartbreak told him

A little after nine that evening, Phineus Marman went out of the house, leaving his son, Chaz, slumped in front of the television. Chaz's schoolfriend, Mercy, had called round and the two of them were watching a one-star film on Channel 4. Actors from Hell and dialogue bad enough to strike a man dumb.

Phineus walked along Fountain Road and crossed over to Margaret Street. He stood on the corner, hands in his pockets like he was waiting for a woman. He stood there for fifteen minutes, shifting his weight from leg to leg, then he turned and walked along Beverley Road as far as Cave Street, eyeing his own reflection in the shop windows. Looked good for his age, slim and straight, still had a spring in his step.

He walked down Cave Street and along Park Road, ending up on Margaret Street, taking the same route Chaz had taken a couple of days earlier. *This is me, Palesa*, he said to himself. *This is what it looks like when I'm not sitting on the fence.* He pictured her as she used to be shortly after she arrived from Botswana. Looked like she was gonna burst with health and vitality and all the things she expected from life. Every man who saw her wanted to whisk her off to his bed. Phineus had to move fast or he'd've lost her for sure; they'd have whipped her away before he'd blinked. Jesus Christ, a man finds out who his friends are when a woman like that comes on the scene.

A car moved slowly along the street behind him and Phineus flexed his shoulders, keeping his eyes fixed on the lights of Beverley Road as the vehicle drew level with him. Could be the cops, he thought. It wouldn't be the first time they'd pulled him over for walking along the street. Didn't see them pulling the white man over for walking along the street. No, never did see that happen, not even once. The accelerator increased and decreased revolutions erratically and the full beam came on, flushing the street with light, sending shadows leaping like huge cats.

Phineus sneaked a look as the silver-haired lady at the wheel switched off her headlights and drove on by. The street settled back into its solitude and Phineus felt a single line of sweat break on his neck and run down his back. *Palesa, baby,* he said inside his head, *it's a hairy old world out here on your own.*

Nine fifty-three. Phineus was standing on the corner of Margaret Street and Beverley Road, his hands deep in his trouser pockets. A scraggy girl with a clot of green stuff around her bulging eyes almost stumbled into him. She stopped and made a wide detour, her spindly legs looking as if they didn't belong. Phineus imagined her thighs ravaged by a storm of needle punctures.

There had been a time when Phineus would have equated the drugged girl with the racists and fascists and drug dealers. It seemed to him now that as a young man he had carried two bags around with him; one for the bad guys and the other for the good. And he had had little trouble in assigning the right people to the right bags.

But increasing age and experience had shown him that these divisions were not enough, that life was not divisible by two. Now he had arrived at a new position. Reality was not at all unequivocal; life was never exactly lifelike. Books and films, the television, all those guys would like you to believe that the images they showed you were how it was. But it never was like that, not really. Nowadays when Phineus felt he fully understood something he got suspicious, started to wonder if somebody had led him there.

In the twenty-first century everybody told lies, or maybe they always had, and he'd only just found out about it. The government, the politicians with their different-coloured rosettes taking bribes from fat-cat businessmen, they all told you what you wanted to hear. The businessmen only had their own interests at heart; wanted us to believe that economic reality was the only reality. The police and the armed forces went around with alternative versions of the law for different-coloured folks. But at least with the police if you were black you knew what to expect. White folks were fed a subtler lie and there were a whole lot of them didn't understand how to interpret it.

And then there was the great bulk of the people, millions of them, their brains swamped by the jingle of adverts and crazy ideas about beauty and religion and drugs and alcohol, pulled this way and that by competing moralities and ideologies, blinded by the money-grubbing antics of millionaire celebrities and sports people. You had to feel sorry for them, mister and missis average, pushing their hypothetical trolleys through the aisles of Western society, collecting a mishmash of bankrupt and redundant ideas all carefully wrapped in brightly coloured paper. From cradle to grave their lives were cosseted by a mixture of blatant and carefully concealed untruths.

Phineus stood on the corner of Margaret Street for another hour. He watched the people go past and played a game with himself, trying to guess where they had come from and where they were going.

Eventually he pushed himself off the wall and made for home. He had not seen the people who attacked Chaz. Tonight they had not shown. But that was all right. He could wait. Eventually he'd meet them face to face.

19

Cicatrices

A man was coming for a portrait at eleven and at one o'clock Katy's reading group was meeting for lunch at the Royal Hotel. She hadn't managed to get the book let alone read it, couldn't remember the title, Kate Atkinson's latest. Still, it wouldn't be the first time she'd bluffed it; some of the women chose books that were quite unreadable.

She checked the studio, made sure the Hasselblad was loaded with film, taped down a corner of the backdrop that had come loose and had been irritating her for weeks. Mr Short, the client coming for the portrait, was a musician who wanted the photograph for a book cover. He had sounded cultured on the phone, well-spoken, using each word precisely, enunciating each syllable. When Katy had demurred he had fallen silent with a sigh. His publisher needed the photograph within a couple of days. If it was a matter of cost he could assure her that there would be no problems in that direction.

Mr Short. Katy smiled as she recalled their conversation. She wondered if she should drop the height of her studio-stand in case the man measured up to his name.

She thumbed through a copy of *Harpers & Queen*, which had pictures from De Beers Diamond Day at Ascot, the rich and the famously rich showing off their teeth and their jewellery. The women wore single necklaces or a bangle, maybe a ring. In those circles nothing was overstated. All you needed was one big diamond. Perhaps a Bertolucci watch to keep track of the time. And a Gucci bag.

None of the people in these photographs would give Stone Lewis a second look. She couldn't imagine any of *them* coming awake in the middle of the night, damp and trembling from the embrace of an erotic dream. Of course not. They had arrived, or perhaps been born into that special sphere of wealth. They were universally admired, the guy who shopped in the Burlington Arcade or the gal in the handmade Italian frock. They were in the running. Why would people like that concern themselves with a tattooed man who waited on tables in a café?

Katy had seen a Bertolucci watch at a shop in Beverley, 18-carat gold, pitted with diamonds. She'd set her heart on it, too. But practical Daniel Madika had put his foot down, decided it was too much for their budget. All of which had resulted in the worst argument of their marriage. If she closed her eyes Katy could hear her own voice demanding of him, 'Am I worth it or not, Daniel? Please don't procrastinate, simply answer the question.'

And it didn't matter how long she kept her eyes closed, her fingers crossed, her husband had not answered the question. Not with words.

Stone Lewis with his haunted face and hungry eyes would not have heard of a Bertolucci watch, and if he slaved away in Eve's internet café for the rest of his life he'd never be able to afford one. He'd think that Katy was worth one, no doubt about that. But he wouldn't be able to find the money. And there, although it was already slipping away, just there in that comparison was one of the fundamental disappointments of life.

The doorbell chimed like the distant echo of a mountain church. She walked along the hall with a ghost of a smile on her face, noticing that the hazy figure of Mr Short through the bevelled and leaded glass belied his name.

Katy opened the door and knew immediately that something was wrong. The first impression was of thin, lank hair badly in need of a shampoo. They spoke simultaneously, he asking: 'Ms Madika?' and Katy pointlessly inquiring: 'Mr Short?'

He smiled at the collision of their voices and Katy attempted to close the door in his face, but she was too slow. He blocked it with his foot and easily shouldered his way into the house. She ran along the hallway and picked up the cordless phone from the small mahogany table but the man was never more than a step behind her.

As she stabbed at the number pad he twisted it from her hand and pushed her back against the wall. Katy lost her balance and fell to the carpet, rolling on to her back while the broad-shouldered Mr Short bestrode her.

Shaking, her mind teeming with images of rape and murder, aware that she was uttering small cries like an injured animal, Katy tried to get back to her feet. The man placed a large foot, encased in a black leather shoe, on her chest. He leaned towards her, increasing the pressure against her ribs and looked down at her.

He had a long face, pale like someone who lived in a cellar. His thin, grimy hair was long, beginning to curl over his collar. He had yellow teeth and receding gums and more than a day's growth of stubble on his chin. And then there were the marks.

Katy had seen scars like them before, around Stanley Pool and Kinshasa. Some of Daniel's cousins were marked in the same way. But they had black skins and their cicatrices were central to a traditional perception of beauty. The wounds were opened on each cheek and pulled apart with a thorn or hook and clay or ash was rubbed in to prevent them healing. This encouraged the growth of keloids and represented the ability to endure pain and prove control over the body.

The face before her was white and there was only a thin scar tissue around the wounds. She vaguely remembered Daniel explaining that keloid growth was encouraged by a darker skin pigmentation, one of the main reasons that traditional European scarification took the form of tattooing.

'Where is it?' the man said, his voice low, confined within his chest.

'I'll show you,' Katy told him. No point in pretending she didn't know what he wanted. The main thing was to avoid being hurt by him; maimed in some way, marked.

He smiled, showing those long yellow teeth, and removed his foot from her chest. He offered her his hand but Katy got to her feet unaided. She made for the stairs but the man grabbed a handful of her hair and hung on. 'Don't get any clever ideas,' he told her. 'I'm not here to play games.'

She walked slowly up the stairs. The man held on to her hair, pulling her head back so she was almost off balance. She led him into the bedroom and stopped in front of the dressing table. 'It's down there,' she said, 'under the corner of the rug.'

With his free hand he took her shoulder, turned her and flung her backwards onto the bed. He stood to the side and picked up a pillow with both hands. He stared down at her for a long time without blinking. Then he offered her the pillow. 'Hold this for me,' he said. 'One move, one sound and I'll use it to smother you.'

Katy didn't doubt that he meant what he said. She nodded her head to indicate her understanding, to show him that she intended to cooperate with his demands. She wanted him to find the Compact Flash, to destroy it or take it away, whatever he wished. She would comply in every respect. She wouldn't cry out or try to trick him. If he needed to punish her in some way she would take that as well, whatever it was, in silence. She wasn't going to be a problem. She wanted the man to be happy. To go away feeling that he had vanquished her, to leave her alive.

He disappeared from sight below the edge of the bed, turning up the corner of the rug to retrieve the Compact Flash. Then he reappeared again, his prize in his hand and a smile on his face.

'So far so good,' he said, taking a hank of her hair and curling it around his hand. He fingered the collar of her shirt, pulling at the buttons until the top two came undone. Katy's hands came up involuntarily, her body defying her mind in an attempt at protection. The man hissed and tightened his grip of her hair and she let her arms fall back by her sides.

He's going to rape me, she thought. And there's nothing I can do about it. She closed her eyes and concentrated on her breathing, feeling the man's hand on her breast, his fingers circling the aureole, pulling and twisting the nipple until her teeth clenched so hard she thought they would break.

Katy had fantasized rape many times as a teenager and beyond. She'd dreamed it, read about it in books and magazines, seen it on film and talked around it with girlfriends. But it had never been like this. Never so quick or brutal. She had not imagined the ease with which the rapist would dissect her, how he would unerringly take what was undoubtedly her and yet leave in the shadow whole swathes of her being that did not suit his purpose.

There was no response from her body. It did not betray her. The surface of her skin dropped its temperature, so that even to her own touch it felt like the skin of a dead chicken. There was no rush of blood to primary or secondary sexual organs. Her brain, though it reeled with conflicting images, contrived a kind of physical anaesthetic. In the forefront there was fear, disgust and, surprisingly, caution. And in the background, almost beyond consciousness, there was her body, her physical sheath, which was being sacrificed to the carnality of a man she thought of as less than human.

He had manoeuvred her to the edge of the bed, turned her over and pushed her face into the mattress and Katy was shaking with fear and loathing. Then, inexplicably, he pulled back. He stopped at the point when Katy thought that his defilement of her was inevitable. From the corner of her eye she watched him pick up the framed wedding photograph from the dressing table. She in her full-length Ralph Lauren dress and Daniel looking as though he'd spent a week in Sloane Square. The man glanced at the photograph and left the room with it in his hand.

She heard him in the bathroom, running water into the hand-basin. The stream of his urine splashing into the lavatory bowl. He flushed it, too, when he'd finished, and pulled the door closed behind him. Katy listened to his muffled footsteps receding down the stairs.

She pulled her legs back into the bed and crawled under the duvet, where she curled up in the dark. Her face was wet with tears, though she couldn't remember crying or even wanting to cry. She explored her face with the fingers of both hands; she touched her arms, her belly, her legs. She pushed her hand between her thighs and felt the hard knot of her sex.

She thought, my God, I'm alive. He has left me alive. He didn't rape me and I'm still alive. And it meant that tonight she'd see her daughter again, and hold her close. That in the weeks and the years ahead she'd be there to see Chloe grow and develop. Perversely, she thanked him, in her mind, for the assault. For realizing that was all it would take. She thanked him for knowing he didn't have to rape her and take her life to gain her silence.

She pushed back the duvet and pulled herself to the edge of the bed. She needed to clean up. To stand under the shower and let the water thunder down on the surface of her body. She'd be no cleaner for it, but she had to make the effort.

Katy examined herself in the dressing-table mirror. Her top lip was cut, but she would be able to mask it with make-up. The scratch-marks on her shoulder were more worrying, but again, she could get away with it if she was careful. There was some bleeding from the lip. It was painful but superficial; a punch in the mouth.

She was alive.

The button had been torn from the right cuff of her red shirt from Paul Smith, but otherwise it was intact.

Katy walked toward the bathroom but stopped at the top of the stairs. Someone was moving down there. There was a tapping sound and a little later the clink of a glass.

It was him. He hadn't left. She'd heard him padding down the stairs but she hadn't heard him leave the house. She had no memory of the outer door closing behind him.

She stood at the top of the stairs and strained to hear.

There was a possibility, after all, that she was mistaken. She prayed that he was not in the house, that her ordeal was really over. Please let it be true, she whispered to herself. Please let it be my imagination.

Katy listened for a long time and heard nothing. She brought her breathing back to normal. She stood so still that she was aware of tiny movements in her own physiognomy, gastric juices stimulated by fear and apprehension rather than the needs of digestion, the quiet inhalations of breath and the pumping of her heart. With her eyes closed she could hear her own blood roaring past her temples, feeding her brain with oxygen. She licked at the wound on her lip and tasted salt. It's all right, she told herself. False alarm. There's no one here but me.

And then she heard it again, the tapping sound, irregular; nothing mechanical about it. Someone was downstairs at the keyboard of her computer. She had to fight all of her own systems; suppress the scream that rushed to her throat and the faintness that undermined her ability to stand. Her mouth ran dry and she watched her hands tremble as the beat in her chest degenerated to a fluttering arrhythmia. There was no doubt about it; the man with the scars on his cheeks was still there.

Katy returned to her room and took the red silk dressing gown from the back of the door. She was still fully clothed but she put her arms into the sleeves and wrapped the skirt tightly around her, pulling the belt until it bit into the flesh of her waist. She walked to the head of the stairs and took ten deep breaths, counting them as she inhaled and exhaled, steeling herself for the descent.

He watched her as she floated down. He was seated at the computer, his legs splayed carelessly, vaunting an outline of his flaccid sex through the stuff of his trousers. He leered as she came to a stop several feet from him. 'She wants some more,' he said, looking around at an imaginary audience.

Katy was perfectly controlled.

She remained impassive as he got to his feet and came over, circled her like a hungry wolf.

'I'm right, aren't I?' he said.

She shook her head, licked her lips. 'I heard a sound,' she said. 'I didn't know who it was.'

He laughed. 'Someone else,' he said. 'Another guy. She's got them queuing at the front door now.' He turned and lifted a glass of whisky from the desk, sipped, and replaced it. Some of the liquid had splashed on to the polished wood of the desk when he'd poured it. 'I don't think so, girl,' he said. 'If your performance upstairs was anything to go by I can't see anybody coming back for more.'

Just take it, Katy reminded herself. Don't give him a reason to go further.

She concentrated on the wedding photograph on the carpet, the glass smashed where he had ground it underfoot.

The computer beeped and he turned quickly at the sound, already on the balls of his feet. 'I've reformatted the hard disk,' he said. 'Just to make sure.'

Katy nodded. It was Daniel's stuff on there. His medical database, his accounts. He'd tear his hair out when he found it was gone.

She looked at the man with the scars and he returned her stare. She couldn't see behind the scars. She couldn't understand who he was or what he wanted. She knew he was connected with the man in the Panama and that he was here to make sure there was no evidence against them. But beyond that scrap of knowledge he was unknowable.

He was the one in control. The man in the Panama was a mechanic, an assistant. This man was the one who had the answers, the one who made the decisions.

And he had the arrogance to leave her alone upstairs after his attack on her. She might have had a mobile up there. He hadn't searched the room, looked in the drawers of her dressing table or her bedside cabinet. She could have opened the bedroom window and called for help. But the man had left her alone up there because he knew that she wouldn't cross him. He knew that she would do anything he asked because she was in fear of her life.

She shuddered. He knew her mind better than she knew herself. He smiled cynically as she thought it, as if in confirmation of his invincibility.

'I'm leaving now,' he said, walking to the door. 'I've got two names for you, people who depend on you.'

He paused, waiting until the weight of his words had got to her. 'The first one's called Daniel Madika, and he's a doctor at the Infirmary. Works real long hours.'

He's been watching me, Katy thought. He knows everything about my life, my family.

'The other one's called Chloe,' he said. 'The piccaninny.'

20

Mixed Messages

Stone read the e-mail from Ginny. He'd never met Sherab, her ex-husband, but had heard a lot about him since he'd been living with Ginny. One of Sherab's parents had been Tibetan and Ginny had shown him a photograph of the guy. He was wearing a white suit, white cowboy hat and tooled boots. This is a guy who calls himself a Buddhist.

Stone left the flat and walked along Spring Bank towards the city centre. Stuart, the local paedophile, was coming back from the newsagent's with a carton of milk.

'They still stealing your milk?' Stone asked.

Stuart stopped and held up the carton. 'I've cancelled it with the milkman,' he said. 'It's never there when I go for it. Or it's on the step but without the bottle.' He was tall and blond with a touch of camp. He'd served time for molesting a six-year-old and when he'd been released the local cops had circulated the neighbourhood with his mug-shot and name and address.

Stone shook his head and walked on. Most people in the neighbourhood were all right, but people like Stuart brought out the worst in them. They'd like to tear him apart, forget all the trappings of civilization and castrate him. Stone talked to him when they met on the street but that was as far as it went. He didn't want to invite the guy into his flat. He'd never considered running a campaign in support of him. Like everyone else, Stone thought it would be better if Stuart moved on. But there was nowhere the guy could go.

At the charity shop he handed over a plastic carrier bag with his old electric razor, which he didn't use any more, a white plastic polar bear, a copy of Carl Hiaasen's *Stormy Weather,* a slow-running watch, a wooden elephant and a presentation box of Tea Tree products. Stone made a point of throwing something away every day. When Ginny was away he tended to go over the top.

Could it be a coincidence that Mrs Robson's Kosovan lodger went missing around the same time Katy Madika thought she saw a murder down by the marina? Maybe. There was nothing to point to a connection. But it was a question worth asking. All questions were worth asking. Sometimes you didn't want to hear the answers.

Several of the tables outside the Euro Café were in use. Stone found one that had been vacated and took a seat. The table had two dirty cups and saucers together with a side plate and the remains of a hamburger with mustard. There was a pool of espresso and demerara, which someone had tried to contain with a paper napkin.

Being a waiter himself Stone was tempted to clear the mess and wipe the table down, but he knew how to be a customer and decided to practise that instead. When you wait table for a living and then find yourself on the other end of the equation you're critical. You know the right way to deal with everything, the way you would do it yourself if you had your apron on, and you quickly move into judging mode to measure yourself up against the party serving you.

The other thing you do is make sure the waiter is relaxed, that he or she knows that you want serving, but that you're basically sympathetic. That's what you do if you feel OK about yourself, if the world hasn't kicked you in the face too many times, or if you've just plucked a high-value banknote out of the gutter. If you're a regular prat or the kind of person who despises all your customers for daring to breathe when you wait on them, then you give all waiters a hard time when it's your turn to be the customer.

It isn't hard to do, you don't have to speak or offer repellent body language. Just silence and a hard stare. You know it'll be enough to ruin the guy's day.

She approached the table tall and straight like a wand. Stone watched her coming towards him, taking in her long legs and her long face, which looked as though it had been chiselled from marble. Her orange hair was cut short and gelled into a spray of spikes. She wore a silver nose-ring.

'Gimme a tick,' she said, loading the leavings of the last customer onto a tray. It wasn't a Hull accent, something from further north, Shields or Sunderland. She'd come down to Hull to make her fortune, or to find love and romance, an adventure. Either that or she was running away from something.

She put on a display walking back to the kitchen, rolling her hips, drawing attention to firm buttocks and calf-muscles that were capable of supporting her body weight for a ten-hour shift. There was a knowing smile around her lips when she returned. She wiped the table with a damp cloth that hung from a Velcro patch on her belt and turned to Stone with a pad in her hand. 'OK, what can I get you?'

'Is the coffee fresh?'

'Could be arranged.'

'I'll take some of that,' he said. 'And when you've got a minute I'd like to talk.'

She raised her eyebrows. 'My boyfriend might have something to say about that.'

'It's not a come-on,' he said. 'You might be able to help with something. Information, about one of your customers.'

'You a cop?'

He shook his head. 'I'm inquisitive.'

'Hey.' The smile came back, bright as a star. 'I can relate to that.' She put the pad away and gave the table another wipe. 'I'll get your coffee.'

Inquisitive was right. For as far back as he could remember the inquisitive had been there. It had been about words, language, throughout the childhood years. He'd hounded words and their meanings, their etymology and derivations, like the other kids of his age had hounded Queen and *Star Wars*. He'd plucked words from the air and carried them home in his head, unwrapped them carefully in the quiet of his room and taken them apart syllable by syllable, letter by letter. He'd laid out the separate parts and regrouped them in vowels and consonants, recombined them in weird and wonderful formations, sometimes coming up with entirely different words and meanings, occasionally coaxing the letters of a single word into a phrase or a complete sentence.

Later, his inquisitiveness had centred around Robert Johnson, so that even now he could quote the words of every song in the bluesman's repertoire. He could bring to mind minute details of the singer's biography and relate the events of his last day as if they had happened yesterday. Every musical phrase was there in his head, only a breath away.

And when he heard Dylan or the Stones or Clapton or Lennon he could stop the record in his head and say there, that's where they connect, that's where the guy is picking up on Johnson, even though he doesn't know it himself. But that's it, that phrase just there, that breath or that interval, straight out of the old man's head.

When they'd put him away in the joint it had moved on to Hammett. Even though the novels weren't officially available, it was possible to get anything if you wanted it. The other cons wanted smack or skunk, they wanted cigarettes or hard-core porn, and whatever it happened to be they'd get it by hook or by crook. Stone wanted *The Dain Curse* and *The Glass Key* and *The Continental Op* stories, and they came in through the same route. *I'm going to the well,* the magician would say. *You name your poison and I'll see you get as much of it as you can take.*

She placed the coffee in front of him and pulled out the chair on the other side of the table. 'I've got five minutes,' she said. 'After that the slimeball'll take it out of my wages.' As she spoke she shuffled a cigarette out of her pack and lit it with one of those lighters you buy in quantity off a guy on the corner of Whitefriargate. Used to be three for a pound but now he's up to eight for the same amount. Free enterprise, see.

Stone watched her inhale and blow the smoke out of her lungs, fixed himself on the way it hung around her in a cloud, seeming for a while to have containing borders before collapsing and drifting off into oblivion. Stone was capable of doing exactly the same thing, of drifting away from the world into the all-pervading obsessions within his head. When Ginny was around she called him back, retaining him in her world, and Aunt Nell did the same thing, had been doing it for so long that Stone could now do it himself. Most of the time.

'My customers?' the waitress said. Her nose-ring caught the rays of the sun and projected them through Stone's eyes, sent them flashing around the pin-board table of his mind.

'One customer,' he said. He brought out a print of the hook-nosed guy sitting at a table of the café. She didn't touch it, left it on the table in front of her and twisted her long neck and spine to get a bead on it. She squinted, smiled briefly, then seemed to fix on it and give it her attention.

That was a mixed message, Stone mused, the way she'd put on the physical display earlier, moving her buttocks like that, rolling her hips; then when he spoke to her she let on she had a jealous boyfriend. So what was going on there? Did she know herself? Or was she acting out some unconscious urge? Her genes on constant look-out, waiting for a way of reproducing themselves?

For years Stone had been unable to read mixed messages, never seeing them for what they were. He'd been unable to see through body language or to interpret social codes correctly. He was getting better at it, but he'd had to learn to see what most other people took for granted. He'd had to learn it by rote, scientifically, whereas most people were given the ability as a kind of birthright. Still learning, he reminded himself. Some days he thought he hadn't learned anything at all.

'The blue suit might ring a bell,' he said. 'Lightweight, looks like linen.'

'Mmm.'

'You don't recognize him?'

'I don't remember the suit,' she said. 'But the nose is a real landmark.'

'D'you know anything about him?'

'He hasn't been in the last couple of days. He was in one day last week.' She squinted at the photograph. 'This is not the best likeness of him, y'know. He's going thin on top. From this you'd think he had all his hair. But he always wears those shoes, no socks. You don't see many guys like that, without socks.'

'Name?'

'I expect he has one, yeah, but he hasn't formally introduced himself. We call him Boris.'

'How old is he?'

'Again, he looks older in the picture, but he's twenty-five, twenty-six.' She thought about it. 'Old eyes, though, like he's seen a lot. Maybe more than he was ready for.'

The manager or owner of the café came out of the building and leaned against the wall.

'Fuckwit's getting restless,' she said. 'I have to go.' She stubbed out the remains of her cigarette in the ashtray, got to her feet.

Stone put his hand on her arm and she looked across the table, locking on to his eyes. He watched her but was aware of the guy in charge glancing at the watch on his wrist. 'Why Boris?' he asked.

'He's Russian, something like that. Polish maybe. Talks English like every word he's bitten off is more than he can chew.'

21

Bruegel

Nell was sitting at the end of the bar in the Queen's with a G and T, Heartbreak beside her with a pint of Riding and a serious expression on his face. 'Even in a place like this,' he said, 'you look around and it's like a Bruegel painting. People're like ants crawling all over the place, running this way and that, all looking after their own interest. So you don't come out and you sit at home in front of the box and it's exactly the same, half the time you're not sure what's going on. They've got presenters on there with shit for brains, half of them haven't been out of school for more than a couple of months. If they've been to school in the first place, which I wonder, the way they carry on. Last night there was this couple, she's got a bare belly and he's got just about enough brains to grin, but he can't do anything else. I watched them for nearly forty minutes and all they did was scream and get excited at themselves. What's the point of that?

'In the old days we had Michael Parkinson and Trevor McDonald, guys like that. OK, so they weren't God's answer and they weren't exactly a laugh a minute either, but most of the time they acted like they were grown-ups. They made you feel that the world was bigger than your own front room.

'What I've heard, the television, everything we get to see, it all depends on this one guy. If this guy likes it the producers get the cash to make it, and if the guy doesn't like it they get zilch. And the guy's not normal, he likes what he likes and what he doesn't like nobody else's allowed to like it either because he's not gonna give out the cash so somebody can make it and push it out on the airwaves.

'One of the things he doesn't like, this guy who's in charge, is Eastern Europe. He's got a block about it, so if you watch the telly it's as if that part of the world doesn't exist. You can see America and Africa, loads of stuff set in Scotland, and France and Spain come up from time to time. But you'll never see anything set in Eastern Europe. Not until this guy dies or retires. I don't know why you're smiling like that, Nell, this is the truth I'm telling you. The whole nation is waiting for this one guy to fall over just so they can watch a bit of decent telly.'

Nell sipped from her glass. She said, 'Did you say Bruegel?'

'He was a painter, Dutch, Middle Ages. He painted these scenes—'

'I know who he was, Heartbreak. Flemish, sixteenth century.'

'Yeah, about round there. There's this woman lives next door to me, one of the flats, her divorce has come through and she doesn't want to know about men any more and she's devoting herself to art instead. I talked to her and she's been educating me. Bruegel was the first lesson. She lent me a book. With pictures.'

'And you think the Queen's on a Thursday night is like Bruegel?'

'Not exactly,' he said. A smile crept over his face and he looked at the ceiling. 'I was talking figuratively.'

'Jesus.'

'In them paintings there's a million things happening, people meeting other people and some of them ignoring each other, there's kids running all over the place and guys and women being ugly and pretty and some of them want to fight and others want to joke or get laid or take a leak. It's like a snapshot you could take in here any night of the week. Everyone's dressed differently and they don't necessarily look like the people in the painting but all the same things are going on.

'What we do is we see what we want to see. I'm here with you and that's what I want to see, so I filter out the other stuff. I don't look at the other women in case you get a cob on, think I'm after poking somebody else. I don't take in everything that's happening in a flash like a camera would, or like Bruegel does. I narrow the world down to the point where it works best for me, to the point where I can manage it.'

'You've been thinking about this, haven't you?'

'Yeah, Nell, I've been thinking about it. I've been looking at the pictures at home and then when I go out the pictures are still there, in my head, and I look around, try to see what the artist saw. This is what you wanted me to do. This new guy at the rock 'n' roll club, Stanley Whatsisface who can't keep his hands to himself but knows about art and culture and makes women want to come across because of it. You wanted me to be more like him.'

'No, I don't.'

'That's what you said.'

'What I said was you could use your brain more.'

'Yeah, Nell, and I've been using it on Bruegel.'

'So I was right?'

'Nell, you're always right.'

'What's that supposed to mean?'

Heartbreak examined the beer in his glass, gave it all his attention as though he was worried it might evaporate.

'When you say I'm always right,' Nell said, 'it's an insult.'

'How's that?'

'Because nobody is always right. It's impossible for a person to be right all the time, so if you say somebody's always right you're being sarcastic, you're saying that they always *think* they're right, that they can't stand to be wrong. Somebody like that has a psychological problem. They're difficult. So it's an insult. You just insulted me. You accused me of being a nut.'

'How many G and Ts have you put away?'

'There you go again,' Nell said. 'Now I'm a drunk.'

'Nell, you're off-beam here. You know that? This is a guy who's crazy about you. I just wanna talk about art and painting and stuff like that, and sometimes I wanna make a joke without thinking too much. Off the cuff, know what I mean? If the joke's on you that's because I want to fool around with you, have a laugh or something. Lighten up after I've been spouting about fucking paintings all night. It's not because I want to insult you or I think you're a nut or an alco.'

'It wasn't very funny,' Nell said.

'Maybe it wasn't. That's because I'm an amateur. I'm not Billy Connolly. Some of my jokes hit the spot and some of them don't. But when I make a joke and it's crap that doesn't turn it into an insult.'

Nell gazed at the rows of bottles behind the bar, the warm glow of the different coloured liquids. There must be dozens of different liqueurs she'd never tasted, some of the names you could hardly get your tongue round. She was tipsy, not exactly drunk, but far enough gone to feel those romantic stirrings. She'd put the lights low when she got home, dig out some blues piano, maybe the Keith Jarrett album.

Heartbreak put his hand on her arm and squeezed. 'You want another drink?' he said.

Nell shook her head. 'It's nearly time.' She looked into his eyes. 'You gonna stay the night?'

22

The Worst Thing

'Alice,' he told her, 'my mum, Alice, I made the chicken dip for? She's got bad legs so I stay with her. Look after her.'

'Nice,' Joolz said.

Mort decided he wouldn't be the first one to break the silence. He thought if she found something she wanted to talk about she'd put more effort into it. But throughout the next five minutes she only managed to sigh four times; three little sighs and a long one that was somehow more tangible than an exhalation of air.

Alice often got depressed and refused to talk, and Mort would be patient and wait, carry on as normal, not make an issue of it. Sometimes it would take all day and she'd only talk again after a long sleep.

'Are you tired?' he asked Joolz.

She glanced towards him. 'That's original.'

'How d'you mean?'

'For a chat-up line. Getting me into bed.'

'I didn't mean that. I thought you might be tired, want me to leave.'

She shook her head. 'D'you have to see to your mother?'

'She'll manage.'

Joolz sighed again. 'Well, then.'

He went over to her and knelt between her legs. He reached up with his mouth and kissed her and she kissed him back with her lips parted. Mort explored with his tongue. He hoped she would do the same and he kept the kiss going for as long as possible, withdrawing his tongue from time to time so she could come into his mouth. But she didn't do it. She didn't object when he probed some more and she sighed when he worked his hand inside her shirt and found her breast and nipple.

But that was the only response he got. Mort was fully erect, his breath coming in sharp bursts, the surface of his body as taut and tender as a fresh bruise. She's here, he told himself, she's giving herself to me. But a contradictory voice just as insistently told him she wasn't interested, that she was going through the motions.

That's what Alice had said about Mort's natural father. One of the few things he knew about him. He'd been posh, not a regular working man, somebody with money and breeding. Boss class. 'But he wasn't interested,' Alice had said. 'He was just going through the motions.'

Mort got to his feet and took Joolz's hand, led her to the bed. Her hand felt small and cold in his. He sat her on the edge of the bed and pushed her back. He stripped off his clothes and looked down at her. She bit her bottom lip and turned her head away as he slid his hand up her skirt.

In his imagination they had been naked together; as he had stripped off his clothes she had thrown hers to the floor as well. It would've been like in the video he'd seen with the lads, something Gaz had bought in the market. But it wasn't to be like that. Mort was naked but Joolz was still fully dressed. 'I want to take your clothes off,' he told her.

'No.'

'I want to see your body.'

'No, just do it.'

She arched her back and pulled off her pants, spreading her legs, displaying her sex.

'Do it to me.'

Mort manoeuvred himself into position, feeling his hard-on dissipating. He went to enter her quickly, hoping that the contact would bring him back to life. But it was too late and his prick shrivelled away like a plastic bag against a flame. He tried squeezing and pulling at it, bullying the thing into action, but he didn't have the conviction to make it work.

She waited. He pulled away and looked at her but she averted her eyes. 'You're going to have to help me with this,' he said, taking her hand and drawing it down towards his flacid cock.

'No,' she said, pulling away. 'Just do it.'

Mort collapsed on top of her. It's not going to happen, he thought. He was aware of the film of grease between his body and hers and didn't know if it was her sweat or his. He should have gone home to Alice, called in at the Chinky on the way and bought a bag full of sweet and sour and double chips.

There seemed to be no way out for him now. He wished that Joolz would fall asleep, that both of them would and then he could wake up and get dressed and steal away in the night. A failed stud.

But that didn't matter either, because he could have had her if he'd wanted. He could have done anything that came into his head. She was his for the taking. The reason he couldn't do it was because he didn't like her, didn't fancy her. She was not the kind of woman he went for. She was too easy and she stank of tobacco. She was skinny and too old. He liked them young.

He slipped off her and turned her away from him, tucking himself into the curve of her back. He kept hold of her breast and lay still, listening to her breath.

The hard-on came back as he was on the point of sleep. He rolled Joolz on to her back and entered her quickly. She was dry but he couldn't wait. He pumped hard and came inside her within a few seconds. When he looked at her face during the last couple of thrusts he saw her mouth was open, her tongue rolled back in there. She made no sound and she didn't move her body in response to his.

It was hot in the room and when he'd finished Mort was slick with sweat. He wondered if he could love her. He wondered if this was the woman who would show him what love was. He wanted to do it again immediately, to undress her and do it the way he'd imagined. He didn't want it to be so cold. He wanted it to be like fire.

The next morning he sorted Alice out in double-quick time and was back at Joolz's flat before she'd got out of bed. He found the remains of a loaf and put a couple of slices under the grill. There was a tiny fridge and a pat of butter in there on a saucer. He couldn't find anything else.

'Just help yourself,' Joolz said.

'I've already eaten,' he told her. 'This's for you. Breakfast in bed.'

She sat up and placed the pillow in the small of her back. Sometime in the night she'd undressed and her shoulders were naked. Bones sticking out like in those photographs the Jews had manufactured in the camps. She reached for her tobacco and rolled herself a cigarette. She laid her head back on the wall and there was a smile on her face. Not exactly a smile, but real close, a look of contentment. The cat jumped on the bed and Joolz stroked her hard from her head to the tip of her tail. The cat purred loudly. 'Tilley wants feeding,' she said.

Mort wanted to be stroked like that, wished he could arouse that response in her. He opened a tin of cat-food and spooned it into the bowl on the floor.

'There's some matches on the table,' Joolz said. Mort got them and tossed them over to her and she caught the box with one hand.

We're a couple, he thought. *Almost like being married.* He wondered if she would control him, if her love would be like a whip designed to tame his wildness. He didn't want her to be like Alice, somebody who would stand by and watch him follow his instincts. He wanted a woman like Joolz who would restrain him, who would dominate and monopolize him, ride him with a tight rein.

He buttered the toast and put it on a plate and cut the slice diagonally as if he were in a café or at a children's party. He walked to the side of the bed and presented it to her.

She said, 'Thank you,' and put it in front of her on the duvet. She didn't eat it, but continued to smoke.

'D'you want a drink?' he asked.

'There's no coffee,' she told him. 'I usually go downstairs to the café.'

Mort sat on the edge of the bed and asked her what she thought about mixed marriages.

'Like Catholics and Jews?'

'Blacks and whites,' he said. 'Or whites and Jews. Like mixing up the races.'

'I don't go with blacks,' she said. 'Or with Jews or Pakis.'

Mort nodded. 'That's the worst thing,' he told her. 'Any woman of mine went with one of those, I'd kill her.'

She stubbed her cigarette out and took a bite from the slice of toast. 'I never have breakfast in bed,' she said.

'What about drugs?' Mort asked. 'You a user?'

She shook her head and kept on shaking it.

'Because that's the second thing,' Mort said. 'Drugs are for liberals and communists. They collapse your willpower, leave you fucking dreaming.'

'What I like,' she said, 'at the weekend, whenever, I get shitfaced on Special Brew.'

'You can do that with me,' he told her. 'We'll get shitfaced together. Go down the Cod, give somebody a fuckload of trouble.'

Gaz brought the Orion round to the door and they got in. Omega sat in the front passenger seat and Mort and Ginner got into the back. Gaz drove over the river and along Hedon Road to Southcoates Lane. He pulled up opposite the White House Hotel, a building that may well have been white at some time in its history, but was now grey, shedding its rendered walls in patches and exposing irregular areas of red brick.

The place had originally been three storeys high but some time in the fifties or sixties they had added another layer of dormer-windowed rooms. The second-floor rooms had balconies with hardwood balustrades, some of them still supporting sections of rail to keep the occupants from falling to the ground.

The building looked unsafe, as if its foundations had long since withered. The grimy windows, the truncated flagpole and the rotting woodwork advertised its neglect and poverty.

'You know this place?' Omega said.

As he spoke, the front door of the hotel opened and a young Asian woman walked down the broken steps to the pavement, accompanied by three small kids. Through the car window Mort listened to her high-pitched voice jabbering at the kids, trying to keep them in line. He couldn't understand what she was saying, thought it must be Punjabi. Ginner had said there were more than fifty languages in India, and that was before you started on Pakistan or all the other places these people came from. Tamil or Urdu, places like that.

As they watched the woman and the kids walk along the street a taxi drew up outside the hotel and two dark-skinned men in traditional dress climbed out. One of them was young and he gave his arm to the older man, helping him up the steps to the door.

Omega said, 'Why use buses when British taxpayers are footing the bill?'

'My cousin's kid,' Ginner said, 'Lauren, they can't get her into school, no places left. There's more blacks than whites anyway, even black teachers supposed to be teaching English.'

Gaz snorted as if he had something to say, but he leaned back in the driver's seat, gazing out at the façade of the hotel.

A gang of five Pakistani teenagers came along the street, cropped haircuts, trainers, loud voices, printed cotton shirts and a readiness for life. As they drew level with the car, Gaz reached for the door handle. 'Let's sort these fuckers out,' he said.

Omega touched his arm. 'Leave it. There's a better way.'

Mort watched the teenagers disappear round the back of the hotel. 'How can they be asylum-seekers?' he said. 'They're younger than us.'

'There's no such thing as asylum-seekers,' Omega said. 'All these people are slipping through loops in the immigration laws. If they can't do it legally they just move away, disappear into the system. They take British jobs and they don't pay taxes.'

'The government lets them do it,' Ginner said. 'Encourages them.'

Mort shook his head. 'But we don't have to,' he said.

Omega twisted around in his seat and looked at Mort. 'That's right. We can sit here and watch them, we can talk about what a tragedy it is, how the country's going to the dogs, or we can do something about it.'

'You got an idea?' Mort asked.

'Firebombs. Couple in the front and a couple in the back. Dead of night, while they're all dreaming. Usually does the trick.'

'What about napalm?' Gaz said. 'Ginner's got a recipe mixing polystyrene and petrol.'

'Soap's better,' Omega said. 'Petrol mixed with soapflakes. That's what we used in South Africa. But we don't want napalm. We want to burn the place down.'

'You talking about Molotov Cocktails?' Ginner asked.

'Something similar,' Omega said. 'I like to put about a third motor oil in with the petrol. Makes a lot of smoke and helps it to stick wherever it lands.'

'We do it at night?' Mort asked.

Omega nodded. 'When they're all in bed.'

Gaz laughed. 'Sweet dreams. The fuckers'll be sorry they tried to take over our country.'

'When?' Mort asked. 'When we gonna do it?'

'Few days,' Omega said. 'I've got a little problem with a woman and a camera at the moment. Soon as I've sorted that one out we'll be in business.'

'Women are trouble,' Gaz said. He engaged Mort's eyes in the rear-view mirror. 'Don't get involved. That's what I say.'

23

Fear

Katy Madika rang to say she was coming round to his flat. She'd been thinking about things, and come to a decision.

'Tell me,' Stone said into the mouthpiece.

'I'll be there in half an hour,' she said. 'You're not going out?'

He hung up and rubbed his hand over a two-day growth of beard. For years he'd rolled out of bed in the morning and reached for his razor. Some days he'd shaved again in the evening, finding the blue stubble unbearable to touch. When he'd been inside he'd shaved his head as well, and he'd continued to do that on the out until he met Ginny.

He smiled to himself, for some reason finding it comical that when he'd met Ginny his hair had made a comeback and now she'd gone away his beard was growing. There was a symmetry there, a correspondence that he could see but not quite reach, like viewing an object in the sea from a boat, the gleam of reality combined with the shimmer of trickery.

Perhaps he'd lost his hypersensitivity to touch at last? It wouldn't be such a bad thing, he thought, remembering the times it had got him into trouble. In school he'd endured a long period – years and years – of being unable to touch the wood of his desk, a handicap that engaged him in elaborate subterfuge to ensure the contact didn't take place, using textbooks and exercise books as a mask, while at the same time ensuring that no one noticed.

And in the joint he'd found himself unable to bear the touch of another human being. This was impossible to maintain, however, and left him time and time again in the washroom or the shower rubbing away an invisible spot that penetrated through the flesh and into the bone.

He added a box of Slazenger tennis balls and some floppy disks to his charity bag by the door.

He wandered through to the backyard where he'd left his book when the telephone rang. A novel by an American woman about a female PI who was beautiful and sexy and intelligent and strong and savvy and streetwise and middle-class and professional. Ginny had read it and said it was awful but Stone thought it would make him feel closer to her because she'd read it before she flew off to America.

He'd carved out a seat for himself between the back gate and what remained of an ancient coal-house, and the rays of the sun found a path through the chimneys and rooftops and flooded the spot with light and heat. The paint on the coal-house door had blistered, an area of a dozen square centimetres had lifted itself away from the wood, almost inviting a finger to puncture it.

When Katy arrived he was drinking a Czech Budvar from the fridge, condensation running in small rivulets down the side of the bottle. He offered her one but she said it was too early in the day. He brought a chair out of the flat and placed it next to his seat in the yard. She was wearing jeans with the cuffs turned up, a high-necked acrylic jumper and a double-breasted cotton jacket. Overdressed for her, he thought. Whenever he'd seen her before there'd been an expanse of flesh somewhere, bare arms or legs, and a general air of cultured sensuality. Maybe she'd become a Quaker since he'd last seen her?

'I imagined the whole thing,' she said. 'No one was killed down by the marina.'

'Is that right?' Stone said. She wasn't the same woman who had kissed him on the lips. That woman had disappeared and left an imposter in her place. He searched her face, tried to read her body-language, but it was like a blank page. Katy Madika had pulled up her roots and gone. What she had left behind was a shade.

'Something's happened,' he said. 'Somebody's got to you.'

She shook her head without conviction. 'I made it up,' she insisted. 'It was a story, I used the photographs to illustrate it. But it didn't happen like I said. No one was hurt.'

'Sometimes in the joint a guy would take a beating,' Stone told

132

her. 'Not an average beating, something severe, maybe put him in the hospital for a while. When he came back he'd be different. Like the guy he'd been before the beating had gone away and left a shell behind.'

'Why are you telling me this?' Katy asked.

'Because that's what you remind me of. You hit somebody hard enough and they die. It doesn't have to be a physical death. Their heart is still beating and their brains are still functioning, but they've gone away. They're no longer with us.'

'I'm here,' Katy told him, attempting a smile. 'I just drove through traffic to get here.'

Stone shook his head, focused on the blistered paint of the coal-house door. 'What happened to your face?'

Her hand went to the cut on her lip. 'It's nothing,' she said. 'I walked into something.'

'Or someone walked into you?'

'I wasn't looking where I was going.'

'I might know who he was,' Stone said. 'The guy who was killed. There's a neighbour of my Aunt Nell's; her lodger's gone missing. Guy from Kosovo.'

'No one died. Really.'

Stone didn't reply. They sat in silence, close but not touching, until the sun slipped behind a cloud. Katy got to her feet. 'I wanted to tell you,' she said. 'I'm sorry about it, but I really did make it up, invented the whole thing. I won't bother you any longer.'

She walked back through the house and let herself out of the front door. Stone remained where he was in the yard. He was still for several minutes, then he reached for the book and opened it at the marker, commenced reading where he had left it. Really bad novel. Hammett had come along and taken murder out of the Venetian vase and dropped it in the alley, and here they were, the twenty-first century novelists, searching through the alleys and polishing their reproduction vases.

Reality is the greatest puzzle of all. The clues you gather about the nature of reality are like the pixels on a computer screen, each one having meaning only in relation to the others. The mind assimilates information like this, one pixel at a time. Only when all the pixels have loaded do you get the overall picture. And even then you have to learn to read it.

Stone had seen frightened people before. Lots of them. You don't spend time banged away from the world without witnessing fear in all its incarnations every day of the week. Fish, coming inside the walls for the first time, were terrified; even guys who'd done a long stretch were scared. And prisons, all of them, were places of secrecy. Everyone had a secret and everyone else was sworn to keep it. If you knew anything about someone in stir you kept it to yourself. The consequences of wagging your tongue could put your life in danger.

Every waking day you'd come to consciousness and you'd know that you were banged away with guys who were prepared to cut your throat for a few pills or a snatch of tobacco. Men who would stalk you from morning till night and sodomize you in packs like demented animals.

Katy Madika was frightened. She had been frightened that first day when her camera was stolen, when she witnessed a murder. But since then something else had happened. If the cut on her lip was an indication, she had been physically attacked, her family, her child threatened.

Stone went inside to the computer and wrote an e-mail to Ginny. He didn't mention Katy Madika or her cut lip or that he'd seen photographs of a murder on the marina. He told her that when he was a child Aunt Nell had bought him more Lego than he'd ever seen in his life, before or since. He'd built a Lego house and then another and finally a Lego village. As the months turned into years the Lego creations continued, spreading from room to room in Aunt Nell's house and next door where he lived with his mother, Sally. Small Lego outposts appeared in the back garden and invaded the shed and greenhouse. A communication system based on green twine was established around the clusters of Lego dwellings, and green twine ran from the bedroom windows of Aunt Nell's house to the greenhouse and the shed and the rockery, and back again into Sally's house, where they snaked up the banister to Stone's room.

'Lego took up the whole of my life,' Stone said in the e-mail. 'Now I never think about it. But I'm still obsessive. Now I can have several obsessions going at the same time. When you come home I'll stop being fixed on the fact that you've gone away because I'll be hung up on the fact that you're here.'

24

Ice Melting in a Glass

Mort put two cigarettes to his lips and lit them. He removed one and passed it over to Joolz. She looked at the juiced end for a moment before taking a long drag.

'I can't stay,' he said. 'We've got a meeting.'

She shrugged. She sat on the bed and drew her legs up under her. She brushed her jet-black hair away from her eyes. She waved at him, a posh wave like the Queen does from her balcony or when she's in a carriage.

Mort returned the wave. 'I'll be back later,' he said. 'When we've finished.' He cast around his mind for something better to say, something that would impress her. 'I'd rather be with you,' he said.

She smiled at the ceiling, narrowing her eyes and letting cigarette smoke seep from the corners of her mouth. He didn't mind that she rarely said anything. Alice spoke all the time, could talk the hind leg off a donkey. Drove you mad with it. That was because she didn't get out, never saw anyone except Mort, sometimes for days at a time. Usually she had a lot to say about nothing; the pains in her legs or what she'd seen on the television. *Oprah*, *Big Brother*, shit like that.

Joolz had a television, there at the end of her bed, but he'd never seen her watching it. She used it like a shelf, kept a large bottle of hair-dye there, lipsticks and creams and scent, Body Shop jars and nail varnish, pink bogroll, which you took with you down the hall and had to remember to bring back.

When he got around to introducing them, Alice and Joolz, it would be fine. Alice would do the talking, more than enough for two of them, and Joolz would supply the ears. Alice talked like she'd invented it. Anyone watching would think she was in charge, but in reality it would be Joolz. She wouldn't mind that Alice thought she was the boss. Joolz would know who was in control. Match made in heaven.

It wasn't as if Joolz was dumb. She could talk, but only when she had something to say. She was that kind of person. Her silence was easy to take because it wasn't empty. If Alice was silent, which didn't happen very often, only when she had a cob on, then you knew what silence was. It didn't recognize anything in the world; there was no birdsong, no distant breeze. Alice produced a silence that was like the aftermath of a nuclear explosion. Joolz created the kind of hush in which you could hear ice melting in a glass.

'You got any bread?' he asked. He fished a twenty out of his pocket and placed it on the bed next to her. 'You could get a few cans in. Something to go at when I get back.'

Her legs went when she got drunk, she needed carrying, lot of physical contact. And she laughed. Mort liked to see her laugh.

The night before he'd dreamed that Joolz was bait. She'd been standing on the corner of Grove Street waiting for niggers and Pakis to come by, leading them into the park where Mort and his mates were waiting. Perfect. He hadn't told her yet. But it was a way she could contribute, improve the environment, help make England great again, something to be proud of.

He tossed the cigarette packet towards her and she watched it fall to the bed. 'Keep you going,' he said. A smile visited her face. Mort the provider, keeping his woman happy.

'How did you get a place like this?'

Omega touched his nose and shook his head. 'Questions,' he said. 'You're all questions. What you don't know you can't tell. Get your head round it. We're involved in a war here. The lives of your comrades could depend on information.'

'I only meant—'

'I realize what you meant, Mort. I'll make sure you know what you need to.'

Mort shook his head, looked out of the window, along the river, could make out the Humber Bridge in the distance, a thin skeletal ghost in the mist.

'What is it now?' Omega said.

'How do I know what I need to? Like I don't know your name because you decided it would be best. OK, I can understand that. But how come you've got my name, and Ginner and Gaz?'

'Because you blurted it out as soon as I met you,' Omega said. 'Would've been better if you'd used false names.'

'How d'you know we didn't?'

Omega smiled.

'OK, but why aren't Ginner and Gaz here? Why only me?'

'The same reason,' Omega said. 'What I want is for you and me to do a little job together. There's no need for Ginner and Gaz to know about it. They'll read about it in the papers.'

'But why me?'

'You're the one with the brains,' Omega said. 'You're brighter than them.'

It was true. Mort had always known it but he'd never been able to explain it to Ginner and Gaz. They'd been together so long that it wasn't right for one of them to be more intelligent than the others. It was OK that Gaz was the thickest, though; everyone accepted that.

'What's the job?' he asked.

Omega was stripping off his T-shirt and walking towards the bathroom. 'Relax,' he said. 'Gimme time to get a shave. Look at the view.'

He left the bathroom door open and Mort listened to water splashing into the sink. This was a posh house. When Omega had given him the address at Victoria Dock village he'd thought it must be an old house, something broken-down like his mother's place or the flats that his mates lived in. But this was new; shiny pantiles on the roof, little wooden balcony outside the front bedroom, burglar alarm on the outside wall. Inside there was wall-to-wall carpeting in all the rooms, pictures like real paintings on the walls, and in the kitchen there was a cooker with a separate hob and a fridge that looked like a cupboard.

'I rented it,' Omega said, standing in the bathroom doorway. 'Short let, three months, but I'll be long-gone before the lease is finished. You don't want to be traced you go for something like this, middle-class area, the neighbours out all day and at night they don't peek through their curtains.' He had shaving foam on his face and neck, his bare chest matted with black hair.

He went back into the bathroom but reappeared again a moment later. 'You ever killed a man?' he asked.

Mort shook his head.

'But you've thought about it, right?'

'If they'd take the hint,' Mort said, 'go back home and leave us alone, there'd be no need. But as it is they don't leave us no choice. It's us or them.'

'You get used to it after a while,' Omega said. 'Killing. It's a matter of duty.'

'You talking about the White House, the hostel?' Mort asked.

'Yeah, some of the people in there won't come out alive.'

'I know,' Mort said. 'They'll be an example, like a message to all the others.'

Omega retreated back into the bathroom. His voice came through the doorway. 'I knew you were bright,' he said. 'Picked you out straight away, soon as I saw you.'

They walked along the riverside path, past the lush gardens of the new houses. Even the streetlights were fancy around here, huge white pearls, two to each pole. Mort wondered what the people who lived here did for a living. Be a lot of Jews, he reckoned, drug dealers and crooked accountants, up-market pimps and Europig councillors.

'Have you seen our website?' he asked Omega.

'Yeah. Good, as far as it goes.'

'Still early days,' Mort said. 'We're adding to it all the time.'

'You need a kids' page. Get them while they're young, before the establishment brainwash them. If we don't do something about it the schools will turn out politically correct robots.'

'Yeah,' Mort said. He'd never thought of that, a page for kids. Maybe Alice could help him, and Joolz. The two of them could do good work. Useful work. 'Good idea.'

'But first I need you to help me.'

'Just say the word,' Mort said.

'There's a woman been giving me some trouble. Needs a warning. White woman married to a coon. I want for you and me to introduce ourselves to the husband.'

25

A Vaginal Citizen

Phineus had his brother, Mike, with him, a man who rarely smiled but who had fathered seven children. Mike worked on the buses and liked to compare stress and suicide rates with other occupations. If you believed statistics – Palesa did, but Phineus wasn't at all sure – then the job of a bus driver was the most dangerous in the country. Bus driving, according to Mike, put you in line for three mortal hazards. Road accidents were one of them; as a bus driver you were in traffic for an average of seven hours every day – up to ten hours with overtime – and after the fourth hour the rate of accident occurrence went up 10 to 15 per cent an hour.

Remarkably, the rate of accident occurrence went down during the first hour of overtime, but during the second hour it went up to 20 per cent, and during the third hour of overtime a bus driver was 25 per cent more likely to be involved in an accident.

Then there was stress, another killer. Bus driving was in the top ten occupations for stress, which led to the formation of ulcers and heart disease, digestive problems of all kinds. It undermined your health and eventually killed you. Phineus, way back in the eighties, had told Mike the joke about stress being when you wake up screaming in the night and find that you haven't been to sleep yet. But Mike didn't laugh, couldn't see anything funny in it.

Third was the suicide rate. If you were a bus driver you were more than twice as likely to top yourself as a construction worker, and three times more likely than someone who worked in the health industry (excepting doctors and mental-health professionals who killed themselves regularly).

Mike himself had not been in a road accident during his twenty years on the buses, and he was in robust health with a strong heart and the appetite of a horse. Remarkably for a man with little or no sense of humour, he wasn't a depressive, and was far too involved in the lives of his seven children ever to contemplate suicide. But he loved to moan. It had started when he was a kid and during his adult life he had developed it into a minor art form.

They were sitting in Nell's Mitsubishi Shôgun, Heartbreak and Nell in the front and Phineus and Mike in the back. Phineus was going over the plan one more time. 'You find a parking place about halfway down Margaret Street,' he said. 'Mike and me'll be standing at the top. The last time I saw them they were driving a light-blue Orion, bit of a heap, number plates so black you can't read them.

'I don't think they'll bother us, just slow down for a while and have a look. They're after Chaz, really, a kid on his own, they're not likely to take on a couple of grown men, especially with Mike being such a big 'un.

'Soon as we see them I'll hit dial on the mobile and it'll ring at your end. No point in answering it, it's just a signal for you to come along the street. If they're picking on us, you put a beam on them and they'll be back in their car and away. But the most likely thing is they've already gone past, in which case you slow down for me and Mike to get aboard and we'll follow them back to their base.'

He looked at Heartbreak and Nell, their faces half turned towards him. 'Got it?'

'I think we can probably work it out between us,' Nell said. 'You're on the mobile anyway, so if we forget some of it, develop Alzheimer's, say, or I have a stroke or Heartbreak has one of his fits, we can give you a ring, get fresh instructions.'

Phineus smiled. 'I'm new at this organizing game,' he said. 'Palesa was the one who did all this stuff in the family.'

'Nell's just taking the piss,' Heartbreak said. 'Extracting the Michael, if you'll excuse the pun, Mike.'

'What?' said Mike, bemused. 'Are we gonna do this or no?'

Nell manoeuvred the Lump into a space between a gold Nissan and a black Mazda, got it up close to the kerb first try. She put the handbrake on and looked over at Heartbreak, see if he had any criticism or praise.

'That time's past,' he said, 'when a woman would get the parking right first time and the guy with her would pat her on the back, tell her how great she was. These days we take it for granted women can drive cars just the same as men.'

Nell did a double-take. 'Heartbreak,' she said, 'if feminism has managed to tuck you under its wing there isn't much left for it to achieve. One or two more declarations like that and the sisters can pack up and go home, start perming their hair again, wear bras, have male offspring.'

Heartbreak shrugged his shoulders. He was wearing a new black T with a slogan on the front: *Do I Come Here Often?*

Nell waited a while, then she said, 'You don't want to say anything else in case you spoil it. That right?'

'I've talked myself into trouble plenty,' Heartbreak said. 'Now I've reached the age I know when to quit. Stop when I'm ahead.'

'I want to ask you one question,' Nell said. 'And I want you to promise to tell the truth. OK?'

'I'm not afraid of the truth, Nell. The truth will make me strong, didn't somebody say that?'

'That's an evasive answer, Heartbreak. If I ask you a question will you tell me the truth? Yes or no?'

'Yes.'

'That little speech about women being as good at driving as men, did you mean it, or was it something you thought I'd like to hear?'

'Both, Nell. Yes, to both of those questions.'

'Would you say the same thing to a guy? If it wasn't me driving, but Phineus, say, or Mike, or your old mate, Deke?'

'You said one question, Nell, now you're coming up with dozens of them.'

'It's all part of the same question.'

'It's not,' Heartbreak said. 'These are completely different questions. I stuck to my part of the bargain, answered the one question truthfully, like I promised. Now you're asking loads of questions, loaded questions, designed to lead me into deep water. This's one of the things about women. A guy wouldn't do that. If a guy said there

142

was just gonna be one question, there'd be the one question and then we'd move on to something else.'

'*One of the things about women.* What does that mean?'

'Don't take it personal, Nell.'

'What does it mean?'

'Jeez. Some women are good drivers and some are bad, like I said. You're one of the good ones. The Lump's not an easy thing to drive, but you handle it real well. I can't imagine anyone else driving it as good as you do.'

'But?'

'There's other things where men and women are different.'

Nell looked straight ahead. The wind changed and the Lump's windows were scratched by rain. 'We're talking anatomy here, right?'

'That, yeah.'

'And something else?'

'Guys don't want to get to the root of everything like this. If a guy says something, that's it, he's said what he wants to say. He doesn't want to say something else. Y'know I wanted to say that thing about women and cars, and that's what I wanted to say. But what you're doing now, chasing it down, making it sound like I wanted to say something else, that's different. That makes women different to men.'

'How?'

'They're more interested in finding other meanings behind the words. Guys don't do that.'

'OK, so we vaginal citizens are more interested in finding out what people mean rather than taking what they say at face value. That what you're trying to tell me?'

Heartbreak sighed.

'Is it?'

'Yes, Nell.'

'And you think there's something wrong with that?'

'Jeez, no,' he said. 'It's one of the things that keeps us distinct, so men can see women and women can see men. All I'm saying here is that it can be frustrating, because we don't see eye to eye on these things. Guys can't understand why women want to pin them down, and women can't understand why guys want to be left alone.'

Nell smiled at him. 'You've wriggled out of it,' she said. 'I thought I had you pinned down there, and you've got yourself off the hook.'

'I've been around a long time,' he told her. 'This's one of the things I've learned to do.'

A car went past and they both squinted at it through the half-light and the rain.

'Could've been blue,' Nell said.

'But it wasn't an Orion.'

She sighed. 'It's times like this I wish I hadn't given up smoking. When you're waiting, hanging around, confined, and there's just space in front of you because you don't know how long you're gonna have to wait for what you're waiting for, then if you have a fag it's a real comfort.'

'You can talk to me,' Heartbreak said. 'Women enjoy talking and guys like to listen to them if they're interested in them. If they don't, they'd rather listen to rain.'

'You're playing with fire, you know. Could end up getting burnt. Anyway, my experience says that men like to talk just as much as anyone else, so long as it's about themselves.'

'We could talk about you,' he said. 'There's plenty I don't know.'

'We could talk about me all night,' Nell said. 'There'd still be plenty I didn't tell you.'

'Give it a go. I'm all ears.'

'Sally's got a new boyfriend.'

'No, Nell, I don't wanna hear about your sister.'

'She met him at her Gestalt therapy class. Really tall with silver hair trained up into a quiff at the front. He's into amateur operatics and he's teaching her to sing.'

'Jeez.'

'It was a duet before I came out tonight. "This Is My Lovely Day". Remember that?'

'Vaguely. It's from a show. Rodgers and thingy.'

'No. It's earlier than them.'

'I don't do earlier than them, Nell. I go back as far as *South Pacific*, maybe *Guys and Dolls*, but even that's hazy. Bill Haley I can remember, Charlie Gracie and Buddy Knox and Little Anthony, they're more my style.'

A light-blue Orion went past and Nell watched its tail-lights for a full two seconds. 'Is that us?' she said.

'The right model and colour and it's a heap. There's three young Aryans in there with their hearts set on purity and perfection.'

'Oh,' she said. Her hands fluttered around the steering column. She jangled the keys, which were hanging from the ignition, wiped a patch of mist from the windscreen and sat back in her seat to compose herself.

The mobile rang. Nell reached for it, but Heartbreak got there first and switched it off. He paused for a few seconds, then said, 'What are you waiting for? Easter?'

'Uh?'

'These guys are getting away, Nell. We're supposed to follow them. That's why we're here.'

'I know. I'm ready now.' She started the engine and eased the Lump out into the street. It leaped forward a couple of times but settled down fairly quickly. The Lump was like a horse that had been badly broken; part of it was wild and dangerous and it needed to test whoever was driving, see if it could unseat them somehow.

At the junction with Beverley Road the Orion had come to a stop. The rear window was splattered with rain but Nell could see the outlines of the guys inside gesturing towards Phineus and Mike on the pavement. One of the car's windows was wound down and an arm and hand appeared, the middle finger raised in an obscene salute to the two black men.

Nell flashed them and the head in the rear of the car swivelled towards her, the eyes locked on hers. Human eyes; not those of a misshapen monster. They were angry, maybe cruel in the moment that they were illuminated by her beam. But perhaps they were capable of reflecting pity and compassion, she thought, intelligence, humour, even love.

The Orion moved away fast, taking a right onto the main road, narrowly missing a bus and giving the bus driver a blast of the horn for his trouble. Phineus and Mike came over and climbed into the back of the Lump. 'That's them,' Phineus said. 'See if you can stay with them, Nell.'

She looked both ways and followed the same route as the Orion, keeping one car between them, anxious not to let the kids in the car know they were being followed. The eyes worried her. Everything was happening fast now and she wanted to concentrate on the action, but the eyes had sparked off something inside her, a half-conceived insight. Demonizing people didn't help, she thought. Hitler, Stalin, all the others who had killed and maimed generations of innocents, it was a mistake to regard them as monsters, as something less than human. When we did that we were conspiring to let ourselves off the hook, denying our own complicity in their rise to power, our own guilt in searching out a strong leader capable of shouldering our individual responsibilities.

The Orion turned onto Spring Bank and Nell let the thought go, concentrated on keeping the Lump on the tail of their quarry. She would come back to her cogitations later, talk to Heartbreak about it, see if she could stir up whatever remained of his grey matter.

They followed the light-blue car along Derringham and Argyle Street, took a left into Anlaby Road and a quick right into Linnaeus Street. The Orion pulled up and parked a good half metre from the kerb and the doors opened simultaneously, spilling three young men into the drizzling rain. Nell kept going, aware that Phineus and Mike, in the back, were ducking down below the level of the Lump's windows.

The three guys they passed were swaggering, the arrogance of youth oozing through their body language. Sure of their invincibility, blithely ignorant of every byway of history, every nuance of human endeavour that did not fit their model of the universe, they crossed Linnaeus Street and entered a darkened house through a door painted red, white and blue.

Nell drove down to Walker Street, turned the Lump around and came back up to within a hundred metres of the Orion. A light showed in the upper front window of the house and occasionally the blurred outline of a figure flitted past the flimsy curtains.

'We could wait for them to come out,' Mike said. 'With a bit of luck they'll appear one at a time. Easy meat.'

'I want to think about the next stage,' Phineus said. 'Tonight was about finding where they live. We've done that.'

Nell shifted in the driving seat, turned to face Mike. 'What d'you mean?' she asked.

'We give them a beating they'll remember the rest of their lives,' he said.

Phineus felt her gaze move over to him. 'Is that what you're gonna do?' she said. 'Beat them up?'

'You got a better suggestion, Nell?'

'Yeah, I have. You go to the police. You tell them the whole story, you give them this address, and you leave the rest to them.'

'The police won't move on it,' Mike said.

'That's not our problem,' Nell said.

'It's my problem,' Phineus told her. 'My boy can't go out of the house.'

'We go with him, then,' Nell said. 'Wherever he goes one of us goes with him. We protect him. We start a public campaign to get these guys off the street. But if you lot go wading in there with baseball bats you're no better than the scum you're beating up. You might kill one of them, end up doing a life sentence.'

Phineus didn't reply. He hoped Mike would have an answer for her, or Heartbreak. There was a long silence.

'You want to do it, don't you?' Nell said. 'All of you. You think you can solve this thing by breaking a few heads.'

Heartbreak put his hand on her wrist. 'Nell,' he said, placatingly, 'nothing's been decided yet. You heard what Phineus said. We wanted to know where they live.'

Nell pulled away from him and faced the street. She scrabbled for the keys in the ignition. 'I'm going home,' she said. 'If anyone wants to stay they'd better get out now.'

'We'll come back with you,' Phineus told her.

During the journey Phineus thought what Palesa would have done in a situation like this. Nell's idea about a public campaign sounded like something Palesa would've come up with. But Phineus didn't know how to do that. And, anyway, even if he did, it wouldn't guarantee to get these shits off Chaz's back. That was the main thing, after all, that was what he wanted to accomplish, for his son to walk the streets without somebody threatening his life.

Nell dropped them off on the corner of Fountain Road. She and Heartbreak carried on along Beverley Road. Phineus didn't notice the leather-clad motorcyclist who followed the Lump as Nell drove it away. Neither he nor Mike had been aware of the bike being wheeled out of the house in Linnaeus Street as Nell had prepared to drive them home.

And a few minutes later, Heartbreak, on his way home to bed, was unaware that the same leather-clad figure was parked in the shadows of Grafton Street, a few doors down from Nell's house. While Heartbreak disappeared along the street, the figure on the bike removed his helmet, revealing a youthful head of thin red hair.

26

Lying in the Flowerbed

Katy Madika was repeatedly raped every night. Her daytime consciousness was dulled, dumbed-down to a level of bare functionality. She maintained her sensory capabilities at a level that enabled her to avoid accidents, to attend to her child and go through the motions of a daily routine. But she was sleepwalking through life.

At night, in bed next to her husband, Daniel, she came awake to the horrors of her world. She was tossed between the murderer in the Panama and the man with the raised keloids on his face. The dreams pulled her in and she had to follow each step of the way. It made no difference that she knew where the dream would lead, that she protested against its inevitability with every nerve and muscle in her body.

There was a cliff face, behind her the open sea. There was a light breeze blowing and a thin sun, which produced no shadows. Katy knew that she would have to scale the face of the cliff, but as she looked at it she could find no obvious path. Straight up would be impossible; there were huge areas of dry soil, like sand, where no hand- or foot-holds existed. To the left and right there were small shrubbed areas, but in each case the path above them turned into an overhang, which was unclimbable without ropes and other mountaineering equipment.

Katy wanted to stay where she was but the waves behind her were creeping closer, threatening to drag her out to sea or to batter her against the wall of the cliff. She made her way upwards and found a cleft or fissure, not visible from below, in which she could fit her body. With her back to one side of this vertical crevice she adopted a sitting position and found she could push herself skywards by bracing her legs and feet on the opposite side.

The effort was exhausting and after some time she stopped to rest, wedged there halfway up the open chimney. It was while she was getting her breath back that the metamorphosis began. The rupture or split in the cliff face in which she was lodged was not what it seemed. Katy had assumed some force of nature, some seismic movement, had rent the material of the cliff apart. But as she rested there she saw this was not the case at all.

Instead there was no cliff, no sea below, no sky above. What remained was unmistakably a vagina and Katy was lodged there, between the outer lips or folds. It might have been that the vagina was huge or that Katy had somehow been rendered down to a miniature of herself. She couldn't decide which and thought either alternative was as bad as the other. At least with the cliff there had been some point in climbing, there had been the possibility of a route to safety. But there seemed to be no escape from her lodging in this huge labial portal.

A scream began somewhere deep inside her as she realized that the metamorphosis had not yet gone through its full cycle. The vagina, which had been the fissure in the cliff face, was still in transition. In fact it was a vagina no longer. It was a cicatrice, a huge scar, and what she had thought to be the labia were the raised keloids that kept the edges of the scar distinct and separate.

Katy was in space, falling. The scar was above her, both of the scars were above her, on the face of the man who would rape her again and again. His fingers were already pushing her thighs apart and reaching towards her sex, inserting themselves inside her, insisting that she submit herself to his appetite.

And she was awake again, damp with sweat, staring at the darkened ceiling of her room. Daniel was sleeping beside her and the silence of the night stretched away into a frozen and deserted landscape.

She dragged herself from the bed and splashed cold water onto her eyelids in the bathroom. She listened to her daughter's even breathing for a while and went downstairs to the living room. Katy sat in a pool of light from the standard lamp and read a chapter from a novel by Carol Shields. When she'd finished it was three o'clock and she could hardly keep her eyes open.

One day in the near or distant future she would go to bed and sleep through the night. There would be no dreams or nightmares. She would not witness the murder of the hook-nosed young man or be pursued by the man in the Panama; she would not be harassed and raped by the man with the scars. Katy Madika would revert to a state of being that was more blessed than she could now imagine.

When that day came, and she fervently hoped that it would, she would once again be a middle-class housewife with a young child, and the time and leisure to play tennis in the afternoons.

She trudged up the stairs and slipped into bed next to Daniel, pulling her knees up to her chin. The room, the house, the street was quiet. Apart from Katy the whole world was sleeping. It was a safe activity. It was how people refreshed themselves, found the strength to tackle the unborn problems of the following day.

Her eyes closed, she listened to her breath coming and going. A blanket of darkness began to envelop her. It was warm and fluid, almost tangible, and it covered her in thick folds like sauce in a mixing bowl. The tautness in her back and limbs ebbed away, and her body and mind became a receptacle for a series of rhythms and time signatures. Consciousness floated above her and was replaced by image and cipher, by symbol and token and fancy.

The sheet was rucked up beneath her, and her neck and shoulders were damp with perspiration. In the dream or in the world, she couldn't decide which, there had been a commotion, screaming, the heavy sound that dead or unconscious bodies make when they fall to the ground.

Her wrists had been tied in the dream and she could still feel the indentures of the rope that had bound them. She reached out for Daniel, to make sure that she was awake, but he was not there. Must be after six o'clock. He'd gone to work.

She pulled on her dressing gown and went downstairs. Yes, there were the remains of his toast and Marmite at the kitchen table. Half a cup of coffee, still lukewarm.

Katy shivered, suddenly cold. She made her way upstairs, hoping for another couple of hours' sleep before Chloe decided it was time to get out of bed. But from the landing window she saw that Daniel's car was standing in the driveway. Her first thought was that he hadn't yet left for work and she stood there for a while expecting to see him return from closing the garage door. Perhaps he would look up and see her there, wave before driving off?

But there was something wrong.

The driver's door was closed. Daniel always backed the car out of the garage and then he got out and left the car door open while he went back to close the garage.

Don't panic, Katy told herself. He'd already left for work, found he'd forgotten something and come back to collect whatever it was, probably his papers by the side of the computer. He'd been furious when he'd discovered the hard disk had been reformatted, obliterating his precious files. *It must have been you, Katy, I don't care what you say. These machines don't reformat themselves.*

Katy took a few steps down the stairs, expecting to hear him in the sitting room or the hall. Muffled footsteps on the carpet, the rustle of paper or the sound of the front door opening or closing. But there was nothing. A silence that became ominous the longer it lasted.

The porch step was hard and cold under the soles of Katy's slippers. The early morning sun was weak and there was no breeze. The blue sky was littered with puffy clouds, white and unbusiness-like, not serious contenders for the making of rain.

'Daniel,' Katy called, hearing the hesitancy in her own voice, not really expecting him to pop his head out of the garage door and chase her back to bed. 'Daniel, are you there?'

There was something of the quality of dream in the sound of her voice, in the bizarre fact of her being out here at this time of the day and in the *Marie Celeste* feeling of her husband's car lying becalmed there in the driveway. But this was no dream. This was real life. Katy Madika was at home and her settled life had begun to go pear-shaped over the past week. Now something else had happened and she dreaded discovering exactly what it was.

'Daniel?'

She moved to the car and opened the driver's door. There was nobody there. She had been able to see that there was nobody there before she opened the door, but still, it had seemed essential to grasp the handle, hear the solid click of the thing coming open in her hand.

Red leather upholstery; luxurious bad taste. A man's car. Daniel's. There was his briefcase on the back seat, something comforting about it. If his briefcase was there Daniel couldn't be far away.

She shut the driver's door and circled the car, hesitated for a moment at the boot. No, she was being ridiculous. In a film, maybe; in some trashy depiction of wise-guys in America. But not in Hull, Victoria Avenue. Not at this end of the street.

She scanned the joins, the precision engineering that picked up the aerodynamic curve of the rear and enabled the boot to close firmly and flawlessly.

Katy turned back to the garage and entered its emptiness. Oil stains on the concrete, Daniel's shelves on the back wall, his tools and collection of cans, WD40, turpentine, half a litre of Antique White paint with which he'd stencilled the giraffe on Chloe's cot.

'Daniel?'

Silence.

'Danny?'

She backed out of the garage and turned towards the house. This was silly. He must be somewhere. A man didn't disappear into thin air like the . . . She stopped at the door of the garage and clutched her lower abdomen. *Please don't let that happen,* she thought. Daniel disappearing from the face of the earth, with no clue to his whereabouts or what had happened to him, was more than she could bear.

Then she saw the shoe.

Lying in the flowerbed. Soft brown leather, he'd bought them in Rome last year while attending some medical conference. A single shoe, abandoned. Ridiculously, Katy Madika thought of Cinderella. She knelt on the path and picked up her husband's shoe, expecting it to be warm, hoping that its warmth would indicate that Daniel was somewhere close by. But it was cold, the leather stiffened by the morning air. And holding it close to her chest didn't dissipate the feeling of deadness around it.

Daniel's other shoe was still on his foot. He was on the narrow path between the garage and the house and his right leg was folded under him, broken above the knee, the jagged end of the femur protruding through the fine weave of his suit trousers.

On her knees beside him, she checked breathing and pulse. There was life there, weak but regular. One of his eyes was closed, the other so bloody and pulped that it wasn't possible to see it. His nose was broken and there was a stream of blood coming from a wound at the back of his head.

His knuckles were grazed and cut and his suit and shirt bore witness in rips and bloodstains to a long and sustained attack.

'Daniel,' Katy said, 'what happened? What have they done to you?'

But Daniel Madika didn't answer. His body remained inert and unresponsive.

'He's lucky to be alive,' the young doctor in the Accident and Emergency Unit said, peeling off his rubber gloves. 'His lung's collapsed and he's in a coma. There are a number of other fractures, some worse than others. That's all we can tell you for the moment.'

'But he'll be all right?' Katy said. 'He'll come through?'

'You should go home, Mrs Madika. See if you can get a friend, someone to stay with you. There's nothing you can do here. Your husband needs sustained nursing care and a degree of luck. If you have faith you might pray for him.'

27

Black Boy Grounded

'What I'm saying is let it cool down.' Phineus's deep tones were ragged from a lifetime of smoking cigarettes.

'By staying in the house? It's been a week.'

'Go out during the day, like everybody else. If you have to go out at night make sure somebody else's with you. Listen, Chaz, you're lucky they didn't mark you. Guys like these don't just want to frighten you; they want to obliterate you. To kill you.'

'It's like giving in to them,' Chaz said.

'It's not giving in, it's being cleverer than them.' The elder man fingered his grizzled beard. 'When they mark you out, son, they keep on coming. If you were white we could go to the police and they'd do something about it. But as it is there's no one going to help except ourselves and our friends.

'You're my only son, Chaz. In the long run we can stop these people and have some kind of life. But in the short run I'm not prepared to lose you.'

'You're making me disappear?'

'A little, yes. I want you to disappear as far as these thugs who attacked you are concerned. If they don't see you they'll forget about you.'

Chaz gazed at the pile of the carpet, feeling as if his life had come to an end. He had slept fitfully in the nights since his attack, unable to escape from a vision of castration. His eyes would close and consciousness would slip away but a few minutes later he would spring awake covered in sweat, his inner eye focused on a hostile universe. He'd crept into his father's bed last night and wept on the elder man's chest, inhaling the ancient scent, which had changed little since Chaz's earliest memories. The pungent, moss-like fragrance of patchouli oil, which his father used as a moisturiser against his dry, ashy skin.

'Why me?' he said. 'Why did they have to pick on me?'

'Because of the colour of your skin,' his father said. 'There's nothing complicated about it.'

'You don't think that's complicated?'

The old man let it go. 'It's not personal, Chaz. That's what I'm trying to tell you. They didn't see *you*. They saw your colour and they used it to justify their feelings of impotence. Deep in the recesses of the racist's brain there is a hopeless egoism and naivety. He thinks that the problems of the world will be solved if everyone is like him.'

Chaz smiled for the first time in a week. It was a wry smile but it was there.

'So I'm still grounded?'

'For the immediate future, the next few days. I need to know you're safe. That'll give us time to think of a way around this stuff.'

Phineus stood at the door of the hospital ward and watched Palesa for a while. She was sitting in a chair by the window, rocking backwards and forwards. She was facing away from him and he could see part of her profile and imagine that she was still young and beautiful like the day he'd first seen her, before Chaz had been born. A blackbird flew past the window and Palesa's head moved along with it bringing the left side of her face into view. There was no consciousness there; only flesh and bone uninformed by will, the last vestige of what remained of his wife.

'How's she been?' he asked a passing nurse.

'As ever, Mr Marmon. She's never much trouble.'

He pulled a chair over to Palesa and sat on it. 'How you doin', babe?' he asked.

The woman looked through him. He'd blocked her view through the window but she didn't crane her neck or try to see around him. She remained impassive, as if he wasn't there.

She was wearing a pink and white flannelette dressing gown with a short belt tied around the middle with a bow. Under that she had a long winceyette night-dress in blue with tiny dogs on it, all sitting up and begging. The skirt of the night-dress showed way below the hem of the dressing gown, giving her an air of abandonment, as though love had given up the search for her.

Since she'd been in the hospital they'd taken to parting her hair on the left side. Palesa had never had a parting in her thick growth of hair, but now it had thinned it was possible. It made her look like someone else.

'Good,' he said. 'We're doing good, too. Me and Chaz. I've been working overtime this week, 'cause they had a conference at the University and we had to go in and make up the beds, clean the rooms for them. But that's all finished now. I'll be back on the early morning stint.

'And Chaz's doin' fine, too, thanks for asking. He wanted to come and see you today but he's got too much schoolwork. Studying away, there. Yeah, he's gonna come up with good results, probably end up in a posh university somewhere. Doesn't wanna stay here in Hull.

'Only one little problem's come up on the horizon. It's not a pretty thing, babe, but I'm gonna tell you about it because I think you'd wanna know. And besides, you might have ideas that'll help us with it.'

Palesa looked down at the back of her hand and picked up some invisible object that had been lurking there. She raised her head and looked over to her right, her mouth open, a thin line of spittle running down her chin.

'Chaz was attacked by some racists the other night,' Phineus continued. 'He wasn't hurt much but he was shook up pretty bad.'

It was when he used the word 'racists' that Palesa shifted her focus. She drew in her breath and moved her eyes around the room. That's all she did. Nothing more. But Phineus thought that the politicized word had somehow awoken memories in her. It was as if he'd given an old actor a whiff of greasepaint. For an instant Palesa looked as though she might rejoin the stream of life.

Palesa had always been disappointed with Phineus's attitude of not getting involved, of leaving-well-enough-alone. But her own philosophy of taking on the State every time a politician told a lie had ended in her present condition. She'd been on her bike, riding into town to see the local MP about the imprisonment of Zoora Shah, when a gold-coloured Vauxhall driven by a seventeen-year-old girl had caught her back wheel. The car hadn't been speeding, nothing like that, and the girl was accompanied by an uncle with a full licence. Everything was legal.

Palesa was still alive, in a way. Phineus came to see her at the hospital every day. 'I've got a plan to make sure they don't attack him again,' he told her. 'We can't stand by and let our children be beaten-up on their own doorsteps.' He waited for a moment. 'Yeah, I thought you'd approve,' he said. 'Sometimes things happen and you have to respond, otherwise people'll walk all over you.'

Palesa strung a few notes together, could have been the opening of the *Internationale*, but it hit an impasse where the same note crashed into the one before it over and over again, like a pile-up on a motorway.

'Chaz said they mentioned Omega,' Phineus told her. 'You know what that is? They're terrorists, girl. They've said they'll kill coloured folk to make a point. And they say in the old days if a farmer wanted to get rid of rats he'd kill one of them and pin it to the barn door, then the other rats would see it there and move on to somebody else's territory.' He shook his head from side to side.

Palesa closed her eyes for a few moments, her lips moved slightly, as though she might be humming a tune, but no sound came from her. Chaz had stopped visiting her at the hospital over a year ago, insisting there was no point. 'My mother's dead,' he'd said. 'What we go to see in the hospital is a shell.'

Phineus said, 'We're still missing you, girl. Chaz doesn't say much about it but he goes quiet sometimes and I know what he's thinking. Me? Every minute of the day some days. Always when I get into that bed of ours. I sleep on my side and imagine you over on yours.'

He sat looking at her for several minutes. He got his handkerchief out of his trouser pocket and wiped the dribble from her chin. Then he leaned over and kissed her on the forehead. 'See you tomorrow,' he said. 'Keep smiling.'

28

Work in Progress

When Stone got to System.ini, Eve Caldwell was already there, her pale-blue eyes flashing in the morning light. She was standing behind the counter with a baby in her arms, looking pleased with herself, as if she'd discovered the key to a foreign language or a cure for cancer.

Baby with mixed blood, coffee coloured; a round face with eyes like huge gems. Eyes that gulped down everything hungrily as if in fear that the world would move on, be unable to wait for the child to assimilate it.

The baby didn't make sense. Eve didn't have a baby of her own, she wasn't a baby kind of woman. And babies usually came with mothers, sometimes with fathers, which was a change since Stone's time in the slammer. Before he went inside babies always came with mothers and never with fathers. Not in cafes anyway. Now, in System.ini there was a space for changing nappies in the men's room as well as the women's room.

That was part of the punishment, because while they had you in there, everyday life on the out continued, and they turned the world upside down, so when you'd finished your time you were so out of date there was no way of catching up.

And where was the mother? The baby's mother? Stone didn't ask, he'd work it out for himself during the next hour or so. Or if Eve wanted him to know who the baby was she'd tell him.

'This is Chloe,' she said. 'Katy's daughter. Have you met?'

'Yes. I thought she was a boy, before Katy introduced us.'

'Oh, she's nothing at all like a boy,' Eve said. And then to the baby: 'Are you, my sweetie?'

Chloe didn't seem interested in the question. She was working out why a cup had a handle, getting the feel of it, wondering if there was a better way of solving the problem of cups. It would be some time before she turned her attention to gender, to working out which side of that equation best suited her.

Eve was trying to enforce a feminine gender on to Chloe before Chloe had any idea of what it might mean in her life. And Eve was herself bisexual, happy and capable of going either way in a sexual relationship. So why was she trying to pin Chloe down before the kid had thought about it? Stone didn't know, couldn't understand, and didn't ask. He didn't share his thoughts with Eve. Not today. He might bring it up tomorrow or the next day. For the moment he didn't want to be distracted from the reason that Chloe was there.

'Katy's at the hospital,' Eve said. 'Her husband was beaten up. As he was leaving for work this morning.'

Stone waited.

'He's badly hurt,' Eve said.

'Why?'

Eve shook her head. 'We don't know. He's in a coma, hasn't said anything.'

Chloe wasn't concerned with this news. She hadn't found a name for everything yet, so language didn't reveal the same kind of complexity to her as it did to other people. To a certain extent she could ignore it, concentrate on the things that interested her. Even news of her father being beaten up and left in a coma didn't interfere with her current preoccupation with cups and handles.

Stone had been like that all his life.

Before he met Ginny he had been stuck with a single version of his life. He was pinned there like a butterfly in a collection. When Ginny came along, after he'd done his time, and began reinterpreting the world for him, a miracle happened. He was released from his category.

Stone loved order and remembered his first realization that things are identified by their names. Almost everything in the world had been pinned down. There were broad categories, animal, vegetable, mineral, but beyond them there were sub-categories and genres, so that the world spread out in a meaningful, patterned existence. Everything was there, substantial, safe, except for the cracks between genres, the fissures that separate reality from fiction, the known from the unknown.

For the whole of his life Stone had loved the known and feared the unknown. But since his release from prison, since meeting up with Ginny Bradshaw, he had begun the arduous task of embracing the unknown.

For most of his childhood he had found it difficult to separate the specific from the general. Team games had been impossible, far too much was happening on a football field for Stone to grasp and hang on to the central tenets of the game. He was tried a couple of times for the school team but it was a miserable experience for everyone concerned. In fact, any activity that meant co-operating with others usually turned out badly.

Later, in adolescence, when he became interested in music, he had to listen to recordings alone in his room. He couldn't listen to Robert Johnson or Louis Armstrong or Chet Baker or Sarah Vaughan or the Beatles or Springsteen or Mary Black or Shirley Horn or Jo Ann Kelly or Dr John or Madonna while other people were in the room. Stone found it impossible to filter out peripheral sounds, so any background noise distracted him. He would put his ear next to the speaker and close his eyes.

When he was invited to parties or if he was in a pub, he would be faced with the same dilemma. Everyone talking to everyone else at the same time. Stone would move up close to the person who was speaking to him, unaware he was trespassing on personal space, unable to perceive that his companion was made uncomfortable by the proximity.

But it was eye contact that got him into real trouble. Eye contact or lack of it. Most people crack the code while they are still children. They know instinctively (or perhaps it's a learning process) that non-verbal communication has rules of grammar and syntax in much the same way as spoken language. There is a reasonable amount of time to establish and hold eye contact. If someone holds it too long they are thought to be coming on, flirting or being aggressive. If eye contact is not established at all, or only fleetingly, then the perpetrator is regarded as weird, uninterested or not listening properly.

As a child and teenager Stone did not grasp the unwritten code of eye contact. He always got it wrong. No one told him how important it was and even if they had, he would not have been able to respond appropriately unless the process was broken down for him into its constituent parts.

What he had learned from Ginny was that when he was speaking to someone or someone was speaking to him, he should usually look at them, but not stare. He should look at them for not less than a third of the time and for not more than two thirds of the time. This was a guideline that enabled him to get through the day without too much trouble. If you look at someone for less than one third of the time they think you are shy or dishonest. If you look at them for more than two thirds of the time they think you like them, or, if you look straight into their eyes, that you want to fight.

The other thing he'd learned was that if you're not talking to someone and they are not talking to you it's best not to look at them at all. Even if someone is facing away from you, they'll feel your eyes prickling on the back of their neck. A good rule to remember.

Stone didn't remember all of the rules all of the time. He was getting better at it, making some headway every day. But he wasn't finished yet, and didn't believe he ever would be. Still very much a work in progress.

Aunt Nell said that was the same for her, and for Heartbreak. Possible exceptions were most of Sally's boyfriends, who seemed to be in the business of contracting rather than expanding their horizons, guys who at some crucial stage of life had chosen to wither rather than bloom.

'There's nothing wrong with being weird,' Heartbreak had said. 'Show me somebody who *isn't* a nut. Christ, I never met one guy in my life who wasn't weird in some way. Sure, when you first meet them they've got this mask, they know pretty well how to keep it hidden. But a couple of drinks down the road and you can see it leaking out. They're into torture or they wanna fuck little kids, there's guys who think they've got the big C or something growing in their heads, women who sit down and cry if you say boo to them. Sometimes I think I'm the only normal guy I know.'

Nell laughed until tears rolled down her cheeks. She had to find a chair and sit down.

'This's my experience of life,' Heartbreak had said. 'I've been around a long time and this is what I've seen. The world is made up of meltdowns. This is why I believe in God. Somebody has got to be looking after the world, 'cause human beings can't manage it on their own.'

'I can't cope with God,' Stone had told him. 'Life's complicated enough as it is.'

Since that conversation Stone had been watching people, to see if he could recognize who was normal and who was pretending. System.ini should have been a good place to do this. People got stuck in front of a cathode ray tube and filtered out daily reality, crossed over into virtual spaces. They were off-guard and it was one of the few times you could look at them without giving them that prickly feeling at the back of the neck.

The problem with it was the tube sucked them in. If you watched you could see them disappear, so you were left observing a shade or a shell. There was nothing to look at when somebody was hooked up to the system. The only time you saw them was when they arrived or when they were paying up to leave.

Stone could see himself the same way. He could sit and surf and at the same time stand back, so his body was at the terminal, his fingers punching the keys, while another Stone, dark and ephemeral, stood at the back wall of the room watching himself disappear.

Katy arrived to collect Chloe. She had rings under her eyes and she avoided eye contact, prepared to look anywhere else in the room. Her features were strained as if she'd been riding in a high wind and small throbbing veins had made their way to the surface of her skin. A little more pressure, Stone thought, and her head would split apart. He imagined it exploding like a bomb, splattering blood and gristle on the walls.

She talked to Eve for a while, her voice high, so close to hysteria that people at the terminals turned their faces away from the screen to clock her. Chloe, who had been entertained by Eve all morning and had seemed incapable of anything but smiles and gurgles, was reduced to a fret as she was stung by her mother's distress and tension.

'How is he?' Eve asked.

Katy's mouth seemed to draw form from her cheeks, making her face sag like a deflating balloon. 'He's not responding, he's got a punctured lung.'

'Do you know what happened?'

Katy's fists clenched and unclenched, her hands fluttered at her sides. She looked out of the window at a bank of high cloud on the other side of the river. 'He's unconscious,' she said. 'They don't know when he's going to come round.'

Eve went to her and clasped her arms around Katy, hugging her close. She emitted a low groaning sound not unlike the call of a lamb and the two of them, for the space of a moment, merged into each other, their individual margins blurring into a new form.

'I'll come home with you,' Eve said. 'You don't want to be on your own.'

'No.' Katy drew back quickly. 'I'll be all right. I've got Chloe to keep me occupied. I need to be quiet.' She fussed with Chloe's pram, achieving nothing apart from a show of bravado.

'It's not a problem,' Eve said. 'Stone can hold the fort.'

'No. Thanks all the same, I'd rather be by myself.' She lifted Chloe into the pram and slipped a pink leather harness around her back, the baby protesting at the top of her voice.

'Well, if you're sure,' Eve said uncertainly, watching as Katy manoeuvred the pram through the door.

'Thanks for everything,' Katy said, looking over her shoulder. 'I'll let you know how Daniel is later.'

And then she was gone. Eve shrugged and showed Stone her palms. The punters at the terminals turned back to the relative ease of cyberspace and a woman at the counter asked him for a cappuccino. Like a film, Stone thought, a scene played out on celluloid or videotape or DVD. Everything should fade now, the images should break up, disintegrate, the screen be reduced to blackness.

But it couldn't happen because the customer wanted a piece of carrot cake with her coffee; she stood there waiting while Stone got the knife and cut off a wedge big enough to keep her happy. She smiled and paid him and he took her money and worked out the change and gave it to her, momentarily confused by her smile, which remained in place. The woman checked her change and put it in her purse, then picked up the tray with the coffee and cake and walked over to a table and sat down.

'I'm going after her,' Stone said to Eve. 'You all right here?'

Eve glanced around the café and nodded her head. 'Don't be long.'

He left and walked quickly along the pavement. Katy and Chloe were no longer in the street. He turned the corner and went past a pub with hanging baskets of plants dripping water to the pavement. He took a zebra-crossing and passed a teenager sleeping in a doorway with a dog. The sun came from behind a cloud and was immediately engulfed by another one. The morning was pale-blue with streaks of red and yellow, and someone had given it all a wash of silver-grey. It smelled of diesel fumes and sour milk and something rotten from the river.

He came up behind her and touched her shoulder and her body jerked into spasm like the dummies they use in simulated road accidents. Her arms flapped as though they had been sewn on.

'Oh my God,' she said, her hand on her heart, her eyes large and staring.

'Who did you think it was?'

She shook her head. She glanced at Chloe, who was sleeping a troubled sleep in the pram. 'I don't know. You gave me a shock.'

Stone waited. He looked into her eyes. He didn't blink.

'What?' she said. 'I don't know what you mean.'

'It's connected,' he said. 'You know what I mean.'

She pushed the pram, continued walking along the road. Stone kept in step with her. She said, 'There's no need to come with me. I'd rather be on my own.'

'Somebody's got to you,' he said. 'This beating of your husband; it was a warning.'

'You don't know what you're talking about.'

'This won't be the end of it,' Stone said. 'People who are prepared to go this far don't stop. They'll be back, Katy.'

He watched her features deflate, thought she might collapse into tears, but something kept her going. 'Everything's all right,' she said. 'You needn't have come after me. Everything's fine. Honest.'

He let her go. 'You've got my number,' he said. 'If you wait until they come back it will be too late.'

He watched her back as she made for home, the curve of her

buttocks rocking from side to side like a small boat on a calm ocean. He shook his head and turned back towards System.ini. Katy was frightened and the fear was close to paralysing her. Stone knew what it could do to a person's head, how it could twist perception and turn life inside out so the nightmares moved into the day and the daylight was engulfed by shadow.

The teenager in the doorway was on his feet now. He had one leg in his trousers and the other one out. He was wearing Y-fronts stained yellow and the crotch was torn and threadbare. As Stone walked past, the boy began to scream and rive at his own face with blackened fingernails.

29

Tossers

'I told you to stop and you just went on kicking the guy.'

'I was into it,' Mort said, laughing. 'Enjoying my work.'

Omega narrowed his eyes and stared at him over the table. They were sitting in the bar of the Spring Bank Tavern a few minutes after the landlord had called time. Mort was nursing the remains of his pint and Omega had already finished his glass of sparkling water.

Omega's eyes were as dead as Christmas spirit, pale, watery blue with thin red veins threading their way through the white.

'I stopped,' Mort said. 'The guy's still alive.'

'For how long? The idea was to work him over, keep his wife in a state of shock. I want her paralysed. Every time she thinks of going to the police, I want her to think about what'll happen if she does. You knew all this.'

Mort sipped from his pint. 'There's a nigger on the ground,' he said. 'I just wanna keep on stamping till there's nothing left.'

'We weren't there for your gratification. We were there to maintain a tactical advantage. I wanted to put him in the hospital for a couple of days, but what you did to him was overkill. It was too extreme, you risked sending her screaming to the police. They'll have to interview her now, ask her questions. If the guy dies there'll be a murder hunt. We'll have to call everything off.'

'I'm sorry,' Mort said. 'I was into it. I couldn't stop.'

'That's not good enough,' Omega told him.

Mort put his glass on the table and showed the palms of his hands. 'What d'you want me to do?'

'You're going to have to be disciplined, Mort. We'll convene a court. Ginner and Gaz and me will listen to the facts and devise a suitable punishment. Few days' time. After we've completed the current operation.'

Mort smiled, not quite believing what he was hearing.

'You think it's funny?'

'I didn't do nothing. I was just getting off on it.'

'You disobeyed an order. Put our whole operation in jeopardy.'

'I didn't know that,' Mort said. 'I didn't realize.'

Omega nodded. 'Right,' he said. 'That's the charge we'll be bringing against you. Stupidity.'

'But yesterday, the day before, you said I was bright,' Mort protested. 'You said I was the intelligent one.'

It was Omega's turn to let a smile crease the lines of his face. 'If you're really bright, Mort, you'll accept the charge and the punishment. Learn from it. Suffer and grow.'

Joolz was playing with the swastika stud in Mort's eyebrow, twisting it to right and left, stretching the skin so he gritted his teeth against the pain.

'Gaz noticed this foreign car behind us,' he said. 'If it'd been a British car we wouldn't've seen it. But Gaz is sharp about cars. It's one of the ways you spot the opposition. Coons drive American cars, those big flashy jobs, or sometimes they have Japanese ones. Pakis drive Peugeots or VW campers, something big so they can pack all their kids and relatives in. Liberals, they have Fiats or Renaults, and social workers have them as well, the little ones, or sometimes they have Italian cars. Commies have Russian cars, and the government lets them into the country even though they don't meet our standards. Half of them shouldn't be on the road.

'Anyway, it's a Jap job, Mitsubishi Shôgun, and five minutes later it's still there. We park outside Ginner's place on Linnaeus Street and this thing comes down the street after us and parks on the other side. Just sits there watching the house. We didn't know what the fuck was happening.

'But Ginner's really calm. He puts his leathers on, and when they move out after about twenty minutes he gets on his bike and follows them. Turns the tables. These guys think they're following us, but now it's us who's following them.'

'All of you?'

'No, just Ginner on his bike.'

'You said "us".' Joolz pulled at the swastika stud in frustration.

'Fuck, that hurts, you know.' He slapped her hand away. 'Ginner is us, he's one of us. We're all one of us.'

'I'm not,' Joolz said. 'Gaz doesn't like me and Ginner's not keen.'

'Ginner likes you,' Mort said.

'I don't think so. And even if he does he wouldn't call me "us". "Us" is just blokes and women don't fit in.' She started fiddling with the stud again.

'These things take time,' Mort said. 'They'll get used to you.'

'I don't care. They're both tossers.'

Mort was quiet. 'There's a couple of Spades in the car,' he said eventually. 'And there's a white guy, but the driver is a woman. It's her car and Ginner followed her all the way home. We're taking turns watching the house, finding out who they are, how many of them. Gaz thinks they might be Irish.'

Joolz didn't say anything. She stopped playing with the stud on his eyebrow and sat with her hands crossed in her lap. Every now and then she'd move her head, look in a different direction, but not at anything interesting. She'd look at the window or the wall or the ceiling, then she'd get stuck looking at the television screen even though it wasn't turned on. The only thing to see there was a grey square and the marks where she'd brushed the dust away with her hand.

Every surface in the room was cluttered with useless objects. If you moved too quickly, a haze of dust would rise up and swirl around until it found another resting place. It was as if she just didn't have the time or the tools to tidy up.

Mort watched her mouth while she rolled a cigarette. The thin lips were never completely closed, there was always a gap between them. Often the tip of her tongue protruded for a moment then withdrew again into the dark abyss of her mouth. She nipped the strands of tobacco from the ends of the cigarette and slipped it between her lips, looking around for a light.

Mort fished a cheap lighter from his top pocket and held the flame to the end of her roll-up. 'I've got some tailor-mades on the table,' he said. 'If you want.'

She inhaled the smoke and nicotine. She didn't speak. There was a hint of a smile on her face, as if she'd remembered something amusing from a long time ago, way back in history before time began. There was a rough, styleless edge to her, as if she was unfinished or she hadn't yet settled on the kind of woman she was going to be.

'What're you thinking?' he asked.

'It's not real,' she said. 'Your war. Following people in a car and them following you. Gaz and Ginner and you beating up immigrants and people who live with them. It's a fantasy, something you've made up in your head. It's not real life.'

'You don't understand.'

'Mmm,' she said through a lungful of tobacco smoke. 'I do understand. You don't have enough to do. You collect your social security and your mother's invalidity benefit and you buy a few ciggies and chips and sweet and sour and then you get together with that couple of tossers and pretend you're onto the main threat to England. Only that threat turns out to be a school kid or an old guy who can't tell his ass from his elbow.'

'We're fighting for our country,' Mort said. 'It's our duty. It's everybody's duty who's a true patriot.'

But Joolz had said her piece. She didn't want to say more.

'We leave it to the government,' he said, 'you know what'll happen? We'll be swamped by an ocean of black faces. It won't be long before there's more of them than there is of us. Like America. Our children'll be slaves.'

'If Ginner and Gaz were in charge of the universe,' she said, 'I'd be a slave.'

Mort knew what it was, why Gaz and Ginner didn't like her. It was because you couldn't read her. She had that poker face, looked like she might be smiling, but then again she might not be smiling at all. Might even be laughing at you. That was unnerving. And then there was the things she said, things you didn't expect. She didn't follow the rules. Always with women, you told them how it was and they'd nod or they'd laugh because they didn't understand. But they'd never question the politics, want to argue the point unless they were commies or feminists. They'd give you an earful about kids or drinking too much or pushing them around, but they wouldn't argue about the movement.

He backhanded her. Didn't think of doing it, just came out of him hard and natural. The back of his hand caught the side of her head and her feet left the carpet for a moment. She crashed into the sideboard and landed ass over tip on the floor. Her lip and one of her knees were cut and bleeding. Mort drew back his foot to give her one in the stomach but changed his mind at the last moment.

He stormed outside and went round the supermarket, filling the trolley with goodies for Alice. Bought ten pork pies, see how long it'd take her to get through them. Had a bet with himself that they wouldn't last longer than a couple of days.

Alice had never questioned the movement. When Gaz or Ginner or anybody came round the house, Alice would listen and she'd always agree. If there was something she didn't agree with, Alice wouldn't argue. She'd suggest making a cup of tea or she'd change the subject. She might tell a joke. But she'd never put one of them on the spot like Joolz did.

With Joolz it was like she was sitting there waiting to pounce. She'd be quiet with her tongue stuck between her lips and Gaz would say something about Omega, how the guy had helped train Palestinian terrorists in Germany. Joolz wouldn't say a word, but she'd shake her head from side to side, that smile beneath the surface of her skin. You couldn't be entirely sure that she was taking the rise out of Gaz, but you couldn't be sure she wasn't either.

Gaz and Ginner hated it because that was one of the things they did; put you in a position where if you kept quiet you hated yourself for letting them get away with it and if you said something they'd make you look paranoid.

She played them at their own game, that's what Joolz did, and that's why they couldn't stand her. Because she did it better than them. They'd never be able to forgive her for that.

Strange thing was that Mort liked her for it. The other women he'd met were passive, like Alice. They agreed with everything because they thought that that was the way to please a man, to keep him hanging around. Joolz didn't seem to care. When he asked her about it, she told him that if he didn't want to hang around he could go.

With Joolz you got more than you bargained for, there was always another layer, something he hadn't suspected was there before. And she was right; if he didn't like it he could go, but when he added it all up he'd be a fool not to hang around. He'd just have Alice then, and Gaz and Ginner, and the world would be a smaller and a colder place.

30

Fetishists

'I gotta go,' Heartbreak said. He was standing on the step waving his arms, gesticulating. Stone thought it looked like his arms were being blown about by the wind, as if they might be lifted up and away and Heartbreak would be left standing there without them. A torso with a bald head, a human lighthouse.

'OK, we'll catch you later,' Stone said.

'You don't gotta go,' Nell said. 'It isn't as if the earth is gonna come to a standstill if you don't go right this minute.'

'The guys are expecting me,' he said. 'They'll be waiting.' He stepped down to the path and edged away in reverse. 'I'll catch you later, Stone. I wanna hear about Ginny, how you doing.'

'You wanna hear about America,' Nell said mercilessly, 'all you gotta do is sit down at the table with us and listen while the man talks.'

'Aw, Nell,' Heartbreak said, 'I've got arrangements.'

She turned her back on him and he bolted for the gate.

'Where's he going?' Stone asked.

Nell raised her eyebrows. 'He's meeting Phineus and his brother. What's he called?'

'Mike.'

'Yeah, Mike and Mike's brother-in-law, Little John. These white kids that've been threatening Chaz. Heartbreak and his cronies see themselves as avenging angels.'

'You remember I told you about Katy Madika?' Stone said. 'Her husband was beaten up yesterday. They put him in the hospital. Could be the same guys.'

'These were only kids,' Nell said. 'Nineteen, twenty years old.'

'They often are,' Stone said. 'Just because they're young doesn't stop them being nasty.'

'I'm sick of violence,' Nell said, 'It makes me puke to think of Heartbreak getting in a fight. A bloke his age should have more sense. If women were in charge of the world we'd do it differently.'

'How, though?' Stone asked, following her through the back door into the yard. 'You gonna leave it to the Race Relations Board? There's an organization that's really stamped itself on the world. The police've never made any difference; most times when they're involved things get worse. And the government are too frightened of public opinion to talk about it.'

'There's still got to be a better way than hitting each other with pick handles.'

Stone smiled. 'People have to defend themselves. If the government won't do it, there's no other way.'

'In my whole life,' Nell said, 'I never found a problem that couldn't be talked round.'

'You can't talk to racists. They don't want to hear. I've had that with Ginny. People who want to kill you because of the colour of your skin, you can't reason with them.'

They sat at the garden table and Nell looked at him, shaking her head from side to side.

'Hi, you two,' said Sally, sailing through her sister's house and joining them at the table. She had her hair in bunches on each side of her head and she was wearing calf-length denims and flatties like a 1950s teenager. She kissed Stone on his cheek. 'Heard from Ginny? How is she?'

'Good,' Stone told her. 'She's OK. Looking forward to coming home.'

'I can imagine. Ex-partners are never much fun, even when you're fond of them.' She flounced around the table and sat next to Nell, suddenly becoming self-conscious. 'Am I interrupting something?'

'Not really,' Stone told her. 'I'm just checking on the old folks, seeing you've got everything you need.'

'Nasty person,' Sally told him. 'We're not old. Me and Nell are sisters, we'll never be old. And just because I happen to be your mother doesn't give you the right to patronize me.'

174

'Sorry,' Stone said, smiling. 'We were discussing the nature of our society, how it's based on violence.'

'Tell me.'

'Young Chaz Marmon's being threatened by a bunch of white kids.'

'Because of his colour?'

'What d'you think?'

'I think it could be his colour,' Sally said. 'But he's gay as well, so it could be because of that.'

'What difference does it make?' Nell said. 'Colour prejudice, gay bashing, they're the same thing with different names.'

'How d'you know he's gay?' Stone said. 'He's only fifteen, something like that.'

'I can tell,' Sally said. 'Women can see it a mile off.'

Nell shook her head. 'He's a little effeminate,' she said. 'Doesn't prove anything.'

'I'd put money on it,' Sally said, examining a split hair from one of her bunches. 'Anyway, you were telling me about violence,' she said to Stone. 'Got anything to drink, Nell?'

'You're walking home at night,' Stone said. 'Suddenly you're trapped by a gang of guys who're gonna beat you up because you're white.'

'These're black guys?' Sally said.

'In your case, yes, Mother. They're Afro-Caribbean or Asian.'

'They'd rape me,' Sally said. 'If it was you they'd beat you up, but if it was a woman they'd rape her.'

'And then beat you up,' Nell said.

'Yeah, probably,' Sally said. 'That'd be part of it.'

'What would you do?' Stone asked.

'I'd run. I'd scream and run.'

'You can't get away. You're trapped.'

'I'd still scream,' Sally said. 'I'd kick and scratch. I'd go for their balls, their eyes.'

'You'd fight?' Stone said.

'You kidding?'

'Nell doesn't want to fight. She wants to find some way round it.'

'I'm not a pacifist,' Nell said defensively. 'The scenario you describe, I'd fight as well. I might even kill if it came to it. But the

175

situation with little Chaz is different. These guys haven't actually hurt him. If Phineus and Heartbreak and their mates beat the kids up, one side is as bad as the other.'

'Yeah, I agree,' Sally said. 'Violence is only the answer after you've tried everything else and it's failed.'

'But if you're an ethnic minority,' Stone said, 'everything has failed already. Your parents, their parents, everyone you know has been abused or exploited or beaten up. When they start on your children, it's the last straw. There's no appeals left.

'This is how our society works. Maybe it's how all societies work. In the old days you were shunned, driven out of the tribe to starve. These days we put people in prisons and forget about them. The guys who run the democracies are always shouting about free enterprise, competition, how it produces wealth and keeps prices low so everybody benefits. But if you look at them working they don't believe in competition at all. They spend most of their time trying to get rid of the competition, building monopolies and running cartels so no one can interfere with what they're up to.

'They move their factories out to Pakistan or somewhere else in the Third World, where they can employ children to do the work at a fraction of the wage they'd have to pay in the West.

'Competition has always involved dirty-dealing, blackmail and violence, even murder. So why are we surprised or shocked when people take the law into their own hands? There comes a point where everyone says no, this thing is not going any further. It stops here.'

'I know all that,' Nell said. 'But I don't want Heartbreak involved. He doesn't think. If brains were dynamite, he wouldn't have enough to blow his nose.'

'He's interested in the therapy of violent acts,' Sally said, talking about her new boyfriend, the singer with the mane of silver hair.

'That means he wants to thump you,' Nell said. 'Get rid of the guy.'

Sally shook her head. 'He's been involved in S and M. His first wife was a masochist but he doesn't do it any more. He says it's one way of dealing with infantile trauma, but it's not the only way. He's into primal therapy now, sucks his thumb and plays with his toes. He's in touch with his inner child.'

Stone laughed for a moment, tried unsuccessfully to turn it into a cough, then smiled. 'I'm sorry; it was the toes. The image.'

Nell said, 'Not another foot-fetishist?'

Sally nodded. 'Yeah, I didn't realize there were so many of them.' She glanced at Stone then switched back to her sister. 'There's different kinds though, they're not all the same. Some of them are into sandals and boots, and others go for rubbers and clogs. He was telling me about a woman who loves dirty feet. There are some who like to be trod on or kicked.'

'Sweet Jesus,' Nell said.

'One thing they all like are casts,' Sally said.

'Casts?'

'You know, what you get in the hospital if you break your leg? They get excited about casts. Apart from that, though, they're a pretty varied lot.'

'This is my family,' Stone said to the spirits in the sky. 'We're Methodists.'

'Lapsed,' said Nell with a wink.

'Nothing wrong with having a good time,' Sally said. 'You don't have to be miserable all the time to have religion. I haven't read that in the Bible.'

'You're right,' Nell said. 'If you're having a good time and no one's getting hurt you're probably on the right track.'

Sally nodded to herself.

'You are having a good time, aren't you?' Nell asked.

'Kind of,' she said.

'What does that mean, sis? Either you are or you aren't.'

'Oh, I don't mind the fetish stuff,' Sally said. 'And I enjoy the singing. It's good to go out with him as well, because he's handsome, you know, all that silver hair, and he's tall, imposing.'

'But?'

'Well, you can't have everything, can you?' Sally said. 'Especially where men are concerned. None of them are perfect.'

'Are you gonna tell us or not?' Nell said. 'The suspense is killing me.'

'Promise you won't laugh,' Sally said.

'OK, promise.'

Sally looked at Stone.

'OK, I won't laugh,' he said.

Sally took a deep breath. She said, 'He's hung like a hamster.'

31

Being Elsewhere

Katy looked at Daniel in his hospital bed. He was wired to a cathode-ray tube, which blipped regularly and barely audibly. A transparent tube disappeared into his nose and followed a route to his stomach. There was a plastic portal with a button stopper on his right wrist, something like the seal on a beach-ball but it was the entrance to a vein. Katy hoped it was more effective than the stoppers on every beach-ball she'd ever come across; there arose an uncalled-for, surrealist vision of her husband slowly deflating.

The room was permeated by a pungent combination of sterile wipes, disinfectant, floor polish and cut flowers. Lilies, the symbols of purity and innocence.

'Daniel,' she said, smoothing the skin of his left hand, 'Daniel, it's Katy. Please wake up.' She imagined there was a switch inside him that had got pushed over to the *off* position. The trick was to discover how to push it back, get the man working again. But how to do it? It was like trying to discover the password to a computer. You could only guess. The more you knew about the other person, the owner of the computer, the better your chances of finding a way through. But how well did she know Daniel? She was only married to him. She was his wife, the mother of his daughter.

'Chloe,' she said, watching his closed eyes for a flicker of recognition. *Chloe* was Katy's password on her computer and for her bank-card; *Chloe* was the code she used for her ISP and her personal Building Society account. 3.8.12.15.5. She tried the numbers on him but he didn't flinch. He had a code of his own, a masculine code that didn't refer to his wife or his child. It would be something to do with his work, *epithelium*, perhaps, or *omphalitis*. But there was no way of knowing, his code could just as easily be a word from his childhood, a remnant of obscure tribal slang known only to the people of Bakonga.

There was an ashy quality to his skin, a greyness about the crew-neck of the hospital gown around his shoulders. In her mind's eye Katy thought of Daniel's skin as black as jet, shining as if freshly oiled. She saw it as he reared above her or as she bore down on him while they made love back in the days of the leper colony in Orissa. A time of innocence for both of them.

Innocence. That shore-line, which, paradoxically, you can never know you occupy because it is only visible from a point where it has passed away. Chloe was innocent, almost unconscious in her child's world. And Daniel as well, wrapped in the soft, comatose blanket of oblivion, was innocent of the reasons for his predicament. Daniel didn't even know that he had a predicament to deal with.

Katy alone was the one without innocence. It was her who carried the guilt. It was her fault, all of it. And if Daniel died that would be her fault too. If Chloe was left without a father it would be the responsibility of Katy Madika. She glanced at the flowers on the window sill. Lily-livered Katy.

She should have listened to Eve Caldwell and Stone Lewis. When she sat in front of Daniel like this and saw his helplessness she couldn't understand how she'd been so recalcitrant, how she'd thought she could take on these people who were capable of killing in cold blood.

Katy looked at her husband. She rearranged the gown over his chest. She touched his face and saw again her pale fingers against the darker pigment of his jawline. She felt profound tenderness for him now and wondered how that equated with the passionate love they had shared when they first met, in those years before the birth of Chloe. Had the passion been boiled down, reduced to this essence she called tenderness? And was it possible to reverse that process, to find a switch within the tenderness that would allow it to revert to the animal energy of passion?

Not without a key to Daniel himself, she thought. He would have to know that the people who attacked him had gone away, that the kicks they rained down on his body had ceased, that the unbearable pain which had caused him to go to sleep was no longer present. 'Everything is all right,' she said, whispering close to his ear. 'There's only me and Chloe; there's tenderness and love, Daniel. That's all, so please open your eyes.'

Coma is frightening. It is the closest we get to that fantasy state of the zombie, the state of the living dead. The person in a coma is not alive or dead, but perched precariously between the two.

For most of us that is a reality at only one period of our life, very close to the end. It is the point we all must visit, however briefly, when our stay in the realm of the material world is coming to an end and everything we know and love must be left behind. Katy saw it as a cliffhanger, that point when you have actually gone over the edge and are still clinging on to a weakly rooted gorse bush. You know the plant is not going to last long and that you are going to tumble into oblivion, lose control and involvement, and yet you hold on, your fingers bleeding and sore, clinging to the last moment of your life, the last couple of breaths, using up any strength you have left for another second of consciousness.

She glanced at Daniel's face. If there was consciousness there it was well hidden in the smooth and blank countenance, in the laugh-lines at the corners of the eyes, perhaps, or the cleft of the chin. The man who lived behind this face was unknown to her, unknowable. There was breath, that soft lifting of the chest, and each pore on the surface of the skin was dutifully fulfilling its limited function and destiny. She realized that he had been shaved by some unknown hand, an auxiliary nurse, perhaps. His body was still producing hair, cells were dying and being replaced by new growth. He was being fed by the tube that went to his stomach and he was excreting that food and someone was coming along to change him. She wondered if he was wearing an adult nappy; if he was still regular or in a state of constant dribble.

His feet were strapped to an L-shaped board to stop the tendons at the back of the calf from permanently shortening.

He was all there. Everything was in place and in more or less good working order. But he couldn't be reached and he couldn't or wouldn't reach out. He was a wonder of creation like all other human beings, but unlike the rest of them there was a pointlessness to him that somehow went deeper than his inability to communicate.

What it was about Daniel that now marginalized him, made him superfluous to the rest of the human community, was his inability to mirror those around him. Katy could still see her husband, but she could no longer see herself in him. It was like standing before a glass and getting no reflection of yourself, a surrealistic effect that left you thinking of an art gallery, made you feel like you might be part of an artistic installation. It sucked life from you, reduced you to the state of an object.

Last night she had brought Chloe into her bed. Throughout a long and sleepless night she had listened to the shallow breathing of the child and felt her responses, even through the curtain of sleep. She could place her hand on the soles of Chloe's feet and push upwards and Chloe would push back, kicking against the pressure with her tiny legs. But Daniel responded to nothing. If she held his hand and pulled a finger back against the joint he didn't flinch. It felt to Katy that she could snap his finger off and he simply wouldn't notice. It wouldn't be a stoic response, an attitude that accepted life was pain and disappointment. Stoicism she could understand and empathize with. Daniel's response, or his lack of a response, would be incomprehensible. Because he had given up and abandoned his body. He had gone away.

She left the ward and wandered down to the hospital cafeteria, stood in line for a cup of powdered coffee and a shrink-wrapped BLT. The silly girl behind the till with a cluster of hairs sprouting on her chin managed to reflect Katy. She hadn't tried to do it and she wasn't aware that she had done it, but Katy galloped it up thankfully. Another woman at the next table looked over with a brief smile as Katy unwrapped her sandwich, and she was reflected again. She was there, in the world, where she had an effect on other people. She existed, however peripherally. She was only invisible to Daniel, her husband, the man with whom she shared her life.

The flickering images on a television screen above her head coalesced into a panoramic view of the Humber. Katy had a mouthful of BLT as the camera zoomed in on the surface of the grey water, concentrating for a moment on the effects of the tides and the evershifting mud-banks that are a feature of the river. In the old days, before the bridge was built, there were a couple of paddle-steamers, which used to ferry people back and forth between Hull and New Holland on the coast of Lincolnshire. Old-timers still told tales about how the ferries could get stuck on mud-banks, often having to wait until the next tide before they could continue their journey.

The camera angle shifted and in the swirling, eddying surface of the water something else took shape. The image was filmed from a distance so everything was distorted and miniaturized but there was a body stuck in the mud, spread-eagled like an image of the crucified Christ, but with one arm still in the water, moving with the current, waving from its watery grave.

The canteen television had the volume turned down so she couldn't hear a commentary, but it was clear that the events being shown were current. A body had been washed up in the river and what she was watching were the attempts of the authorities to recover it. A man in military fatigues and a crash helmet was swinging from the winch of a helicopter, hovering above the mud-encrusted body.

Katy got to her feet. She left the sandwich with one bite out of it on the table and dialled Stone Lewis's number on her mobile. When he answered she said, 'Switch the television on.'

'I'm watching it,' he said. 'Where are you?'

'The hospital. In the canteen.'

'I'm on my way. Be there in about twenty minutes.'

'No,' she told him. 'There's no sound here.'

'What?'

'I'll come to you. I'm leaving now.'

She put the phone down and as she walked out of the hospital and looked around for a taxi, her mind raced and reeled in a progression of pirouettes that mirrored the images on the television screen behind her.

It all came tumbling out of her when she got to Stone's flat. She hadn't known that it was dammed up inside, waiting to come rushing out like an express train. She told him about the visit of the scarfaced man, how he had cornered her up in the bedroom, ripped her shirt and taken the Compact Flash card. She described how she had heard him downstairs and how she had gone down and found him reformatting the hard disk on the computer.

'It was enough of a warning,' she said. 'He didn't have to go for Daniel as well. I'd never have said a word to anyone. And now Daniel is not going to wake up. He'll lie in that bed in the hospital and eventually they'll let him die. Chloe'll grow up never knowing her father.'

Stone Lewis sat and listened to her. He didn't interrupt. He'd switched the television off but he had a small radio with the sound turned low, tuned to Radio Humberside. When she finished speaking he said, 'This body they've found, it might not be the guy you saw, the hook-nosed one.'

She looked at him. 'What do you mean?'

'Most likely it is,' he said. 'But don't bank on it.'

She nodded. 'My life doesn't depend on it.' She bit her lip. Her involvement with the hook-nosed young man, the photographs she'd taken, they had involved her life in a very real way. Daniel's life was now in the balance because of the day she'd seen the hook-nosed young man down by the Marina, and even Chloe's life had been threatened by the man with the scars. She waited for a moment, then she said, 'But it is him. You'll see.'

They waited for an hour with no further news and Katy got to her feet. 'I should go to the nursery,' she said. 'I have to collect Chloe.'

Stone put his finger to his lips as the recording of Queen's 'These Are The Days Of Our Lives' was faded before it was halfway through.

The announcer's voice said, 'There's more news just in on the body that was found in the river this morning. The body was that of a man in his middle forties and police say they have not yet been able to identify him. They are appealing for the friends or relatives of a large man with black hair and a moustache. The man was wearing a white gabardine raincoat with a folded Panama hat in the pocket.'

32

Red Meat

They walked along Greek Street and turned up towards Anlaby Road, cars parked bumper to bumper outside the endless rows of terraced shams. The moon was coming up and Mort put his arm around Joolz's shoulders.

She turned her face towards him, sensing correctly that he wanted to kiss her. He tasted of whisky. Nice. Pork-pie in there as well.

'How long's she been like that?'

'Alice? Last few years. She was normal like you and me, then she started getting fat. She couldn't get out of bed. Next thing she's got these varicose veins and there's clots forming in her legs. She had a stroke. The doctor told her she had to lose weight or she'd be dead and then she started eating serious. Everything she could get her hands on. Next time I look she's got these elephant legs, no ankles left. Then her bowels disintegrate, which is when she got the colostomy bags.

'He asks me, the doctor, if I'm gonna supervise her diet. I'm supposed to make sure she eats lettuce every day, herb tea, no meat or fried stuff. Chicken, she can eat that, hundred grams a day. But I can't do that. I give her what she wants. Now her brain's going, that's why she keeps her mouth open. Forgets to shut it.'

'Couldn't she go in a home?' Joolz asked. 'Somewhere they look after people?'

'She doesn't want that,' Mort said. 'She likes being at home. It's her independence.'

A streetlight flickered and died and they walked in silence for a moment. 'Mortimer,' Joolz said, trying it out. 'I thought Mort was your real name.'

'Alice called me Mortimer,' he said. 'It's on my birth certificate. You know what it means?'

'Something to do with death,' Joolz said. 'Like in mortuary.'

'No.' He shook his head, let a smile creep around his face. 'It means everlasting. Mortimer, it means imperishable, immortal. That's why Alice chose it.'

They got a taxi and Mort asked the driver to take them to the Cod.

'I don't wanna go there,' Joolz said.

'That's where I drink.'

'I know, and bloody Ginner and Gaz'll be there. I just wanna be with you.'

'The clock's running, folks,' the cabby said

Mort held his hands up. 'OK, you name it,' he said to Joolz.

She shook her head. 'Somewhere nice.'

'There's the Altisidora,' the cabby said. 'Bit of a ride but it's nice.'

'No way,' Mort told him. 'That's halfway to York.'

'You want to stay in town,' the cabby said, 'there's the Bluebell, opposite the old custom house.'

Joolz smiled. She said, 'Yeah.'

When they arrived Mort paid the cabby and led the way down the narrow alley that took them to the Bluebell. Fairly quiet for a Friday night. A few old geezers playing dominoes at one table, three married women out on a spree at another. A young man wearing a blazer and tie with jeans and trainers sitting on his own, waiting for the girl of his dreams to come through the door. A couple were just leaving so Mort went to the bar for the drinks while Joolz recolonized the free table.

'This do you?' he asked, sliding a Pils over to her.

She took a drink from the neck of the bottle. 'S'nice. I liked meeting your mum. D'you think she liked me?'

'Yeah. She thought you was OK. You made her laugh.'

'It must be terrible, never getting out. Forever stuck in that bed.'

'She keeps cheerful. I look after her.'

Joolz fell silent. She made a roll-up and stuck it in her face, waited for Mort to set it on fire. She took a couple of drags and another swig from the bottle. 'D'you mind not going to the Cod?'

He shook his head. 'This'll do me.'

'I don't mind Ginner too much,' she said. 'But Gaz gets on my tits. He hurt me when we were together.'

'How d'you mean?'

'He hurt me.'

'Yeah. But how?'

'First I didn't wanna do it. So he held me down. Punched me round the kidneys till I let him in. Then he did it bareback, said I'd probably have one of his kids.'

'But you're not?'

'No.' She shook her head. 'I'm on the pill, but that's not the point. If a woman doesn't wanna do it you shouldn't force her. That's the old days, when that happened. Or in a war or something. But this is now, Mort. Mortimer.'

'I've never done that.'

'You hit me,' she reminded him.

'It was a reaction,' he said. 'I didn't go for the kidneys.'

'Cut my lip though. Could've knocked me out.'

'I wasn't thinking. Stuff happens.'

'That's the worst thing,' she told him.

They walked back along Whitefriargate, looking in the shop windows. Mort put his arm around her shoulder.

'I could tell you something about Gaz,' he said. 'It'd be like getting your own back, only you wouldn't be able to let on I told you.'

'What?'

'Promise you won't let on.'

'I won't let on. You can trust me.'

'When we was fifteen, Ginner went with this slag off Calvert Lane. This was just after his mother'd run off to live with a guy in Gloucester. He was the first one to do it with a real woman. Before that we used mucky magazines, or we'd do gang-wanks watching porn videos.

'Anyway, this slag said, because Ginner told her about the gang-wanks, she asked him if he ever used red meat.'

'Oh, God, I feel sick.'

'I don't have to tell it,' Mort said.

'You can't stop now.'

'I dunno where Gaz was, but Ginner told me and we went out and bought a piece of steak.' Mort laughed. 'I used one side and Ginner used the other. He said it was exactly like the real thing. Almost no difference. And I'd never had the real thing so I couldn't tell but I knew it was better than using your hand.'

Joolz shook her head. 'What happened to the steak?'

'Alice had this boyfriend at the time. Stanley. I gave it to him, told him my mate had stolen it from the butcher's. He grilled it for his supper with some frozen peas and oven chips. Said it was the best steak he'd ever tasted.'

Joolz laughed and punched Mort's arm. 'You're having me on.'

'No, straight up,' he said. 'Old Stanley went on about it for weeks, asking me if I could get him another one.'

'This was supposed to be a story about Gaz.'

'I'm getting there,' Mort said. 'So we told Gaz about it, and he hadn't never had a woman and didn't wanna be left out. "I can't believe you did it without me," he said. "Red meat, yes?" And he ran off to the shop to get some.

'Later on he catches up with us and he's raving. "What's wrong with you?" we ask him. "Didn't you get the meat?"

'"Oh, sure, I got the meat," Gaz says. "But it doesn't work. You bastards set me up."

'"Worked well enough for us," Ginner told him. "We had a good time, right, Mort?"

'"And it cost me," Gaz said. "I didn't know meat was so expensive. It was a total waste of money."

'"Hang on," I told him. "It worked for us. You must've done something wrong. We used rump steak."

'"I couldn't afford that," Gaz said. "I looked at it but it was too much money."

'"So what did you use?"

'"There was this lamb chop," he said. "But it had a bone in it and I thought it might be dangerous."

'"So is that what you bought?" Ginner said. "Should have worked fine."

'Gaz shook his head. "If it hadn't been for the bone I'd have bought it," he said. "In the end I got a hundred grams of pork mince. It was disgusting. I didn't even get a proper stiff. And the mince is everywhere, down the back of the couch and there's some of it trod into the carpet. I had to bring the woman-next-door's cat in to clean the place up."'

33

Night Callers

That night Nell sent Heartbreak home early. Her sister, Sally, was quiet next door, probably out at a rehearsal with the boyfriend. Nell played the *Abbey Road* album. When it got to 'I Want You' she thought she'd play the track again when it was finished, but it went on too long for her mood and she let it go. She could hear what Stone meant about it and there was that small crippled magician in Lennon that forced you to look in all directions at the same time. But there was a wilderness in her tonight that didn't want to play with the world. Her mind was bent on solitude, and she needed to find some serenity within the confines of her house, to sip at the small cup of privacy that gave her strength to face the world.

She washed her hair and took a long soak in the bath, plucked out unwanted hairs and pared toenails and fingernails, applied face-cream to her temples, cheeks and neck, rubbed a little into the wrinkled skin of her elbows.

She was critical, of course, but she didn't go over the top. At fifty-seven years of age her body was no longer her greatest asset. Character and personality were what she had to rely on now, and she was still surprised to find they were more pleasing than a smooth skin. It would have been nice if she'd looked after her teeth better, back in the early days, when they didn't seem as if they needed it.

She put on a brushed cotton nightdress and went into her bedroom. All in all her body was hanging together better than a lot of other people's. She could still ride her bike and give Heartbreak a run for his money when the fancy took him. 'You're in a better state than

England,' she told her reflection in the mirror. A country trying to move and stand still at the same time.

She propped up her pillows and read a magazine article about American dentists taking one-day courses so they could perform liposuction operations. Apparently vaginal rejuvenation was all the rage over there. Vanity surgery was the new buzz word and the brave new world of Western capitalism was still beavering away at its citizens' insecurities.

Nell shuffled down in the bed and reached for the switch of her table-lamp. She closed her eyes and let herself be enveloped by the darkness, a series of dreams and memories already queuing at the periphery of her consciousness, waiting for the day to exit before they moved into the vacant space. Far away, over the rooftops, a lone tomcat called out in the night.

For a while Nell didn't know if she would sleep. It wasn't that she was in two minds, but more that she was two different people. And everyone in the world was the same, she thought. The first, a being who is uncomplicated, designed for public consumption, someone who is eager to conform to the expectations of others and so presents a face that is reduced, restrained. But there is always a second self buried behind this public face, someone who is individuated, consecrated with a fate that muddles and combines strands of existence into a unique life, different from the life of anyone else on earth or who has ever lived on the earth.

We live for others and for ourselves, and most of us keep these two strands of our existence separate. We feel there is a relationship between these two existences but we rarely know what that relationship is. We think our search is for simplicity but when that simplicity is achieved we find it is not what we want. It is from that basic simplicity that we wish to escape. Our real need is for a more radical complexity that will show us a path towards meaning.

Everyone Nell had ever known had put their lives on hold from time to time, some of them for ever. Her sister, Sally, had had her life on hold, waiting for the right man to come along, for about forty years. The result was a heart that had dried up, a cultivated neuroticism and an alcohol dependency problem. Heartbreak had had his life on hold on and off for even longer. All the times he was in prison he was waiting until he got out, and when he was out he had everything on hold until he got enough money to retire from being a villain.

The trouble was, putting your life on hold didn't stop you living. It just stopped you noticing that you were living. In the end you had an achieved existence, whether you believed in it or not. It might be different to what you had expected it to be while you were living it, but it was still there. It had still happened. Life was what happened to you while you were busy trying to avoid it.

For a while Nell couldn't tell if she was dreaming or not. She didn't know if the sound she heard came from within a dream or if what had jolted her awake was a noise in the real world.

She was staring into the blackness of her room, straining to keep her breathing at a low level. Sally sometimes came home pissed and knocked things over but Nell didn't think it came from next door. It had been a sharp crack and it was over quickly. Like a door being forced.

Now there was silence, as if the outside world was colluding in a plot against her, holding everything audible in suspension.

Her head was heavy, her mind sluggish from sleep and she didn't want to face the possibility that someone was in her house. She couldn't imagine why anyone would break in, anyway. Not for a five-year-old television and an antique music system.

The neighbourhood was highly populated. A single sound in the night carried no significance. There were cats on the prowl, owls on the hunt, bats shifting and whirling in a blind search for food. The darkness supported all kinds of activities that were no threat to a woman in her own bed. The luminous hands on her clock showed the time as two-fifty-six, and as the silence lengthened, Nell felt her eyes close and unconsciousness come back at her in small, rhythmic waves.

From the main road there was the insistent whine of a siren, some emergency vehicle rushing through deserted streets. Then silence again, and in the stillness the memory of the siren was distorted. It could have been an alarm produced in her own head. A subconscious signal that she should not give way to her drowsiness, should investigate the disturbance that had brought her out of sleep.

Nell froze in the bed, every nerve in her body subjugated to the functioning of the inner ear. The creaking of the third step of the staircase was nothing to do with imagination. There was a loose board there that she had meant to fix for the past couple of years, and someone had put weight on it. There was someone coming up the stairs to her room.

The step creaked again. Two of them. Nell was out of bed and racing across her room to close the bolt on the door, at the same time screaming at the top of her voice. She let the shriek come, feeling the strength of it ripping at her vocal cords. As she grasped the bolt to lock the intruders out, the bedroom door opened inwards with force, slamming her back into the room. She felt the corner of the bed against her legs and grasped at air as she fell over backwards, cracking her head on the floor.

In the half-light she made out the figures of two silhouettes standing over her. One of them drew back and aimed a kick at her head. She rolled over and took the force of the boot on her shoulders. She screamed again, letting it rip, hoping to wake the whole neighbourhood.

'Nigger lover,' one of them said. She took a boot in the stomach, and in spite of herself, felt a rush of vomit flood her mouth and dribble down her cheek.

Nell went into the foetal position, protecting her head with her hands and arms. It was instinctive. No one had taught her what to do when a couple of thugs came into her bedroom and wanted to kick seven kinds of shit out of her. She took blows to her shins and forearms, and one got through to her face, felt like her top teeth had come through her lip. There was another one, particularly vicious, which caught her at the base of her spine and she lost focus for a time. She was aware that her body was beginning to unwind but she couldn't do anything to stop it. Her willpower abandoned her for a time, like part of her stepping out of line. It was as if her body was made of separate sheaths, each supporting the others in a shared dependency, and one of them became dislodged after that kick to the spine, sending the others into a chaotic independence incapable of supporting consciousness.

She heard the banging of the front door downstairs and Sally's voice come floating up towards her. 'Nell, are you all right? What's the bloody noise up there? I've called the police.'

And then the bedroom ceiling light was switched on and Sally was in the room and the two guys were rushing down the stairs. Sally was wrapped in a short velvet dressing gown, her bare legs as white as bleached cotton. Nell looked up into the pity in her sister's eyes and felt a tear come into her own. She didn't weep for the pain or the injustice or for anything that had happened to her that evening. She wept because Sally was there when she needed to be and because there was no one else in the world that she would rather have seen at that moment.

Stone arrived at quarter past five in the morning. Sally was ready to leave and he talked with her for a few minutes in the hospital corridor. 'They were young guys,' she said. 'Two of them, dark clothes. They had crash helmets.'

'You didn't see anything else?'

'I think they got away on a motorbike. Sounded like that, but it could have been somebody else on the bike. I only saw them for a moment.'

Stone shook his head. 'How is she?'

'They think she'll mend. She's not making a lot of sense. Talking about how you shouldn't put your life on hold and how psychiatrists are making a fortune out of people who want life to be simple.'

Stone went into the side-ward and pulled a chair up to the bed. Aunt Nell smiled at him. Her face was small and there was a huge muff-like dressing covering her chin and part of her mouth. Her forearms were swathed in bandages and the left one looked to be supported by a splint.

'How're you feeling?' he asked. She didn't reply and he shrugged. 'Silly question. I didn't bring grapes or flowers, the shops aren't open yet. D'you need anything?'

'You could tell Heartbreak. Don't get him out of bed, though, he might have a heart-attack. Wait until after nine, then tell him to get round here and keep me company.'

'Did you see who did it?'

'No. Two men. I got the impression they were young.'

'Why you?'

'They called me a nigger lover.'

'Did they have an accent?'

'No, they were locals.'

'That narrows it down, then.'

'Don't get involved, Stone. Leave it to the police. I don't want anyone else getting hurt.'

'Don't worry,' he said. 'Try to sleep. I'll send Heartbreak round when it gets light.'

34

Bombs

They made the bombs with 2-litre juice bottles, which Gaz had stolen from outside the Clarendon Hotel on Londesborough Street. Two thirds petrol and one third motor oil and Mort told the others how Omega had shown him to set the rag-wick by melting candle wax into the top of the bottle.

First the rag was soaked in candle grease and put into the neck of the bottle, keeping one end in touch with the petrol and oil mixture. When it had cooled down and was stiff he took some of the wax and moulded it in his hands, pushing it into the neck, around the folds of the rag.

'The next bit is dangerous,' he explained. He took the pan with molten wax and poured it slowly into the neck of the bottle, sealing the remaining crevices and gaps.

'If the melted wax comes into contact with the petrol there's a good chance it'll go up in your face.'

'What's the flash-point of petrol?' Ginner asked.

'Dunno, but it's somewhere around the same as the melted wax. You don't wanna find out.'

'What happened to you last night?' Gaz asked.

'I was with Joolz. Took her to see Alice. We had some Chinky and a couple of beers.'

'Get your end away?' Ginner asked.

'Might have.'

'It's the only thing she's good for,' Gaz said. 'Might as well use it.' He laughed at that and Ginner joined in. Mort cracked his face, let them see they weren't getting to him.

'We did for the old biddy who was following us,' Ginner said.

'The one in the Shôgun?'

Ginner nodded. 'Got her out of bed and worked her over.'

'Where was I?' Mort asked.

'You was poking the slag,' Gaz told him. 'We came round for you, and Alice said you'd gone out for the night.'

'You could have come to Joolz's place.'

'We went on the bike,' Ginner said. 'Safer. Next time it'll be you and me.'

'And I'll stay at home with the slag,' Gaz said, giving it teeth, showing where he'd lost a couple of the front ones.

Mort wanted to tell Gaz to quit calling Joolz the slag but he didn't know how to do it. If he came out with it now they'd take the rise out of him, and then Gaz'd make more jokes about it. The thing with Gaz was, you couldn't talk to him if somebody else was there. Even Ginner. Especially if Ginner was there. You had to get him on his own and it had to be quiet and easy, catch him in one of those moods where he was prepared to listen and not be jumping in with his own cracks. A time where he was impressed by you, because you'd shown him something he'd never seen before.

Any other time was useless. When there were people around, it was impossible to talk to him. He'd turn everything into a joke, which with Gaz meant having somebody as a scapegoat. At the moment the scapegoat was Mort because Gaz was jealous of him because Mort had Joolz and Gaz didn't have a squeeze of his own.

Mort didn't understand that because Gaz could have had Joolz if he'd wanted. He was the one who'd found her. But Gaz only wanted her when Mort had her. Or if he didn't have her himself then he didn't want anybody to have her. Sex and women, they were the most complicated things in the world.

If you had guys together everything was OK, it was only when sex came into the picture that the world turned upside down. Mort and Gaz had had good times in the past, they had been the best of friends. Gaz wanted that to go on; he didn't want anything to interfere with it. And Mort wanted that as well, only he wanted Joolz to be included.

If it came to a showdown, if, for some reason, he had to choose

197

between Gaz and Joolz, he'd choose Joolz. But he couldn't tell Gaz that. Gaz wouldn't understand; he'd take it as an insult.

Mort walked over to the kitchen work-bench and looked at the eight bottles lined up on the Formica top. 'We all know the routine for tonight?' he said, taking four of the bottles and placing them inside his rucksack.

'Meet at the hostel at half-past-one,' Gaz said. 'And we bomb the fuckers.'

'We hit the back of the place and the front at the same time,' Mort said. 'We have two bombs each and we work as a team. One-thirty on the dot we all light up and four bottles go through the windows. Soon as we've done that we do the same thing again with the other bottles.'

'Then we're out of there,' Ginner said. 'You and Omega in his car, and me and Gaz on the bike. We're away in different directions. We don't meet up again until tomorrow.'

'Don't forget the most important thing,' Gaz said.

Mort and Ginner looked at him, waited.

'Enjoy yourselves,' he said. 'We're not going to a funeral.'

35

Katy's Car

'Ideas grow out of conduct and experience,' the Kosovan said. His accent was rough but he reached for and found English words with relative ease. 'In my country there are many ideas because we have lots of experience in a very short time. We have seen the conduct of our enemy when they burn our houses and we have seen the conduct of ourselves when we defend our women and old people. When we avenge the death of our children.'

'Revenge is an idea,' Stone said.

The man nodded, a smile around his mouth. 'This is what I told you,' he said. 'Ideas grow out of conduct and experience, and then they are turned back into conduct and experience. We observe, we reflect, and then we reply in kind.'

Stone agreed. His time within the walls of HM prisons had given rise to many ideas. The process was still continuing for him. Almost every action in his life was based on an idea transformed by past conduct and experience.

Shaban's sister touched her cousin's arm. She spoke to him in their own language.

'She says I must pack my things,' the man said. 'We'll miss our flight.'

'But how can you be sure that Shaban is dead?' Stone asked. 'The body in the river wasn't him, was it?'

'No. The man in the river was older, heavily built. We haven't seen the body of Shaban, but he is dead nevertheless. My cousin was going to be a witness at the War Crimes Tribunal in the Hague. He could identify a Serbian commander who killed and raped Kosovan villagers. There were two other witnesses and both of them have been killed; one in Paris and another in Mitrovica. They will release the commander now.'

'You think Shaban was killed by Serbs?'

He shrugged. 'Who else? If they didn't do it themselves they put out a contract on him. They have friends everywhere. *Fascisti.*'

The woman spoke again and her cousin translated. 'She says the same, that we will not see the body of her brother. But we know that he is dead. When Serbs feel threatened they hunt us down and kill us.'

Stone offered his hand and the man took it and put his arm around Stone's shoulder. He was rough like a soldier and he said that Stone should come to Kosovo and help them out. 'You could be a hero,' he said.

The woman took his hand and Stone looked into her eyes. There was an emptiness there, pools of dark light that gave away nothing. It was as if there was no depth to her, as if everything that she was lived on the surface. It couldn't be so, because everyone had depths. Shaban Brovina's sister must have depths as well, but she had blocked all access to them. She didn't want the world to touch her. Her experiences in the future would be external ones. Her private, inner world had been shattered by the loss of almost everyone she had known in her life.

An essence of the Kosovans travelled along with Stone as he left Mrs Robson's house and cut through Salisbury Street to Victoria Avenue. He couldn't shake them off, the way they defined themselves and their country in an accented tongue; the way they defined their enemy.

How Shaban's cousin used the word 'we', so that it brought the whole of his fellow countrymen alive inside him. And when the sister used the same word, how that 'we' predicated a 'they' who were totally alien.

This was the way personal pronouns were used in prison, and during his time there Stone had thought it particular to that place. The 'we' of the cons and the 'they' of the screws. But it applied across the spectrum of society. To be a man or a woman in the modern world meant precisely that; to be a body at war between the limiting definition of selfhood as an 'I', and the extended infinity of an awareness of everyone as a universal 'we'.

Katy Madika didn't open the door. She spoke through the wood. 'Who is it?'

'Stone.'

He stood back while she fiddled with the lock, waited until the door cracked open and her pale face appeared from the gloom of the hallway. 'What do you want?'

The baby was on her hip, seemingly oblivious to the fact that her mother had been reduced to a caricature of herself.

'How's Daniel?'

'The same.'

Stone found his sympathetic mask. It wasn't an effort. She awoke compassion in him. He felt his warmth going out towards her. This was someone he had known for a few days and it felt as though he had known her all his life. What had happened to her had loosened the woman's social constraints. She communicated like a child, bypassing the codes of normal parlance.

He was aware that her experiences and her fear had combined to drive her to the edge of sanity; that she was hanging on for the benefit of her daughter, Chloe. But he knew, also, that there was little he could do to help. Her battle was with her own mind, and so far she was winning. Hanging in there.

'Can I come in?'

She turned and led him into the sitting room. She waved towards the sofa, inviting him to sit.

'My aunt was attacked,' he told her. 'She's in the hospital.'

'Like Daniel?'

'She's conscious.'

Katy shook her head.

'The man with the scars, when he came here, did he say anything racist? Was Daniel beaten up because of his colour? Or was he just warning you to keep quiet.'

'I don't know any more,' Katy said. 'He called Chloe a piccaninny.'

'Anything else?'

Katy closed her eyes. 'He stamped on our wedding photograph,' she said. 'Crushed it under his heel, broke the glass. What's this about, Stone?'

'The man you photographed on the dockside,' he told her. 'His family think he was a victim of ethnic cleansing. There's a young black boy, Chaz Marmon, who was baited by some racist thugs. Sounds like the same people who beat up my aunt. Called her a nigger lover. Daniel was beaten after Scarface came to see you, took the Compact Flash and threatened your family. All these things are related.'

'I'm not sure what you're saying.'

'I need to borrow Daniel's car,' he said.

'Why?'

'It's personal. I want to find the man with the scars.'

She looked at him, examined his eyes. Chloe reached out a tiny hand and pulled her mother's bottom lip away from her mouth, adding momentary disfigurement to Katy's list of calamities. 'Just a minute,' she said. 'I'll find the keys.'

He could have showed the photographs of Shaban Brovina to the man's sister and his cousin. In other circumstances they would have been glad to see their relative, the hook-nosed young Kosovan, sipping coffee on the Hull waterfront, or walking along by the side of the marina. Stone didn't show them the photographs because they were part of a series, which ended with the young man sprawled over an antique cannon, his lifeblood spilling to the cobblestones.

One of the men who had killed him, the large man with the Panama hat, was dead, washed up in the river. Both of these lives were written to the account of a nameless face with deep vertical scars on his cheeks. When this Scarface had arrived in the city he had brought death with him, and the ability to injure and to spread fear and loathing. Daniel Madika was lying in a coma in the same hospital as Aunt Nell. Another surgeon in Cottingham had also been attacked. Young Chaz Marmon had been threatened and was confined to his room while his father and his friends went out hunting racists.

Stone leaned back in the deep-red leather upholstery of Daniel Madika's black BMW and felt the surge of power from its engine. There was a confrontation on the way.

He pulled the car up against the kerb in Linnaeus Street and waited. Aunt Nell had described the house and he picked it out easily. Sitting cool in a BMW, playing something from Africa, the Soweto String Quartet's *Renaissance* CD. Stone was only superficially cool. He instinctively got everything wrong, but since his imprisonment he no longer worked instinctively. He thought about his responses, he felt his way around each problem. When he was absolutely sure, then he moved.

Scarface and these thugs had to be connected. While other people were being intimidated and maimed Stone could keep his distance, but now that his Aunt Nell had been worked over he was involved. The best way to find Scarface was to watch the young racists. Either Scarface would contact them or they would lead the way to him. It was just a matter of time.

The house had been left to fall apart. No one had spent money on it for years. Perhaps it was a squat, Stone thought, an absent or dead landlord, or someone with so much money they didn't need to bother with it.

The rich were an unknown quantity, they didn't follow the rules because they didn't have to. Their main function seemed to be to make sure everyone else followed the rules. Organizing the little people to keep their houses in order, pay the mortgage, make sure they're insured for everything, that there are no loose slates falling off the roof, denting the rich man's car or slicing someone's brain in half, filling up another hospital bed.

There were curtains at the windows, tattered but drawn tight on both floors. Together with the grime on the glass they made it impossible to see inside. You might think the place was deserted, but houses like this were always occupied. Inside it would be warm, the sweet smell of piss and sweat like a physical presence in every room.

Stone didn't need to go inside to know what it was like. He had been in a dozen places like this. There would be damp patches on the walls and ceilings, and peeling wallpaper from the sixties or seventies. Maybe some psychedelic swirls from an acid-inspired artist. And in and around the squalor and degradation of the building's interior there would be a constant plethora of dreams. Of love and hatred, of power and abuse. There would be the fantasy of untold wealth, and the changes and opportunities that it would bring.

In this particular house there would be the fear and paranoia engendered by Nationalistic longings, by the constant striving for an imagined perfection of Englishness based on blood and skin colour and an unreal perception of courage and moral superiority.

This kind of heady mixture could only result in tragedy. Based on an icy and insubstantial premise and nurtured on a cocktail of home-brewed idealism and false camaraderie, the recipe led to a glass of frustration and anger and the loss of life and limb.

When the detail of a person's life is meagre or unsatisfying, when there is a dearth of beauty or truth, they evolve a pattern, a plot, they begin to impose meaning and a sense of inevitability on the randomness of their lives. They confuse error and nostalgia, ignorance and poetry, and construct an imaginary landscape that feels like destiny.

Stone didn't except himself. He knew better than anyone of his own flights of fancy. He stopped at compiling a programme for mankind, though. Because that always ended in death for someone, often for thousands, sometimes for millions.

Stone Lewis didn't want to be involved in activities that led to the death of innocent men and women. Not again. He didn't want a destiny. He wanted a quiet life. A silent life.

But in the space he occupied at this moment, behind the wheel of Daniel Madika's black BMW, the silence was only separated from chaos by a thin membrane of time.

The door of the house opened and a guy in his early twenties came out. He stopped with the door held ajar for a moment while he spoke something back into the house. Then he closed the door and walked along the path. There was a silver stud through his eyebrow and his black hair was gelled and in need of a cut. He had black jeans, black trainers, and he walked a little flat-footed. He stopped at the kerb and waited, holding a green khaki rucksack in his right hand. Something strange about the way he was holding the bag, like it had eggs in it or something else that might get damaged easily. A cream cake? A kitten?

Within a minute a red taxi came along the street and the guy waved it over. He got in the back and the driver did a three-point turn and headed for the main road. Stone turned the ignition key of the BMW and followed.

The taxi went over Drypool Bridge and turned into the Victoria Dock development, pulling up outside a large house that fronted onto the river. The guy got out of the cab and walked to the house, pushing his thumb against the doorbell. He looked incongruous in these new surroundings. He'd seemed to fit in Linnaeus Street, but these new designer houses were not built with this kind of guy in mind. The people who lived around here wore trainers in the mornings when they went jogging but the rest of the day they wore regular shoes.

The door was opened from the inside and the young guy slipped through the gap. It was dark in the interior of the house and Stone was a good 50 metres away, but for an instant, when the door opened, the light caught the face of the man who was living there. It could, of course, have been a trick of the light, or a case of Stone's retina helping him fulfil his expectations. There was always room for error, and you had to be prepared for that.

36

Mythical Monolith

Heartbreak and Deke arrived at the house a couple of minutes after midnight. Deke was an old friend, sixty-five years old now, but upright and fit and still looking for a fight. Heartbreak tapped on the door and walked in. 'You ready?' he asked.

Phineus shook his hand and clapped him on the back. 'Yeah, we can go. How's Nell?' He looked over Heartbreak's shoulder and nodded at Deke.

'Philosophical. Bruised. It could've been worse. They thought her spine was damaged at first but it seems OK. They weren't finished with her. If Sally hadn't come in they could've killed her.' He looked down at Phineus's feet. 'You going in your socks?'

'Funny. I've got my hooves here.' He knelt to pull on his boots.

'I used to be like that,' Heartbreak said. 'Holes in my socks. I'd throw them away, buy another pair.'

'I hate socks,' Deke said.

'That's not a hole,' Phineus said. And after he'd examined it, 'I didn't know that was there.'

Heartbreak laughed. 'Your toe's sticking out. Y'know how to darn?'

'Palesa used to do all that. I'm too old to learn it now.'

'You're never too old,' Heartbreak told him. 'When we get back I'll show you. Piece of cake.'

'Let's walk,' Phineus said. 'Mike'll pick us up on the corner of Margaret Street at half past.'

'Who else is coming?' Deke asked.

'Mike's brother-in-law, Little John. Remember him?'

'Vaguely. Big guy with a neck like Tyson?'

Phineus nodded. 'Useful to have around.'

There was a high moon and the houses were dark, the people inside settling down for the night.

'What about washing?' Heartbreak said. 'Y'know how to do that?'

'Yeah,' Phineus said. 'I know you gotta get behind your ears and the parts you don't show your mother.'

'Not yourself,' Heartbreak said. 'Jeez, I'm talking clothes here; washing your kecks, all that, ironing shirts.'

'We've still got the washing machine. I bung everything in there with detergent. All our clothes are the same colour now, but they're clean.'

'You should do 'em in batches; whites one day, coloureds the next. One day a month you stick in the things that're really filthy.'

'I know the theory,' Phineus said. 'I don't have time to do it right. Chaz has a couple of T-shirts he washes by hand, designer stuff. Says he doesn't trust the machine.'

'I go down the launderette,' Deke said. 'Talk to students, ask 'em what they're studying. Tell 'em about the old days. Some of them lasses swear like troopers. Supposed to be educated.'

Mike and Little John were sitting in the front of Mike's Cavalier about 20 metres down Margaret Street. He flashed his headlights and Heartbreak followed the others along the pavement and waited until they'd climbed in the back. 'Where'm I gonna sit?' he asked.

Phineus and Deke squeezed up and Deke patted the seat next to him. 'Plenty of room for a bony little ass like yours,' he said.

Heartbreak got in and closed the door. Mike turned round and shook hands with them. Little John, who had put on some weight, couldn't turn around in the seat, but he put his hand over his shoulder so everyone could shake it. His head was shaved clean and Heartbreak couldn't see where that finished and his neck began. Neck and head together amounted to a huge domed probe growing out the top of his shirt, the tiny ears like redundant wings. It was over thirty years since he'd been in a boxing ring but he looked like he did back then; a Buddha-like poise, his coach's voice a blur in the background, as he waited for the bell.

Mike drove through the town and along Anlaby Road to Linnaeus Street. He parked on the same side of the street as the house and switched off the lights. They listened to the creaks and groans as the car settled down and the engine cooled. Little John said, 'I've got a couple of baseball bats in the boot, three lengths of two-by-two and a lump hammer.'

After a couple of minutes he added, 'It's all I had.'

'Should do the job,' Deke said.

Heartbreak nodded in the dark, feeling the dryness at the back of his throat. 'What's the plan?' he said.

'I don't wanna talk to them,' Phineus said. 'I want for my boy to go out on the street. That means keeping these guys off it. They have to learn the lesson.'

'So we beat them good,' said Little John.

The silence stretched to nearly a minute before Phineus said, 'What we waiting for?'

Heartbreak reached for the door handle, but as his fingers closed over it there was a movement in the garden of the house and one of the guys wheeled a motorbike along the path.

Mike said, 'Hold it, what's happening here?'

They watched as the man with the motorbike straddled it and adjusted his helmet. Another one came out of the house and locked the door after him, tucking the key into his breast pocket. He carried a couple of Tesco bags, one in each hand, and when he got to the bike he put a bag in each pannier.

'We could take them now?' Little John said.

Mike shook his head. 'Not in the street. Let's see where they're going. We're looking for three of them, right?'

'Yes,' Phineus said. 'They might take us to the other one.'

The second guy sat on the pillion and the bike indicated and pulled into the road. Mike waited until they had turned right at the T-junction, then he reached for the ignition and followed the same route. 'I'm on you, whitey,' he said.

Deke tapped him on the shoulder. 'What's with whitey?' he said. 'You call me whitey behind my back?'

Mike laughed nervously. 'Sensitive,' he said.

'I say something about your colour and you're the one's sensitive,' Deke said. 'But you expect me to take it lying down.'

'You don't like the way I talk you can get out of the car,' Mike said. 'Take the rest of the night off. We don't need you, man.'

'Hold it,' Phineus said. 'Nobody's getting out of the car. What's wrong with you two? We're trailing a couple of racists, teach them how to live and let the other man live as well, and you two are falling out over the colour of your skin.'

'Ain't no colour to his skin,' Mike said. 'That right, Deke?'

'White's as much of a colour as black.'

Mike kept the motorbike well ahead of him. He said, 'You know what it means to be white, Deke?'

'You gonna tell me? Out of personal experience?'

'What about you, Heartbreak?' Mike's eyes flashed in the rear-view mirror. 'You ever think about that?'

'It means we're top of the pile,' Heartbreak said. 'We got the power, but it doesn't mean we got to abuse it. Stone told me once that race is nothing to do with biology, it's a social construct.'

'Whiteness,' Mike said. 'It means you're not black, it means you've got no colour in you. You're white, like driven snow, you're innocent, the chosen of the Lord. What it means to be white, is you give all the rest of us a problem, because we're not white. White men, they're not different, they're just what is, the standard that the rest of us is judged by. And we can't ever match up because we're nothing like white. We're different shades of colour; some of us are downright black, like we just walked out of Hell. Sound familiar, Deke?'

'You haven't finished, then?'

'No, I haven't finished. For most of my life I've been thinking about this stuff and I never got a chance to come out with it before. You know what I been doing the last twenty, thirty years? Little John, here, and Phineus, they've been doing it, too. You know what it is that us black folks have been doing, Deke? We've been coming to terms with our racial identity. Some of us have come to terms with it more than others. We've been working it out, trying to understand what it means to be black. Why it is that we're such a problem in the world.

'And it doesn't work. It doesn't work because we're the only ones doing it. Black people are doing all the work and whitey don't even think about it. When was the last time you wrestled with your racial identity, Deke? Heartbreak? Did you think it might be important for you, as representatives of the dominant race on the earth, to consider what it meant to be white?'

He left it there, concentrated on the road as he drove over the bridge.

'You've got a point,' Heartbreak said. 'I'll get on to it tomorrow.'

Phineus and Deke laughed but Heartbreak put his hand on Deke's arm. 'No, I mean it. Tonight we've got a job to do. But tomorrow I'll have time on my hands. How'm I gonna understand the world if I don't think about these things?'

'OK,' Phineus said. 'I'll give you something else to think about. White people, lot of black people, too, they're all the time trying to organize the black community. It's on the television, the radio, in the newspapers, how we've got to solve the problems of the black community, come to grips with it.

'Nobody ever talks about the white community like that; it's the black or the Asian community, as if there's this thing, this massive thing that exists.

'Truth is, though, it doesn't exist at all. If it existed the whites would have one of their own. But the whites don't have one of their own because they know they are all different, all individuals, and they live in small groups, working-class estates, middle-class neighbourhoods, they don't all live together.

'And it's the same for blacks and Asians, we live in scattered communities that are different to each other. So I'm interested in understanding these and I don't want to get involved in organizing on behalf of one mythical monolithic Black Community.'

Heartbreak whistled between his teeth.

Deke said, 'These guys on the motorbike aren't the only ones being taught a lesson tonight.'

'You live and learn, Deke,' Mike said. 'White men've been teaching me how to live since the day I was born. This's just ten minutes of your time.'

37

Father Figures

Stone waited. He sat in the BMW for an hour, then he got out and walked along the riverside path. This whole area had been a working dock not so many years before. A day like this there would've been a thousand men running deal from the timber ships as they came in from Stavanger and Trondheim. Their hard bodies browned by the sun and their shoulders ripped and straining under weights that would have made a horse stagger.

Sally had had a boyfriend who was a tally-man on the old Victoria Dock and Stone carried a vague picture of the man in his head. Short and squat with a greasy coat, a collarless shirt and large black boots. A mouthful of black teeth. Syd, he was called, wore a brass ring on the third finger of each hand, swore they were made of gold.

Earlier, in the latter part of the nineteenth century, Wilson Line ships had transported millions of emigrants from Scandinavia to the New World, landing them at Victoria Dock before putting them on trains to Liverpool and Manchester where they were shipped to America. The trade was cramped and unhygienic and there were reports of human shit running down the sides of the ships and battles with the local sanitary authorities.

But it was all in the past now. There were virtually no reminders of the labour and commerce that had taken place on this land. The architects and builders had rubbed it all out and drawn in a riverside village with its bowling green, play park and community centre.

It was a neat trick. You cut out everything that had happened before, dismissed all the peripheral distractions and concentrated on the job at hand. There was a killer in the house with the wooden balcony and the pantiled roof; the man with scars on his cheeks. The young guy who was with him was probably one of the pair who had beaten up Aunt Nell.

These two and their friends were responsible for the death of the hook-nosed young man in the photographs, Shaban Brovina, and for the beating of Daniel Madika and the harassment of Katy. They were driven by racial hatred and intolerance and now they were up to something else. While he waited for them to make their move, Stone Lewis began the process of putting everything else out of his head. Focus, he told himself, forget who you are, where you came from, ignore irrelevant details like the history of the Victoria Dock.

He controlled his respiration, taking short deep breaths. He held the picture of those two vertical scars in his mind's eye, kept it before him like a banner. When another thought intruded he waved the banner and chased the thought away. He allowed nothing else in; no Ginny, no *I Want You-oo-oo*, not even the shrunken face of Aunt Nell in her hospital bed.

He paced the neighbourhood. Up and down the riverside path, then deeper into the estate, always keeping one eye on the house with the wooden balcony. Occasionally he would walk out of sight of the house for a few moments, knowing it would come back into view before the occupants had time to leave and disappear. It was like a game of cat-and-mouse without the mouse taking an active part.

One by one the house lights went out until there were only a handful of houses showing signs of life.

For a time Stone Lewis had thought that Syd, the tally-man, with his mouthful of black teeth, had been his father. Sometimes he thought back to that time, to determine how old he was and what it was he wanted to call the man. Was it 'Father' or 'Daddy'? Did he have a word at all, or was it just a childish concept? An attempt at conformity? To have a father of his own as some of his friends at school had fathers that belonged exclusively to them?

After Syd there had been Shooter Wilde, another of Sally's boyfriends. And Shooter had been a father of a kind for a long time. It was only when Shooter turned on Sally that he turned also on Stone and revealed himself not as a father, but as a mortal enemy.

Stone sometimes thought that his whole life had been a search for a father. He was inexplicably drawn to the realms of powerful and dominant men, and, particularly in prison, had found himself more than once as the object of sexual lust. It was no easy job trying to explain to a brawny, sexually aroused psychopath that you wanted affection and regard, and that getting fucked was not something you had imagined as part of the equation.

Since meeting Ginny, Stone had begun to learn to live his life with its pluses and minuses, and to skirt around the holes left in his soul by the damaged or missing parts of his personality. He no longer looked for a father, but he did walk through periods in his daily life when there was an inexplicable ache within him. And occasionally he would meet a man, usually older and always charismatic and dominant, and the ache in him would dissolve and float away.

An owl threw itself from a rooftop, dive-bombing prey in a nearby garden, and at the same moment the lights in the house with the wooden balcony went out. Stone sighed, wondering what to do next. He turned towards the BMW with the vague intention of sleeping behind the wheel until morning. Now that he had run his quarry down he didn't want to take the chance of losing him.

But the door of the house opened and two figures emerged into the night. One of them looked like the man he had followed here. Stone couldn't see his face, but he could make out the silhouette, complete with rucksack. The other figure was taller and he walked with purpose in his stride, carrying a suitcase in each hand. Stone glanced at his watch; ten minutes after one.

The tall figure put his bags into the boot of a grey Maestro. He got into the driving seat and pushed open the passenger door for the guy with the rucksack. Stone strained his eyes to see the man's face in the dim glow from the car's internal light, but he was too far away and could make out next to nothing. As the Maestro's engine was powered up and the car moved out of the village, Stone ran for Daniel Madika's BMW and gave chase.

The Maestro travelled slowly, keeping a couple of miles per hour under the speed limit. At traffic lights he slowed up, even when the lights were green, and he indicated purposefully at every corner. There was little traffic on the roads at this hour, and Stone kept well back, hoping that this careful and fastidious driver would be too busy with his signalling and his observance of the Highway Code to notice that he was being tailed.

Eventually the car entered Southcoates Lane and pulled into a side-street, which went around the White House Hotel. Stone parked the BMW on the main road and edged his way down the side-street, keeping as close to the houses as possible, utilizing every shadow, alley and doorway to keep himself hidden from the two figures who were sitting in the grey Maestro by the side gates of the hotel.

38

Silhouettes

Gaz thought he'd buy a bike of his own. Sell the car and get another loan, look around for a British bike, something you could trust that would last. There were plenty of tossers around in beaten-up old cars like his Orion, but a motorbike gave a different impression.

He had his eyes on a Triumph Thunderbird, which would make Ginner green with jealousy. He'd get new leathers at the same time and a crash helmet painted with the Union Flag.

Man of iron.

British man of iron.

Another thing about a bike was it was healthier than a car. With a car you sat inside and smoked fags and if you had the lads in with you you breathed all the air that'd been inside them. Specially Mort stinking of Chinky spare ribs and that barbecue sauce they use. But on a bike you were outside on two wheels, breathing fresh air. And the air was coming at you fast, even when you were on the pillion, like now, with your head down below Ginner's shoulders. A bike made you feel real; the air grabbing at you as you thundered past. Compared to this, cars were tame, cars were sad, they were for tired, old people, those who had given up on life.

And Gaz wasn't one of them. Gaz was in the front rank, a conscious politician, building the kind of country he wanted to live in. Politically correct wankers and lily-livered liberals could sneer as much as they liked, it was their world at the moment, but there were big changes on the horizon. There were iron men at work in the land, at work all over the world, and as sure as the earth travels around the sun their time would come round again.

Ginner braked and half-turned to catch Gaz's attention. With his gloved hand Ginner pointed to the mirror on the bike's handlebar. Gaz looked at the mirror but couldn't see anything. He tapped Ginner's shoulder and yelled, 'What is it?'

Ginner slowed down until the bike was travelling about ten miles an hour. 'Car behind us,' he said. 'Been with us since we left home.'

'Can you lose them?'

'Yeah. Should think so. Hang on.'

'Not too fast, though,' Gaz said. 'We don't wanna get stopped.'

Ginner revved the engine and let the bike shoot forward. They took a right along Great Union Street and followed the curve of Mount Pleasant, over the Wilmington roundabout and along Stoneferry Road. Gaz glanced behind and saw that the car was still with them.

Ginner turned into Chamberlain Road and picked up speed along Laburnum Avenue, turning back on himself when they hit the main road and rejoined Mount Pleasant. When he got to Hedon Road he pulled into a dark cul-de-sac with a cinder track drive, drove to the end and switched off the engine. 'Did they see us come in?' he asked.

'Dunno,' Gaz told him. 'They stayed with us for a while, but you probably outgunned them.' He looked around. They were in an abandoned timber yard. Broken pallets strewn around the place, the remains of a mattress in one corner, a tidy pile of empty bean-cans and a brick hearth white with wood-ash. The whole area enclosed by a slatted fence about 5 metres high.

'Give 'em a few minutes to get lost,' Ginner said. 'And we'll be on our way.'

They waited in silence, heard the car that had been pursuing them zoom past on the main road. Gaz took his helmet off, reached into his pocket and put a cigarette to his lips. He lit it with a transparent lighter and tilted his head backwards to blow the smoke towards the sky. 'It can't be the old woman,' he said. 'She'll be nursing her head.'

'It'll be her mates,' Ginner said. 'Couple of spades and the skinny white bloke.'

Gaz took a drag of his cigarette. They'd need sorting as well, these people who thought they could follow him around. Unbelievable, really, people who didn't have a right to be in the country, following him around, stalking him on his own patch. Gaz would have a problem with anyone limiting his freedom, even people who were pukka, from inside the movement. But he was never going to take it from a bunch of freeloading sun-speak aliens.

Mort and Ginner were always going on about how men were nothing on their own, how the task was to build a society that was bigger than the sum of its parts. How individuality should be submerged into the greater glory of the State. Gaz paid lip service to the ideas but he didn't know how to square them with his longing for heroism. He couldn't understand how, if the State was supreme, we would ever achieve a nation full of heroes.

You'd need the State, though, no doubt about that. For discipline. For order, and to give direction. And a strong army. Because as soon as the revolution came, there would be foreign powers trying to take it all away from us. And we'd need to fight, anyway, to get the Empire back.

There was an eas-o-teric side to the argument; a change took place when everyone did the right thing at the right time and it allowed a mighty spiritual warrior to come and guide the ways of men. Something like summoning a genie out of a bottle, only the mighty spiritual warrior would be the essence of England, not some shitty little pimp in a turban.

There was the brief purring of a car engine, but the sound was cut off almost immediately as a pair of headlights rolled around the corner of the yard, loose gravel and small cobblestones spitting out from the tyres of a Cavalier.

Gaz felt Ginner's body tense and the bike shifted under them. All four doors of the Cavalier opened and the men spread themselves on either side of the car. There were five silhouettes. One of them opened the boot of the car and handed out baseball bats and long square batons. None of them spoke and they brandished their weapons in both hands, like ancient warriors captured in the glare of a dying sun.

Ginner began to get off the bike but Gaz held his shoulder. 'We don't have time for this,' he said. 'Be ready to start the bike when I say.'

Ginner exhaled loudly but he didn't resist. If you put something to him earnestly, made sure there was authority in your voice, he'd go along with it. He'd give his all as well, do everything necessary. If he had to choose somebody to be in a tight spot with, Gaz would choose Ginner every time. With Mort there'd be questions; while the gates of Hell were closing on you Mort would start a debate about tactics. Ginner was the opposite, he was a foot-soldier, he'd obey orders, do what had to be done without reservation.

Gaz reached into the pannier and came out with one of the fire bombs they'd made earlier in the day. The tang of petrol fumes and candle wax filled his nostrils. The silhouettes of the men from the Cavalier had taken a few steps forward but they hesitated when they saw what Gaz was holding in his hand.

He straightened the rag wick and lit it with a flick of his lighter. The flames threw dancing shadows on the back of Ginner's leather jacket and Gaz's face was reflected in the gloss of his friend's helmet. He looked at his own helmet but left it where it was on the cinders, realizing they were out of time.

'Now,' he said quietly. 'Move fast and get close to their car.'

Ginner kicked the starter and the twin engine roared into life. He played with the accelerator, shattering the neighbourhood with vibrations loud and powerful enough to drive a tractor through a waterlogged field.

When he released the clutch the machine screamed forward, the cylinders spinning crazily, metal and rubber stressing and rupturing, and Gaz raised himself from the pillion, his fire bomb held aloft and his eyes fixed on the dark outline of the Cavalier.

The armed and silhouetted figures of the men who had come to face them faltered for a moment, startled by the sudden movement and the ear-splitting storm of the racing engine. Gaz was aware, from the corner of his eye, that one of them was coming forward to intercept the bike. A madman who thought he could stop powerful machinery with mere muscle.

Gaz lobbed the fire bomb at the windscreen of the Cavalier at the same moment as he realized that Ginner was leaving the bike. The thick-set man with a 2-metre pole caught Ginner on the neck, just below his helmet. Ginner let go of the bike and toppled over on to the bonnet of the Cavalier almost at the same instant as the fire bomb exploded into the car's windscreen.

Gaz saw the sheet of flame as the petrol and oil exploded and he grabbed for the handlebar of the bike as the machine stood up on its back wheel. There was space in front of him and for a moment he saw with absolute certainty that he was going to make it, that he was within an inch of bringing the bike under control and making his rendezvous with Mort and Omega and the bombing of the wog hostel.

A smile crossed his face as the bike came down onto two wheels, but as he twisted the throttle, the back of the machine skewed away from him and went into a zig-zagging, ragged, sliding motion. Gaz touched the brakes and the bike left the ground, began a long slow somersault that never felt right. Gaz didn't know how it was going to end and he couldn't pinpoint the moment when the thing had started to go wrong.

The bike slammed itself into the side of the slatted fence that surrounded the yard and Gaz heard the bone of his own head split open and the blood and the juices, whatever it was that was in there, all make a rush for the exit.

39

The Barbecue Sprinkler

A quiet street on the east side of the river, time coming up to half past one in the morning and two men, both of them associated with extreme violence, were sitting in a grey Maestro. Stone couldn't work it out. There were mainly family houses in the street, all of them in darkness, their occupants sleeping peacefully in their beds. The broken hotel was also quiet, a couple of lights at landing windows, but no movements inside, no voices or sounds of any kind.

This was the same scenario that had led to Aunt Nell being attacked in her bed the previous evening. Perhaps they were here to intimidate another Aunt Nell, some old lady sleeping in her bed in one of these houses. But if that was the case they'd have to take on Stone Lewis as well, and with Stone in the picture they wouldn't find their job as easy as it had been yesterday.

A man and the moon. When he'd been small Stone would say, 'A *boy* and the moon.' He'd lie awake at night waiting for Sally to come home from the pub, his ears cocked for the sound of her high heels clipping along the pavement. Sometimes she'd go to a party or a one-night-stand at some guy's house and the time she was supposed to come home would go sailing past.

Stone would get out of bed and sit by the window in his pyjamas, watch the deserted street and listen to the neighbourhood cats taunting each other. No one else alive in the universe, all the streets like this, the towns and cities emptied of human life. Nothing happening. Nothing going on. Just a boy and the moon.

'What about the bloke they fished out of the river?' Mort asked.

'Useless.'

'Was that you? Did for him?'

'Peter Packard,' Omega said. 'Supposed to be a professional. He helped with the Kosovan lefty I told you about. Then he tells me about a woman who's been taking photographs of us. That's fine, though, because he's got her camera. Doesn't notice that she's taken the Compact Flash out.'

'She's still got the film?' Mort asked.

Omega shook his head. 'Not any longer. And I don't have to worry about Peter Packard either.'

'You threw him in the river?'

Omega shook his head from side to side. 'There you go again, Mort. Asking questions.' He glanced at his watch then reached for his gabardine coat on the rear seat, each pocket bulging with a firebomb. 'You got yours?' he asked.

'Yeah.' Mort held up his rucksack.

'Matches?'

'I'm all prepared. I know what to do.'

'And your friends?'

'I don't know where they are,' Mort said. 'They should be here.'

Omega shrugged. 'OK, let's do it.' They left the car and walked into the grounds of the hotel, the man with the scars draping his gabardine coat over his shoulders as though taking a stroll before dinner. 'I'll take the front,' he said. 'You go round the back. And don't hang about. We do the job and get out of here fast.'

Mort shook his head as they separated. His mouth was dry and there were pinpricks of tension in his eyes and at each of his temples. This was a trial, a kind of initiation. But he was focused; failure didn't exist, even as a concept. This was the deed that would take him away from the pain of his life. The deed that would lead to glory. Far off, still too distant to hear, there were the stirrings of a symphony. When the flames reached their pinnacle the music would have swelled to deafening proportions and the spirits of all the great Englishmen of the past would be singing along in the chorus.

Stone could have followed either of them. It was something connected with the rucksack that made him follow the younger man around to the rear of the hotel. The moon slipped behind a cloud and the shadows disappeared. For a moment Stone lost sight of the guy. He stood and held his breath and when his eyes refocused he saw the young man standing on a square of flagstones outside the back windows of the hotel. There was a door off to the side, at the corner of the building, flanked by a couple of large metal containers, the kind used for waste food, kitchen refuse.

By clinging to the wall Stone could get close to the guy, his progress masked by the waste containers. Within a few seconds he was crouched behind one of them, barely two paces away from the man, able to hear his breathing and make out the swastika stud above his eye.

The man went down on one knee, muttering under his breath. He took a couple of bottles from his rucksack and stood them next to each other on the flagstones. He dug deeper into the bag and came out with a box of household matches. He put the matches on the flagstones next to the bottles and shook his head. Something was wrong.

He took one of the bottles and put it back into the rucksack, smiling now as if he had remembered something important.

Stone still hadn't worked it out. It looked as though the guy was going to have a drink and a smoke. It wasn't until he struck one of the matches and transferred the flame to the rag at the neck of the bottle that Stone realized what was happening. The flame flickered uncertainly at first, then took hold and illuminated the scene.

The guy picked up the bottle and looked at the window above his head. He took a couple of steps back from the building and turned, the hand with the firebomb raised, ready to launch at the window.

Stone felt the brick wall of the building behind him. He put his feet against the first waste container and propelled it towards the guy with the firebomb. The small wheels took it for perhaps a metre before it toppled over, striking the man on the shoulder, making him drop the bottle between his feet.

The explosion was spectacular. It wasn't particularly loud but it gave rise to all the colours of the spectrum in a confined space and time. The bottle cracked open where it landed and the dark liquid splashed upward in a fan, covering the guy's legs and crotch. They both watched it. Stone glanced at the guy's face for an instant and saw him looking down at his legs and thighs in that instant before the mixture of petrol and oil ignited.

He could have been watching a film, scanning a tabloid headline, anything. There was no fear there, no appreciation of what was about to happen. There was only a fixed fascination, perhaps a tinge of surprise that things had taken off in a different direction to the plan.

Then it blew.

The legs and lower body of the man were engulfed in flame that roared and howled with such anguish that his own cries were smothered. Within seconds the man's hair was alight; he was a human torch, his arms flapping aimlessly, his mouth an open gash as his skin crusted to charcoal and his eyes melted back into his head.

The second bottle blew, the one in the rucksack. But the man was already far too well done.

There were times in Aunt Nell's yard when Heartbreak would be cooking chicken on the barbecue, yelling for the sprinkler when the flames licked their way out of the coals and turned the meat black. That was how it was with this guy at the back of the hotel, his clothes turned to rags or melted away and he was a piece of chicken underneath, his flesh seared and bubbling, his mouth an image of agony. Stone looked around in the dark, felt his way around the brick walls, but there wasn't a sprinkler in sight. God could have turned the taps on in Heaven but He didn't bother. The guy wasn't important enough.

As he went down in flames, first to his knees and then crumbling forward onto his face, there came the sound of breaking glass from the front of the building. The ground floor lit up like a lantern. When another window shattered, the contents of a second firebomb added to the flames inside the building.

The man with the scars came around the side of the hotel and headed for his car. He looked briefly at the still burning body of his partner and ran off along the path. Stone chased him for a few paces but gave up and returned to the rear door of the hotel. He would've liked to get hold of the guy, push his head through the windscreen, pay him back for what he'd done to Katy and for the murder of the hook-nosed young man from Kosovo. But it was more important to raise the alarm in the hotel.

The back door wouldn't open, and although he found a side

entrance to the building that was also locked fast. He raced up the ancient metal fire escape and got in on the first floor, running along the dimly lit corridor banging on the doors and shouting at the top of his voice. There was an old man sitting cross-legged at the end of the corridor, emaciated, with brown leathery skin hanging in folds on his body like an array of necklaces. The old man put his index finger to his lips and shook his head but Stone took him by the hand and led him back towards the fire exit. As they went, the doors on the corridor opened and a succession of Kurds, Afghans and Marsh Arabs, some of them with children in tow, left their squalid and dingy apartments and followed.

Stone extricated himself from the old man and while the procession of refugees went down the steps to safety, Stone went up to the next landing and brought out another crocodile of sleepy-eyed and bewildered asylum-seekers. A couple of Albanian teenagers, a one-eyed Nigerian, a Punjabi Sikh and a heavily pregnant Ghanaian woman with a red turban and no shoes. They joined the first group, close to but apart from the crumpled body of the man who had burned to death. A couple of the men edged closer to the body, trying to identify it, but they moved away as soon as they realized what it was. There was a deep silence around it. It was as if it was hollow, just a brittle outer casing that might be damaged by sound. In the mixture of religious faiths and beliefs now gathered around it, the dead sheath of the man seemed strangely material. A corpse; a piece of meat. Carrion.

It was only when he had cleared the next floor, and the sirens of the fire engines and ambulances pulled up in the street, that Stone slipped away, not wanting to explain to the police how he happened to be in the neighbourhood.

40

Nemesis

There wasn't room to park the black BMW in Daniel Madika's driveway because the space was taken up by a grey Maestro.

Stone left the car by the side of the road and walked up the drive. He placed his hand on the bonnet. The engine was still warm.

The house was in darkness, the sleeping street quiet. The moon was an eagle-eyed watcher high in the sky.

Stone took a moment to compose himself before edging his way along the narrow path that ran between the garage and the house, the path on which Daniel Madika had been beaten senseless just a few days earlier.

He emerged at the rear of the house. There was a long, narrow garden with fruit trees and neat borders and an ornamental pond with a fountain and a mock waterfall. At the bottom was a shed with the orb of the moon reflected in its windows.

Closer to the house was a concreted area with a circular drying rack, festooned with baby clothes, a couple of sheets and a sleeveless cotton dress cut to the exact shape of Katy Madika. The washing hung from dark-blue pegs, fluorescent in the moonlight.

By standing behind the washing Stone could see into the interior of the house through the patio windows. The man with the scarred face was sitting on a blue upholstered chair by a small inlaid table, a bottle of malt by his right hand. In his left he held a half-full crystal glass. He was alone, motionless, his head cocked as if listening to the night.

Stone watched him. The man could have been the resident of the house, the husband, sitting up late to ponder a domestic problem or to enjoy a moment or two of solitude while his wife and child slept upstairs. There was no hint that the man had only recently, less than an hour before, fire-bombed a hotel full of men, women and children.

Or perhaps it was this that occupied the man's thoughts. Maybe he was enjoying a post-fire-bombing scotch, a personal celebration of a job well done.

And why here, at Katy's house? Had the violence, the terror he'd wreaked on the people in the hotel turned to lust? Was it a case of an awakened libido looking to maintain and extend its presence through the night? Would he, after finishing his drink, tread the dark stairs up to Katy's room?

Stone shook his head. The man's motives were unknowable. He might be using the place as a stopover with no intention of disturbing Katy Madika's sleep. He might suspect that the police would be stopping vehicles on the road after the hotel went up in flames. Or it could be that he intended to burn down Katy's house as well, while she and Chloe slept in the upper rooms.

But whatever was going on, Stone had to stop this man. He was a danger to everyone.

During his time in the prison system Stone had accustomed himself to looking at men. Before that he had watched women with an obsessive passion, and since his release he had reverted to looking at them again. He loved to watch Ginny and when she left the house he would stand at the window and take in her movement along the street. Even now, while she was away, he could bring her to mind, let his eye rove over her insubstantial image.

But he'd learned how to look at a man. To read his body language, to discern the degree of danger that he might represent. Size and weight were often incidentals in a personal scrap. The main factor was willpower or determination, how single-minded you could be, how much tenacity and resolve you were prepared to commit to bringing the other man down.

With a man like the one sitting in Katy Madika's living room there were other factors to consider. He was a professional, and he was hard. He had a broad, solid forehead and he'd worked to build his biceps and the muscles in his back and legs. He was fit. He wouldn't be short of breath and would quickly recover from any punches Stone might throw at him.

It would be madness to walk in there and face up to the man bare-handed. The guy liked violence. He had killed and he was motivated by some twisted political obsession. Stone wouldn't've minded being a hero but it seemed more important to him to live long enough to see his girlfriend come home from America.

He retreated slowly down the garden, avoiding the pond. At the shed he looked back and could still see the scarfaced man sipping his malt in the soft glow from a table-lamp. There were two cycles in the shed and little room for anything else. A garden sieve and a hose-pipe carefully wrapped around a wire drum. A plastic sack of peat and another of pebbles, probably for the pond. A pair of Canadian rigger gloves in orange and yellow were hanging from a hook on the wall. The only object that approached the status of weapon was a small border spade. It was fairly new, the stainless-steel blade bright and the ashwood shaft covered with its original varnish.

Stone took it in his hand and weighed it, found its centre of balance. He carried it to the house and found the back door open with a smashed lock. It led into a utility room with a quarry-tiled floor and a central drain; a washer and spin-dryer stood at the far wall.

The internal door from the utility room took him into a hallway. Straight ahead was the sitting room he had seen from the back garden. To his right the hallway led to the front of the house and the stairs to the upper floor. He could see Chloe's pram standing inside the front entrance.

He walked into the room with the lighted table-lamp and looked at the empty chair where the scarfaced man had been sipping his malt a couple of minutes earlier.

Stone spun around, expecting to see the man bearing down on him from behind the door. But there was nothing. No movement. No sound. The crystal glass was on the small table, two fingers of malt left behind.

Without thinking but feeling his heart and mind racing, Stone went down the hallway and opened the front door. Part of him expected to see the grey Maestro making its way along the street with Scarface at the wheel, but the car hadn't moved. There was no one in the driving seat. The street was deserted.

He walked back to the house and stepped into the front hall, closing the door behind him and leaning against it, his eyes fixed on the stairs. When his breathing returned to normal he took the first step, straining every nerve in his body to anticipate the meeting with this man who had always been ahead of him.

There was a light switch on the wall but Stone left everything in darkness. Light would only expose him, while the scarfaced man would remain in the shadows. He trod softly on each step, slowly ascending to the upper floor where Katy and her child were sleeping, unaware that their home had been invaded once again by the killer who had put Daniel Madika into a coma.

The first door opened into a bathroom. Pink fittings, cork floor, tiles up to the ceiling. The bath was fitted with a faucet and the shower door was open, concealing no one.

The second door led to a storeroom; boxes of books, a monitor and a spare computer keyboard, suitcases, several pairs of shoes and a desk piled high with old vinyl LPs, Steve Earle's *Guitar Town* sitting on top. Along one wall was a chaise longue stripped of its upholstery, ready and waiting for a recovering job. Some of Katy's discarded frocks were lying across its backrest.

The hairs on the back of Stone's head prickled as he opened the third door. He paused for a moment, grasping the handle, wondering if his nervous system had detected something that the rest of his senses had failed to identify. But there didn't appear to be anything sinister or dangerous once he'd opened the door and stepped inside. It was Chloe's room. The wallpaper embossed with the faces of children, black, white and Asian, toothy and smiling countenances from around the world. Chloe's cot stood in the centre of the room, empty. Stone placed his hand on the sheet, feeling the impression left by her small body. It was cold, slightly damp.

The last bedroom was dominated by a large double bed. The curtains were half drawn and the moon cast a strange greenish light through the windows. When he pushed open the door Stone took in a wall of wardrobes to his right. Behind the door, next to the bed, was another cot and in it he could make out the tiny head of the sleeping child.

He edged himself around the room and stood at the foot of the bed, his back to the windows. Katy Madika was lying in the centre of the bed on her back. Her eyes were open, staring. There were no sounds apart from the breathing of the child and the animated, suppressed gasps coming from her mother.

Stone spoke in a whisper. 'Where is he?'

As a reply Katy glanced to her left. She moved her eyes without shifting her head. But there was nothing there. The edge of the bed finished and there was a small bedside table and the outer wall of the house. Stone took two steps and looked down into the dark gap between bed and wall.

As he stared into the abyss the scarfaced man rose up before him with a scream like a bandsaw. He rushed forward, a hooked crowbar, gripped in both hands above his head. Stone ducked instinctively and used his spade to ward off the blow that would surely have split his head apart. The man took stock and came at him again and they locked together, their weapons bouncing off each other in a parody of a medieval joust.

The child in the cot awoke and joined in the cacophony.

Scarface fought like a wild animal. There was no aspect of defence in his movements; his objective was to destroy Stone or perish in the attempt. Stone wanted to disarm the man, or at least push him back to a position where he could feel he was making some headway. But all Stone could achieve was to remain standing, feeling all the time more and more beleaguered by the man. It was as if Stone's failure to submit to Scarface's blows only drove him to come with renewed force.

Gradually Stone was pushed back to the wardrobe and pinned in the corner against the wall. Scarface rained blows down on him with the crowbar and Stone warded them off more or less successfully with the shaft of the spade. In a moment of inspiration, while Scarface was adjusting his grip on the crowbar, Stone drove the handle of the spade into his belly. Scarface groaned and sank to his knees and Stone had time to step out of the corner, hoping to squeeze the man's throat with the shaft of the spade until Scarface relinquished his hold of the crowbar.

But the intruder recovered immediately and swept the crowbar out in an arc around him, catching both of Stone's shins and bringing him down in a heap on the carpet. Stone felt the spade spin away from him as he fell in front of the window.

He rolled over on to his back and cast about for the spade but before he could find it Scarface was standing astride him, the crowbar raised above his head. 'So long, sucker,' he said, a grin animating his face.

There was no way that Stone could avoid his fate and he closed his eyes, hoping for a clean kill.

In the same instant he heard Katy scream and opened his eyes for an instant, quick enough to see her standing on the edge of the bed, swinging a bolster at the head of the scarfaced man. The guy saw it coming, too, but a fraction of a second too late. He adjusted his weight and tried to turn the crowbar on Katy but wasn't quick enough to ward off her blow.

Stone saw his chance and as the bolster connected with the guy's head, he twisted over, causing Scarface to lose his balance.

The crowbar went through the window first and Scarface followed it. It was as if he was reluctant to let go and was pulled through the shattered glass.

Katy's legs went and she slipped off the bed, her bare feet landing on Stone's chest. From the cot behind the door came the long, high-pitched call of the traumatized child.

Stone got to his knees and peered through the broken window. Below on the tarmac outside of the garage the broken body of Scarface was lying face-down. His crowbar had bounced away from him and embedded itself in a composted flowerbed.

A light came on in a neighbouring house.

'What does it look like?' Katy asked, moving towards the cot.

'I think he's dead. He's not gonna move.'

She sighed and collected Chloe into her arms. The child stopped crying and buried her head in her mother's breast.

'I can't stay,' Stone said. 'I was never here.'

As he moved towards the door Katy sat on the edge of the bed. She placed Chloe, on her tummy, across her lap. She picked up the spade and wiped it clean of fingerprints, polishing the shaft and the blade with the cover of her duvet.

'The door handles,' he said.

She gave him a smile. 'Don't worry. It's all taken care of.'

41

Some Kind of Setback

Daniel Madika's bulky body filled the narrow hospital bed. The blanket was pulled down, revealing powerful shoulders and a chest dotted with small white discs to monitor the slightest change in his body's responses. His eyes were closed.

Stone put his back to the door and stood facing the man for a couple of minutes. He wanted to tell him that the world was a safer place, that it was all right for him to come out of his coma, to return to his life. He wanted to tell him that Katy and Chloe were waiting for him and that the threat from the man with the scars and the other thugs who had beaten him half to death was now over.

But he couldn't tell Daniel Madika those things, because they weren't true. This was the new world in which wherever you are might not be too bad but anywhere else would be better. Even though the man with the scars was dead, his mission would continue elsewhere. The young guy who had burned to death and his friends on the motorbike had been stopped in their tracks, but others like them would be thrown up by the system. Wherever there was ignorance and exploitation there would be a search for scapegoats. Men in powerful national and international positions would ever be willing to divide and rule, to turn one section of the population against another in order to hide their own misdeeds. And there would always be men and women who could not understand others outside of their own confined group and who wanted to destroy all that they did not understand.

Daniel Madika wasn't listening anyway. He was deaf to anything that Stone had to tell him. His mind was in neutral, waiting for better news, or for an elaborate and fantastic fabrication that would enable him to re-grasp the details of his life.

Aunt Nell was looking better. The tiny and withdrawn face she had presented the day before had already been banished. 'They didn't kill me,' she said. 'But they got me thinking.'

'You'll be limping for a while and nursing the bruises.'

'Bruises schmuises,' she said, squeezing his hand. 'But you know, Stone, I wasn't frightened of dying when it was happening. The worst thing would be if they took my sight, or if I had brain damage, or if they took my leg off. But death doesn't hold those kind of fears.'

Stone made a face.

'I was thinking about it again, yesterday, after you came to visit. There's something complete and completed about death. There's a kind of beauty to it. It's not something to be frightened of. We should go out and embrace it because it unites us with the infinite, at last we come face to face with eternity.'

'Maybe there is some brain damage,' he said.

'I was being serious.'

Stone shook his head from side to side. 'I wasn't up close to it like you,' he said. 'But death doesn't feel like that to me. I mean, whichever way you look at it, it's got to be some kind of setback.'

Nell smiled. 'Yeah, I'm not ready for it, either. Still got things to work through with Heartbreak and your mother.'

He gave her a plastic bag full of books. 'I don't want them back,' he said.

Nell smiled.

When he left her Stone took the wrong turn in the corridor and didn't realize his mistake until he came to the ladies' lavatory. He turned around to retrace his steps and find his way out of the hospital. Ahead of him now, and coming towards him, was an ancient woman with a walking frame. She placed the frame in front of her and shuffled her way into it with tiny feet, her wrinkled head going up and down from floor to ceiling like a chicken pecking at grain. Once she'd reached the frame she would lift it again and place it an arm's length in front of her. It was slow progress, but effective, and the woman was no learner; her movements had the rhythm and precision of long practice.

When she was about 20 metres from the lavatory another ward

door opened and an equally old lady hit the corridor on a pair of crutches. This second woman was tall and thin and she'd hitched up her nightgown to enable freer movement, revealing a single leg. When she got it right, the crutches enabled her to take long, swinging strides, giving her an air of flight and speed that would easily leave the one with the walking frame behind. But she was new to the crutches and uncomfortable with them. The right one kept slipping out from under her and all movement would stop while she balanced herself on the one leg and managed to get the crutch into the right position for her next move.

They drew level with each other and turned their heads to make eye contact. The woman with the frame looked away and fixed her eyes on the door to the ladies' lavatory, which was now about 10 metres away. The thin woman with the leg followed the other's gaze. They glanced back at each other for a moment and simultaneously set off at a rush, each determined to get there first.

Crutches took the lead immediately, making a couple of metres, while the wizened one with the frame was still shuffling forward and had not covered half the ground. But the situation was reversed when the thin one lost her right crutch and looked for a moment as though she wouldn't be able to retrieve it.

'I was first,' the one with the frame said as she passed the now stationary thin woman. 'It's a queue.' She had a piping voice, abrasive and harsh, and it ricocheted off the walls with indignation.

'First come, first served,' the tall thin woman said as she got her crutch into position and swung past the little shuffler. But she lost her crutch again and grimaced angrily as she wrestled to regain it.

Stone got out of the way, his back to the wall, as the two of them came rushing towards him with the paraphernalia of swinging crutches and wildly wobbling walking frame. They looked and sounded like something out of a school sports-day and Stone made himself as small as possible as they went past him in a fury of willpower and perspiration.

The one with the frame got there first. She smiled evilly as she locked the tall woman out and left her hammering on the door with her crutches.

42

Who Was That Man?

The wheelchair had flat tyres and with the bulk of Alice sitting in it Joolz had to strain herself to get it moving. On the flat it was OK and along a straight length of the hospital corridor it zinged along. But when they came to a ramp she had to ask someone to help. Even then it was hard work, Joolz and the little fat bald guy both putting their back into it and Alice gripping the arm-rests like she was going to be shot out of a cannon.

She had imagined that the mortuary would be dimly lit, that it would be cold in there, quiet and spooky with an abundance of echo. And the feeling that, although the bodies were all dead, there might be the odd spark of life about, the constant possibility of a tap on the shoulder.

But it wasn't like that. The temperature was the same as everywhere else in the hospital and they had fluorescent lamps hanging from the ceiling on long chains.

There was a cop in uniform and a tall fruitcake in a white coat. They'd been on training courses, learned how not to smile when there was a dead body and relatives in the same room. Both of them believed that nothing like this would ever happen to them. They were like most of the people Joolz met in her life. They had this idea that everything in the world was nailed down, that it was all sorted and that nothing would happen to them unless they planned it. They'd get married and have one-point-two-five children who'd grow up to take care of them in old age and supplement their pensions. They had no idea that a storm was raging and by the time it had blown itself out there would be nothing left.

The body was in a chilled pull-out cabinet like something you might keep vegetables in, or dairy produce. Joolz had never been to Madame Tussaud's but she imagined that the models there looked like this, some of them. The stillness of death, none of the vitality of living flesh. They'd put a white cotton cap on his head and his shoulders and arms were covered with a gown, but you could still see the burn marks on his neck and the top of his chest. And his forehead was black, crusted where the flames had licked upward to consume his hair.

Alice broke down. Her round head seemed too heavy for her neck and it started wobbling from side to side. She came with a thin cry, a prolonged, high-pitched warbling like you hear native women doing on the news. Joolz had thought it was a ridiculous sound to make but when Alice did it she changed her mind. It could be useful to get something wound up inside of you out into the world.

She remained quiet herself, contained. Mort had only wanted to live to be thirty-five. And he was nowhere near it.

The cop asked Alice if this was her son and Alice, between gasps to get her breath and a stream of tears, said that it was. Joolz looked again. She could see the similarity in the face, which, strangely, seemed to be the only part of him that wasn't burnt. But it wasn't Mort. Mort had been more than this. Mort had been authoritative and eager, he'd been a thinker and looked after his mother and he'd been set to change the world. This was alien. Mort would have had nothing to do with this useless, disgusting husk in the cold cabinet. He would have found out where it came from and had it repatriated.

Alice was hungry and Joolz trundled her down to the hospital cafeteria and left her with a plate of three-meat Chinese stir-fry and egg fried rice. On a side plate she had a pork-pie and a slice of Black Forest Gateau with a pint of Coke to wash it down. She didn't smile but the food seemed to calm her nerves, eased her breathing back into a recognizable rhythm.

While Alice was tucking in, Joolz went to have a look at Gaz and Ginner. The policeman wouldn't let her into the room, but she could see just as well through the glass. It wasn't as if she wanted to talk to them.

'The fat one's fractured his skull,' the cop said. 'The other one's *compos mentis* but drugged up to the eyeballs.'

Gaz's head was swathed in bandages and he was propped on the pillow looking clean and peaceful with his eyes closed. If she didn't know it was him, Joolz might have walked on by without recognizing him. Ginner had his eyes open but he was staring into space. His face was burnt, the skin raw and angry on his cheeks and nose, and he looked as if he'd been crying for a long time and as if he'd been tortured. His eyes were rimmed with red and his lips had receded and rolled back into his mouth. They'd put some cream on the burns and the angry flesh was glistening. He had an oxygen mask but had pulled it away from his face and left it dangling around his neck.

Joolz couldn't think why she had found them so threatening. They were like children.

'They're looking at life sentences,' the cop told her.

Joolz nodded. She already knew that. They'd been found in possession of fire-bombs and it was the same mixture that had set fire to the hostel and killed Mort. 'There must've been someone else involved,' she said.

The cop shook his head. 'There was the guy who got the asylum-seekers out of the hostel. He's disappeared without trace. But these two are the ones responsible for the murder.' He rubbed his hands together as if warming them at the flame of truth. 'D'you know them?'

'I know who they are,' Joolz said. 'Mortimer was my boyfriend.'

'Mortimer?'

'The one who was killed.'

'Oh. Sorry to hear that. You must be in shock. Haven't you got someone to talk to, a friend?'

'I've got Alice. Mortimer's mother.'

'That the one in the wheelchair?' he asked. 'The invalid? What's going to happen to her now her son's gone?'

'Alice'll be all right,' Joolz said. 'I'll take care of her. Mortimer would expect me to do that.'

The cop smiled. A kindly smile. Joolz wondered how old he was under his uniform. She reckoned he wasn't much older than her. He was more secure, though, sure of himself, but that was because he had a regular job and a posh accent and he was a man.

'D'you get to talk to them?' she asked, indicating his two prisoners.

'Not much,' he said. 'They don't have a lot to say.'

'The fat one,' she said, 'Gaz, could you give him a message?'

The cop shook his head. 'Not supposed to,' he said. 'Is it important?'

'Just say I was here,' Joolz said. 'And I'm gonna get him a hundred grams of pork mince.'

The cop half smiled. 'Not a hidden code, is it?'

Joolz blinked her eyelashes at him. 'He'll understand,' she said.

43

Plots

Ginny gave up her freedom and sense of proportion as she shuffled aboard the plane at LAX. It was like being swallowed by a giant toothpaste tube, waiting to be squeezed back out at the other end. She reflected that the same technologies were probably employed by the designers and makers of both planes and toothpaste tubes. She'd been allocated a window seat and she could look back at the concourse and imagine Sherab, her ex-husband, gazing wistfully out at this machine that was going to fly her back to her lover in England.

Ten days back in his company had reminded her over and over again of the reason she had left him for Stone Lewis. Sherab was suffocating. His insecurities were so raw and uncontrolled that he required constant assurances in almost every area of his existence. To live with him Ginny had had to sacrifice all self-interest and place herself at the service of his fragile ego.

That in itself would have been all right if it had made Sherab strong, if in some way her efforts had been healing. But throughout their brief marriage Sherab had got weaker, his need for reassurance reaching obsessive proportions. If he couldn't find a can of beans in the kitchen he'd interpret it as wifely rejection: 'If you really loved me you'd make sure you did the shopping properly.'

The plane stopped for an hour in Atlanta, birthplace of Martin Luther King Jr. Ginny thought she should visit the King Center and pay homage to the memory of a man who had given his life in the struggle for racial equality. But she'd never got around to it and sitting in a plane at the airport might be as close as she'd ever get.

There had been a time during the last months of her marriage when she'd studied the assassination documents and seen that James Earl Ray, the man who died in prison for the deed, was a patsy. Ray had been a criminal whose career was marked by sheer ineptitude. Once when burgling a house he'd been discovered and in his panic fallen out of a first-floor window. Another time he'd held up a taxi-driver at gunpoint to steal eleven dollars and then tried to escape down a dead-end alley. In prison he'd lived by renting second-hand magazines to other cons. He could no more have organized the assassination of Dr King than he could have stayed away from criminal behaviour.

More passengers boarded the plane at Atlanta and a tall, tacky Cary Grant lookalike took the seat next to Ginny. He cleared his throat and looked at the outline of her legs beneath her skirt.

She closed her eyes and thought of England.

The engines revved and the plane began that headlong lunge down the runway that never fails to remind you of human frailty. Ginny took a breath and kept her eyes closed until the roar of the wheels on the tarmac ceased. The nose of the airliner pointed skywards and the huge bulk of the thing pulled away from the earth, heading for the clouds and a different life on the other side of the Atlantic.

'Are you going to the UK?'

Ginny looked at the man. She'd been reading Marquez's *One Hundred Years of Solitude* and the language and dream-like time sequences of the novel had enclosed her in a bubble, insulated her from the world and her immediate surroundings.

'Yes,' she said. 'If I'm on the right plane.'

He smiled. He was tall and slim, wearing designer glasses and a well-cut light-blue suit with a darker shirt and no tie. A curl of wiry hair protruded from the top of his shirt. A leather briefcase rested on his lap, the initials DR embossed in the lower right corner of the lid.

'Oh,' he said. 'An English accent. Curiouser and curiouser.'

'What kind of accent did you expect? Mandarin?'

'No,' he said pensively. 'Asian, but not Chinese. Thai, perhaps.'

He's not a complete philistine, then, Ginny thought. 'I'm English,' she said. 'But my parents were Vietnamese.'

'And you read Spanish,' he said, indicating the novel, which she had placed on the pull-down table in front of her.

'I like the language,' she said. She didn't tell him she was fluent in French as well as Spanish and that, although she didn't read or write German and Russian, she could get by conversationally in both. People, strangers, don't want to hear about your talents, they want you to help them relax, put them at ease. In England you're not allowed to say you're good at something. If you do that you're committing the cardinal sin: admitting that you're bad at being English.

'David Rose,' he said, extending his hand.

'Virginia Bradshaw,' she told him formally. His hands were long and bony, cool to the touch. Not working hands. Although his hair was dark there was one lock in the middle of his forehead that was white. This gave him a badger-like appearance, which wasn't attractive unless you were an animal lover.

He asked questions. Where did she live? What was her job? What had she been doing in LA? It was like an examination but Ginny didn't mind. After ten days of Sherab telling her who she was and what she was like, it was refreshing to have someone *asking* her to define herself.

'How did you get from Vietnam to England?'

'I was a refugee orphan,' she said. 'I don't know what happened to my natural parents. The Bradshaws adopted me, brought me up in Hull.'

'Where did they find you?'

'Saigon. My adoptive father was a Scot but he'd been in the East when he was young, in the Navy. Someone wrote to him about me.'

The hostess arrived with a trolley and David Rose offered to buy her a drink but Ginny shook her head. 'I'll have a Bud,' she told the hostess. 'And a single malt.'

David Rose ordered a coke for himself and Ginny could see he was silently amused by her ordering two drinks.

'Go on,' he said. 'You were talking about your parents.'

'My mother was from Rosedale, in Yorkshire. Dad died when I was sixteen. Mum and I spent a couple of years propping each other up and then made different lives for ourselves. She works in a circus now, training animals. I went off to the States and got married.'

'And it didn't work out?'

She smiled. 'Understatement.'

He waited. He looked across her out of the window at the clouds far below. His eyes were grey, only a tinge of blue in there, right in the centre of the pupil, radiating outwards in tiny veins. He had wrinkles in his face, but not too deep. 'And now?' he said. 'Is there someone else?'

Ginny nodded. 'I'm living with a man called Stone Lewis. In Hull. We share a flat.'

Several creases appeared on David Rose's forehead. 'Not far from me,' he said. 'I'm in Leeds.' He looked at her for longer than necessary, his gaze flicking between her eyes and the rest of her face, his features earnest and thoughtful. Being stared at in this particular way didn't change Ginny's pulse rate. If anything, she wanted to giggle.

'I expect this new relationship is good?' he said. 'Just what you were looking for?'

'Better than that,' Ginny told him. 'I don't think I knew what I was looking for; I only know that I've found it.'

'So there's no room in your life for a recently widowed architect from Leeds?'

She shook her head. There was no way of knowing if he was a recently widowed architect or just another married man on the lookout for some spare. Whatever, it was a good line. If he used it regularly he'd do all right.

Amazing, though, how they had this capacity to move in without having a clue about who they were moving in on. They'd met less than an hour ago and on the basis of a few exchanged trivialities he was ready for a relationship, whatever he meant by that. Everyone she met was desperate in one way or another; they were lonely or dissatisfied with their partners or their job or the mix that life presented them with. The old, traditional values that had kept people tied to their families and classes and tribes had withered away, but the new consciousness was failing to deliver the right mix of security and freedom. Most people were still looking for salvation outside of themselves. Sex or drugs or God, some kind of flag to wave or an ethnic minority to crush.

Ginny didn't want another man in her life. It wasn't easy living with Stone and the complications of his obsessive nature, but it was real and Stone needed her and appreciated having her around. She wasn't sure about love, after the debacle of her marriage, but if there was such a thing, it was ephemeral and fragile and needed to be discovered again every day. You couldn't rely on it being there when you woke up in the morning, even if it had been shining brightly the night before.

She was stopped and searched by Customs at Manchester International. The officer, a small oily woman with a face like a hawk, fingered every garment with a slow, deliberate detachment. She opened Ginny's make-up bag, spilling lipsticks and mascara, eyeliner and foundation into a small plastic tray and used a pencil to ferret through them. She looked at her passport twice, scrutinizing the photograph and feeling the texture of the pages and the binding, as if she hoped to find a flaw.

Ginny switched off, went into patiently waiting mode. She was carrying nothing illegal, all her papers were in order. None of her white friends had ever been stopped by Customs and when she was younger she'd worried about being searched every other trip. Now she took it in her stride. So long as they didn't get around to a strip search, which had happened once and still made her cringe when she thought about it.

David Rose had gone when she emerged from the Customs Hall, despite his cheery assertions that he would wait for her. Ginny didn't mind. In fact, it was a relief not to have to relate to a man who saw himself as recently bereaved, someone who consciously placed himself at the centre of his own imagined universe.

She slept on the train, dreamed of her old friend, Juliet. In the dream Juliet was still alive and wanted to show Ginny a sexy new dress she'd bought, outrageously revealing, with a neckline that forced her breasts dangerously upwards, like they would be thrust out at any moment. Juliet had been like that. Living on the edge until one day she fell off it and disappeared.

Ginny fixed her face with the aid of the small make-up bag that travelled everywhere with her, combed her hair and smoothed the creases of her skirt as best she could. When the train pulled into

242

Paragon station she walked along the platform with the other passengers, pulling her suitcase behind her on its tiny wheels.

Stone was standing by the gate, his hands in the pockets of his chinos. He was wearing his black leather jacket and straining his head, trying to pick her out in the crowd. Ginny quickened her step, tried to rise above the other passengers so that he would see her. He was concentrating on those people who were closest to him, and occasionally he would look to the end of the platform where the stragglers were, old people and young couples with babies. She could feel his vision sweeping over her and then going back again, scrutinizing the faces of those close to him in case she somehow went past without him seeing her.

Then something else happened. It was as if she had entered his consciousness. She was still 40 metres away and she saw him swallow. He swivelled his head in her direction and locked on with his eyes. He smiled. For a moment he looked away, he turned his body and glanced behind him, at nothing in particular, the backs of the passengers who had already gone through the gate.

Then he turned back to her and began walking in her direction, the space between them receding at double the pace. Ginny's heart was pumping loud enough for her to hear it above the sounds of the station. Stone was running and she ran towards him, her suitcase trundling and bumping along behind her.

She threw herself towards him and felt his arms take her up. In the moment those last days with Sherab in America fell away from her and her body was filled with a lightness and freedom she had almost forgotten.

And then everything was Stone Lewis; the smell of him, the sound of his voice, his arms and shoulders, his fingers brushing the tears from her cheeks, his own eyes shining with relief and genuine affection.

'How was it?' he asked. 'I didn't think you'd come back. Jesus, it's good to see you. What d'you wanna do? Go home? Have a drink? Christ, you look wonderful.'

She laughed and kissed his eyes, wrapped herself around him, tried to get to an imaginary spot on his neck where no one else in the world could reach. She ran her fingers through his hair and closed her eyes and sucked in a long lungful of station air.

When she surfaced there was Stone's face, composed now, apart from his eyes, which were bigger than normal. And they were the only people on the platform.

On the other side of the gate there was a middle-aged woman whom no one had met, struggling towards the taxi stand with two large bags.

'I'm going to need a drink,' she said. 'But let's go home first, get rid of my luggage.'

Stone took hold of her suitcase with one hand and her waist with the other. Didn't seem to mind that he had none left for himself.

Later, lying close to Stone, their bodies glued together with a warm film of perspiration, she said, 'You know what it is I like about you?'

'I'm almost solvent,' he said. 'That and my immaculate sense of style.'

She punched his arm. 'The last ten days with Sherab, his ex-girlfriend, his mother, I realized they've got a plot going. And today it was the same, Sherab at the airport, this David Rose character on the plane, the Customs woman, they've all got a plot. You're one of the few people I know who side-steps the plot and gets involved in the details.'

'I don't have a plot?'

'You might have several plots for all I know. You might have plotted to get me into bed this afternoon, like I was trying to get you here as well. But that's not what I mean. It's as if there are two different kinds of people; people who are plot-based and people who aren't.'

'And what's the plot?' Stone asked.

'It's the plot of the society we live in,' she said. 'Rags to riches or the idea of equality, winning the lottery, overcoming all obstacles and gaining your heart's desire.'

'You saying I don't want to be rich?'

'Well, do you?'

'Not particularly,' he said. 'I could use a little bread occasionally. I'd like to travel more.'

'But you're not going to bust a gut to get it.'

'Maybe not. I'm not ambitious enough.' He shifted his weight on the mattress. He put his head on one side and thought about it for a couple of minutes. 'How about this: We put our clothes on, go down the pub and get that drink?'